"I don't want to cause you any trouble..."

Paula's voice trailed away under John-Henry's unwavering stare.

Don't you know you already have? He could feel his resolve crumbling; it had started that first day, when Paula had walked into his office and asked for a loan.

Since then, among other things, he had acquired a half interest in a lame racehorse, formed a conspiracy with an eighty-two-year-old woman against her granddaughter, and caused an uproar at the bank by departing from customary procedures.

And now, it seemed, he was falling in love!

ABOUT THE AUTHOR

The expert touch of wit and whimsical humor, a trademark readers have come to expect in Risa Kirk's stories, is again evident in this, her seventh Superromance novel. A native Californian, Kirk's love for horses is obvious in this heartwarming tale.

Books by Risa Kirk

Don't miss any of our special offers. Write to us at the following address for information on our newest releases.

Harlequin Reader Service
P.O. Box 1397, Buffalo, NY 14240
Canadian address: P.O. Box 603,
Fort Erie, Ont. L2A 5X3

Send No Regrets

RISA KIRK

Harlequin Books

TORONTO • NEW YORK • LONDON
AMSTERDAM • PARIS • SYDNEY • HAMBURG
STOCKHOLM • ATHENS • TOKYO • MILAN

Published February 1991

ISBN 0-373-70441-0

SEND NO REGRETS

Author's note: With apologies to those horse lovers who know that real racehorses never train with cookies, and certainly not before or after an actual race. (We may know that, but has anyone ever explained it to a broken-down, also-ran, lop-eared Thoroughbred named No Regrets?)

CHAPTER ONE

BECAUSE SHE HAD CALCULATED so carefully, Paula Trent was early when she pulled her ancient little Volkswagen into a parking space in front of the imposing Hennessey Bank in downtown Oklahoma City. She had left the house in plenty of time; appearances were so important, especially when one was asking for money, and she hadn't wanted to be even one minute late. But now she had ten of them in which to fidget, forget her meticulously prepared speech, and in general become more of a nervous wreck than she was already. What if the bank said no to her request?

They won't say no, she assured herself, rubbing her cold hands together. Inclining her head, she peered up through the car windshield at the brick building in front of her.

But what if the answer was no?

It won't be, she told herself, and wished she had a stick of gum, or a cough drop, or anything that would make it easier to swallow over the growing lump of fear in her throat.

Maybe she should just start the car, drive away and pretend she had never come, she thought. Now that she was actually here, it seemed pure folly to have made an appointment with an investment banker. If the sight of the building alone struck such terror in her heart, how much worse would it be when she was confronted with the head of the bank himself?

Oh, what had she been thinking? she wondered in sudden despair. Selling cookies for a living had seemed like a good idea at the time, but now it seemed ridiculous, like something kids might do on a Saturday morning on the sidewalk in front of the house, with a plank table and a sign lettered in crayon: Homemade Cookies, Only a Dime.

Wincing, she sat back. If she kept on this way, she was going to make herself sick. She had already been over it a thousand times; she had no choice. She knew what she had to do; now she had to steel herself to go in and do it.

"Easy for you to say," she muttered, and rubbed her hands together again. Her fingers were icy, and she couldn't blame it all on the brisk air. Oklahoma weather could change at the drop of a hat, but she hoped that it would stay mild for a while longer; if her plans went according to schedule, she would need all the balmy days she could get.

That reminded her again of the reason she was here. It was almost time to go inside, and she used the rearview mirror to check her appearance. When she saw how pale she was, and how frightened her dark eyes looked, she shoved the mirror back into place. Despite her efforts at makeup this morning, she looked colorless and scared, and if she sat here much longer, she knew she wouldn't have the courage to go into the bank.

Well, she had to go in, whether she wanted to or not. She couldn't just drive away, no matter how frightened she felt; too much was at stake. All she had to do was remember the facts she had learned, she told herself. If the man inside laughed in her face and told her that no one sold cookies for a living, she'd remind him of Maggie

Rudkin, the Pepperidge Farm lady. And if he told her she was a silly housewife who had nothing better to do than cook up schemes because she was bored, she would set him straight.

Thinking about it, Paula's mouth set. Oh, she could tell Mr. Banker a thing or two, she thought. For one thing, she was not a bored housewife. Randy had walked out on her last year, just after their eighth anniversary. Since then, she hadn't been a housewife at all.

And she had never been bored. She'd always had a job—that is until a couple of months ago, when the real estate office where she'd been working closed up shop. She had been going to school at night to get her license, but she'd had to drop out of school, too. Without a job, or husband to help pay the bills, she couldn't afford the tuition, and all because Randy had felt—what was the word he used? Oh, yes, constricted.

Well, now he was *un*constricted in California, or so she'd heard through her lawyer. He'd gone to make his fortune, but apparently things hadn't worked out quite the way he'd hoped. Much to his surprise, she guessed, the streets there had not been lined with money after all, but with other people looking for work.

She couldn't spare any sympathy for him. She'd been looking for work, too. When she realized that Randy had taken all the money with him, she hadn't panicked; oh, she had been furious all right, but not scared. After all, she reasoned, she had her job. And even when that fell through, she wasn't worried. She was young—well, she was thirty-two, but that wasn't old—and she wasn't afraid of work. She was sure she'd find something.

She hadn't, however, found anything. And she'd looked. And looked. And *looked*. When the want ads didn't turn anything up, she had gone to the Unemployment Agency for help, but it seemed that she was either overqualified or underqualified for every job they had available. Finally the only thing left was waiting tables at some greasy spoon for minimum wage. She hadn't balked at the idea of being a waitress; desperate for work of any kind by that time, she had rushed over to the diner, terrified that someone else would get there first.

Someone had. Paula needed the job to pay the bills; the girl who got it wanted to buy designer jeans. The gum-snapping, smart-mouthed teenager she saw leaving turned out to be the owner's niece. He was sorry, but family was family, right? *That's* when she panicked.

"Don't worry so, my dear," her grandmother, Heddy, had told her. "Something will turn up."

Paula loved her grandmother, who was usually so wise in all things. But right now she had no faith in old-fashioned homilies, however well-meant. Her situation was getting grim. She hadn't had time to build up her savings again before the real estate office had closed, and she didn't have much of her severance check left. And, despite Heddy's robust health she was, after all, eighty-two years old.

Shuddering, she remembered Heddy's bout of bronchitis last year. Her grandmother had weathered that successfully, but Paula still had nightmares about pneumonia. She didn't know what she would have done if Heddy had had to be hospitalized. Heddy had her Social Security, but there was no other insurance. Paula felt responsible for her grandmother because she and Heddy only had each other. Paula's parents died five years ago, within months of each other, and her only brother had been killed by a drunk driver the night he turned twenty-one. If Paula didn't take care of her grandmother, no one else would. Without a job, and little prospect of one despite all that searching, the future seemed bleak indeed.

That was when she had thought about selling cookies for a living. Everyone she knew raved about her cookies; people were always asking her to make up a batch or two for parties, or meetings, or bake sales, and she had always been happy to oblige. At first, the idea of charging for her baked goods had embarrassed her. But after two months of unemployment, her pride seemed a very expensive luxury. She kept thinking how she would feel if something awful did happen, and Heddy had to go on welfare.

Feeling anxious and desperate, she had taken to walking the floor again at night. She'd started that when Randy left, trying to figure out what had gone wrong and when, and whether it was her fault, or his, or if in fact anyone was to blame. The speculation had been futile, especially after she got word that Randy wanted a divorce. She decided right then to give him one. By that time, she wouldn't have taken him back again. She'd never forgive him for walking out on her. After all her fruitless soul-searching, hearing about the divorce had almost been a relief.

She had just started sleeping again at night when she'd lost her job. Sometimes it seeemd to her that one event merged into another. She had no sooner begun to adjust to the fact that her marriage had gone wrong, before she had to worry about more practical things, like whether she was going to lose the house, and how she was going to pay for car insurance, or buy groceries, or any of a hundred other things.

Heddy, bless her, had offered to help as much as she could. But her grandmother didn't have much money, either, and in any event, Paula could never have taken money from Heddy. *She* was supposed to take care of her grandmother. After all, she was the one who was young and strong and resourceful; it was up to her to figure out a solution.

And she had hit on one. The cookie idea had come to her during one of those long, sleepless nights. After she'd sat up several more nights working out the details, she'd tried the plan out on her grandmother.

"It's a wonderful idea, Paula!" she said enthusiastically. "You make the best cookies in town, and you've got a good head on your shoulders. I know you'll be a success."

Paula wasn't so sure. Sadly, she said, "I don't know, Grandma. I wasn't so successful with my marriage, was I?"

Heddy's mouth had tightened. "That wasn't your fault. If that Randy had the least amount of gumption, he wouldn't have walked out on you like that. How could you fix it if you didn't know what was wrong?"

Paula hadn't answered right away; she got up to put on the water for tea. She and Heddy were sitting in her little kitchen, with the scarred table and the chairs that needed refinishing. Randy hadn't been the handiest man in the world, and he disliked doing chores around the house. Paula had to nag him just to get him to mow the lawn. Now he wasn't here even to do that.

"I don't know, Grandma," she'd said, from the stove. "Maybe I should have realized something was wrong."

"You did realize it, as I recall," Heddy pointed out stoutly. "And you asked him and asked him to talk to you. He never did, did he?"

"No, he always said everything was fine."

Heddy's tone became even more crisp. "Well, then, I wish you'd stop thinking you've got to take all the blame.

Randy has some responsibility, too, you know. You did ask him. If he didn't want to tell you, that's not your fault.''

"Yes, but—"

"No buts about it," Heddy interrupted, folding ample arms over her cushiony stomach. "Now, I've said it before, but I'll say it again. You're many things, Paula— most of them wonderful. But as far as I know, you haven't learned to read minds yet. What did Randy expect?''

Heddy looked so affronted it made Paula smile. Coming back to the table with the pot of tea, she set it down and then gave her a quick, affectionate hug. Heddy was always so supportive and sympathetic; sometimes she felt as though her grandmother was her best friend.

"I think you're prejudiced," she murmured.

"So what if I am?" Heddy said complacently. "I'm eighty-two years old. I've earned the right to my own opinions. Now, tell me more about your cookie business."

So Paula had told her what she'd worked out. After going to the library and poring over books on small businesses, she had quickly realized that she couldn't work out of her own kitchen; if she wanted to succeed, she had to commit herself to a store where she'd have room for commercial ovens, and big counters to work on.

"But that takes money, doesn't it?" Heddy said doubtfully. "Do you have that kind of cash?"

Paula shook her head. "No, I'm going to have to ask for a loan."

"At a bank?"

Heddy looked so horrified that Paula had to laugh. "Of course at a bank! Where else?"

Heddy belonged to the old school of cash-and-carry; she had never understood buying on credit, or the reasons why anyone would trust those little plastic cards when everyone knew real money was better. Growing up influenced by that attitude, Paula had the same philosophy. She had always paid her bills and she'd never borrowed a dime. But this was different. She had to have a loan; no matter how she figured it, there was no other way.

"Have you...have you gone to a bank?" Heddy asked, still looking uncertain.

"Not yet," Paula said, reaching for the folder she'd put on the counter. She extracted a newspaper clipping from it and handed it to her grandmother. "But I have an appointment with this man to talk about it."

Heddy took the clipping. "John-Henry Hennessey, of the Hennessey Bank, Oklahoma City," she murmured, reading the caption below the picture. "Where did you get this?"

"From an article in the *Daily,*" Paula told her. "It said that Hennessey is an investment banker."

Heddy handed back the paper. "What's that?"

Paula hadn't known either, until she looked it up in the library. "Someone who invests in other people's ideas."

Her grandmother still seemed doubtful. "And he'll invest in yours?"

"I hope so," Paula said fervently, staring at the clipping. She couldn't believe she'd had the good fortune to stumble across the article. She didn't usually read the financial section of the paper, but for some reason she'd turned to it that day, and John-Henry's picture had immediately caught her eye. The accompanying article said, because so many of Oklahoma's banks had failed a few years back with the drop in oil prices, the Hennessey

Bank—one of the survivors—was considering new investments in the hope of stimulating the state's economy. Although the column hadn't been very detailed, the information it did provide was all she'd needed to convince her to make an appointment with John-Henry Hennessey. That, and the picture of the bank's owner, she thought.

Even though the photo had that grainy newspaper quality, she had felt that John-Henry Hennessey was the man to approach for her loan. She liked his name, his face…everything about him. Of course, she couldn't tell much from his picture. But a man named John-Henry had to be down-to-earth, didn't he? And even if he was awfully handsome, with thick dark hair that curled back from his forehead, and a square chin in which she could discern just a suggestion of a cleft, she was sure he would at least listen to what she had to say. After all, the article said that he was interested in new businesses, and she certainly qualified there. She couldn't have felt newer at this than if she had been six years old and thinking about setting up her first Kool-Aid stand.

To her amazement, things had worked out perfectly. She had looked up the bank's number, and then it had taken her another two days to screw up enough courage to make the call. She nearly hung up when a frighteningly efficient-sounding woman answered the phone, but somehow she managed to ask for an appointment without stammering. The secretary put her on hold for what seemed an interminable length of time, but then, sounding surprised herself, came back on the line.

"Mr. Hennessey can see you at eleven o'clock on Tuesday," the woman said. She paused. "I hope that will be convenient."

Convenient! Paula would have accepted if she'd been told he could only see her on the Capitol steps for two minutes at five o'clock in the morning.

"That will be fine," she managed to say politely, and then let out a whoop of delight as she hung up the phone.

SHE DIDN'T FEEL like whooping at the moment, now that it was five minutes to eleven on the appointed Tuesday. Realizing she had sat here daydreaming long enough, she licked her lips, glanced at the forbidding-looking building again, and got out of the car.

The breeze whirled her cream-colored coat around her as she emerged, revealing a glimpse of forest-green wool jersey—the new dress she'd bought for the occasion. She hadn't wanted to spend the money, but she knew how important first impressions were, and she wanted to look exactly right.

Not that it had done much good, she thought, remembering the pale face she had just seen in the mirror, but she had taken more time with her makeup than she usually did. Most days she just wore mascara and lipstick, if she remembered to put them on; today, she had given herself the full treatment: blush, shadow, the works.

Deciding to check her appearance one last time—for courage—she bent quickly and looked in the car's side mirror. To her relief, the breeze had whipped up some color in her cheeks; now if she could just get inside the bank before the wind made a mess of her hair, she'd be all right. With no money for a haircut, she had let her hair grow down to her shoulders in a soft bob, and she kind of liked it that way. Today she hoped it made her look sophisticated. Pulling her coat firmly around her, she grabbed her purse, and went inside for her appointment with Mr. John-Henry Hennessey, investment banker.

MR. JOHN-HENRY HENNESSEY, investment banker, was, at the moment, standing by the windows of his office, staring blankly down at the street, five floors below. He looked taller than his six-foot-one, and, because he was on the lean side, he wore clothes extremely well. In this city—this state—with heavy Western and Indian influence, he seemed a rarity. Not for him the dress cowboy boots with the silver toetips; not for him the string tie topped with a polished hunk of agate or turquoise. He didn't wear a Stetson, and his belts were plain leather. Even so, he managed to turn many a woman's head when he entered the bank every morning promptly at nine-thirty. To his credit, he rarely noticed the admiring glances that came his way. With black hair and deep blue eyes, he looked as though he belonged in the movies rather than in the chair of the president of an investment firm; in fact, during his travels, quite a few advertising executives had offered him starring roles on their commercials. Even in those other days, he'd usually just laughed.

This morning, however, he wasn't laughing. Gazing somberly down at the street, his mind on other things, he saw a woman in a cream-colored coat step out of an ancient little Volkswagen parked by the curb. She was too far for him to see her features clearly, but he watched as she paused to check something in the side mirror of her car. Then she turned and hurried inside, disappearing under the awning that led to the gilded doors of the bank. Probably one of the secretaries, he thought, and turned away from the window with a heavy sigh.

He was forty years old today, supposedly a milestone in a man's life, and all he felt was profound boredom. He knew his mother, Henrietta, was planning a small celebration at home tonight despite his request to ignore the occasion, and for a moment he toyed with the idea of simply not showing up. But that would be unthinkable. His mother would be hurt and embarrassed. All the bank officers had been invited, as well as the mayor and several other important people. No, he had to go.

And be bored to death. The thought came out of nowhere, making him cringe. What had made him think that? This had been his life for five years now, ever since his wife Camilla had died, and until recently, he'd been perfectly content with his decision to come into the bank. After the accident, he had buried himself in the dry details of investment banking. The Hennessey, known throughout the state for its very conservative approach, had seemed the perfect haven.

Haven? he thought, and grimaced. Now that was an odd choice of words; what was the matter with him this morning? He was still thinking about it when the intercom on the desk gave a discreet buzz.

"Yes?" he said, without turning around.

His secretary, Mrs. Adams, answered through the speaker. "You wanted me to remind you of your appointment with Miss Trent, Mr. Hennessey."

John-Henry frowned. He didn't remember anyone named Trent. But then, this wasn't the first time his memory had failed him lately. He hadn't had his mind on business these past few months. It was an effort to keep track of details when he felt so weary of it all. Was it only his birthday—or was it something else? Maybe he needed a vacation, he thought suddenly. He hadn't been away from the bank since Camilla died.

Without warning, as sometimes happened to him, images of Camilla flashed into his mind, and just for an instant his beautiful, spoiled wife was with him again. As always, he pictured her with her head thrown back in laughter, as it so often had been, her swanlike neck stretched, so that delicate blue veins stood out under her milky-white skin.

With an effort, he shook the images out of his head. Usually he could put what had happened out of his mind, but for some reason, Camilla's mocking laughter always returned to him on his birthday.

Feeling impatient with himself, he glanced at the clock in the corner of the opulently appointed office. Good; it was almost time for his appointment with Miss Trent, whoever she was. At least she would be a distraction, he thought, and went to sit down behind the desk. Abruptly he stood up again. Meeting people sitting down seemed such an obvious power play.

"Use power wisely, John-Henry, or it will use you. Misuse is just as bad as abuse and remember—one day Hennessey banking will be in your hands."

He could remember his adoptive father, Claude, saying that to him on so many occasions. A smile flitted across John-Henry's handsome face. Then his smile faded. Not that it had mattered to him back then. Why hadn't he realized how important some things were until it was too late? Claude had been one of those things.

John-Henry had never known his real father, but it hadn't mattered much because Claude had made him feel like a son. His mother had married Claude when she was twenty-three and Claude in his sixties, but despite the age difference, they had truly been a family. Claude had been dead many years now, but John-Henry could still remember him clearly. Not very tall in physical terms, but a giant in stature, Claude had been unfailingly kind and generous. He had also been a stern disciplinarian, when necessary. The odd thing was, John-Henry thought, it hadn't often been necessary. There had been something about Claude that had made him want to obey—at least when he was younger.

Recalling those halcyon childhood days with the father who doted on both him and his mother, John-Henry smiled fondly again. He had always felt so proud and grown-up when Claude brought him down to the bank with him for a few hours before they went to lunch at the club. From the age of seven, he had formed his first impressions of the bank while waiting for Claude outside the big office. He had wandered around counting the polished black-and-white floor tiles, and he had slid down the marble bannister when no one was looking. The building had been old even then, almost as old as his father.

John-Henry's expression became sad. He had always been glad that Claude hadn't lived to see his marriage to Camilla; he knew how disappointed Claude would have been in him. He knew, because he was so disappointed in himself.

But he didn't like to think of that time, or what had happened, and because he needed to distract himself, he glanced at the clock again. The meeting with Miss Trent shouldn't take long, he thought; he would have plenty of time to get to the club for lunch. He'd promised to meet his friend Charles Rasmussen—Charlie—at the courts at noon, and he was glad they had decided on a few sets of tennis before they ate. He was so restless that he needed some strenuous exercise before his afternoon appointments.

But would tennis help? he wondered. Lately, he'd been inclined to shake things up around here, to take a flier on some wild venture just for the hell of it. He had granted that interview with the *Daily* a while ago, and had indicated that the bank was open to new investment possibilities. That had caused enough of a stir in the ranks. His mother, of course, as well as his officers, would be appalled if they knew what he was really thinking these days; Henrietta herself would be sure it was a sign he was returning to the "old ways," as she called them.

He sighed. That was one reason he had maintained the status quo, much as it chafed him. He'd caused his mother enough grief in the past, and ever since Camilla, he had promised himself that he would toe the line. Thinking that the line was getting increasingly wearisome, he was just sitting down again when his secretary buzzed.

"Miss Trent is here, Mr. Hennessey."

"Thank you, Mrs. Adams," he said, calm as ever, without a trace of the inner turmoil he still felt. "Please show her in."

A FEW MILES AWAY, at Remington Park, the city's major racetrack, Otis Wingfield, hands in his pockets, rocked back and forth on worn-down heels. It didn't matter that he was far away from the action and the more prestigious stabling closer to the track. He beamed proudly at his companion and said, "Well, what do you think, Heddy, my girl? Isn't he a beauty?"

Heddy Bascomb adjusted her glasses and peered at the horse the groom, Fernando, was parading before her. Today, as always, she was wearing a flower-print dress under her coat and sensible shoes, with her purse clutched in front of her ample stomach. Two years older than Otis, she regarded him as a "younger man." He was as short and round as she was, and just as sharp. Or so she had thought, until he'd brought this horse out.

"Well, I don't know, Otis," she said. "He looks a little off on that right hind to me."

Otis squinted. "Well, a'course he's off on the right hind, Heddy," he said tartly. "That's the reason he's goin' so cheap. If he was sound, do you think they'd be sellin' him?"

Heddy could be a little sharp herself. Trying not to think what her granddaughter, Paula, would say if she knew what her grandmother was up to at this moment, she gestured to the groom to turn around and lead the horse by again.

"I'm not a fool, Otis Wingfield," she said. "I know why they're selling him. I just don't know if I'm prepared to buy. What if we fix him up and he still can't run?"

Otis drew himself up to his full five-foot-two height and looked Heddy right in the eye. He had once been a jockey—sixty-odd pounds, and about the same number of years ago—before he had turned to training racehorses instead of riding them. "If I say he can run, he'll run," he stated adamantly.

Heddy still looked skeptical. "With that strained ligament you told me about?"

Otis glanced around, as though afraid he might be overheard. It seemed unlikely to Heddy, since they were the only ones out along this particular shedrow. But she leaned forward obligingly anyway as Otis whispered, "I don't think the ligament is a problem, Heddy," he said, and paused. "I think it's a gravel."

"A gravel!"

Wincing at her tone, Otis put an agitated finger to his lips. "Shh. Do you want everyone at the track to hear?"

Heddy wanted to get this settled. "Otis, there's no one within a mile of us except Fernando, and he doesn't speak much English," she said bluntly. "Now, what in the world is a gravel?"

When Otis beckoned her forward again, she sighed heavily, but obeyed. "A gravel is just that," he said, glancing here and there for spies. "A tiny little piece of stone that somehow worked itself up inside the foot, causing pain."

Heddy pulled back. "Can you get it out?"

"It has to work its way out."

She narrowed her eyes. "And in the meantime, what happens?" she demanded. "Do we just wait? How long does it take, Otis? Will we all be dead and buried before this horse can run again?"

Looking wounded, Otis said reproachfully, "Now, Heddy—"

"Don't you 'now, Heddy' me! I can read the *Daily Racing Form,* and it says that horse has only been in the money once!"

"In three starts, that ain't so bad," Otis retorted. "He was just gettin' the feel of the track, and he got bumped the first time out. Come on, Heddy, love. Don't you trust me?"

It wasn't that. If Otis had told her the horse would win blindfolded and barefoot on a muddy track, she wouldn't have hesitated to put her money on his nose. But *buying* a racehorse was not the same as betting on him. She could just imagine what Paula would say.

"Well, I don't know, Otis," she said, staring hard as the groom again trudged by leading the animal. The horse was undoubtedly one of the ugliest equines she had ever seen: raw-boned, platter-footed, walleyed, and lop-eared to boot. He was a horrible shade of gray; he had no mane to speak of, and his tail looked like a bottlebrush that had seen better days. But all that was cosmetic, Heddy knew. Some of the most unsightly horses in the world were the best runners, the famous Exterminator being just one. That horse had been so stringy and lean that they had called him "Old Bones," or the "Gallop-ing Hatrack." But he hadn't been lame on that right hind, Heddy thought, and frowned.

She didn't doubt that Otis could make the horse well enough to run again; her old friend had been one of the best horse trainers in the country in his hey day. Even today's brash young trainers admitted that Otis had probably forgotten more than they'd ever have time to learn. But owning a horse wasn't something to be under-taken lightly, especially when the horse was a runner. And especially when the runner wasn't exactly the pret-tiest horse she'd ever seen. Oh, my, what would Paula say?

Well, she'd just have to keep it a secret, that's all, Heddy decided. Opportunities like this one didn't come around every day. If the horse had been sound, she and Otis could never have afforded him; even now, his price was still high.

Longingly, she looked at the gray again. He might be her last grab at the old gold ring, she thought. Even though she felt tip-top, she wasn't getting any younger, and that concerned her at times. She'd had that darn fool bronchitis last year that had been so hard to get over, and she knew Paula was worried it might happen again.

And Paula was worried about too many things these days, Heddy thought with an inward sigh. Ever since Randy had walked out, it had been one blow after another. Oh, Paula tried to put up a brave front and pretend everything was all right, but Heddy knew how much that cost her. Paula should be thinking about herself and her own future rather than how she was going to take care of a meddlesome old grandmother. The last thing Heddy wanted was to give up her little cottage and go into an old folks' home, but if she had to, she would. She would not be a burden on Paula, no matter what. Paula deserved her own chance at life; Heddy had had hers.

Or maybe hers wasn't quite over yet. Thoughtfully, Heddy looked at the horse still being paraded by the patient groom. She had never believed in letting fate whisk her about—not without trying to take some control. She'd always believed in taking matters into her own hands. She might not be able to do anything about getting old, but she could have a say about what happened when she got there. At least she could give it a darn good try. And wouldn't Paula be surprised when she and Otis handed her a check for her share of a racing purse? Heddy wanted to laugh aloud with delight at the thought.

"You *sure* this horse can run?" she asked.

Otis looked at her indignantly again. Hadn't he already told her so? "As sure as I'm standin' here. Now you can ask one of them fancy young fellers their opinion, if you want, but—"

"No, no, I believe you," Heddy said quickly, seeing she'd hurt his feelings. "It's just a lot of money, that's all."

Otis hooked a thumb under his suspenders, giving her a wink. "But think of those racing purses, Heddy. Just think of those!"

"Let's get him well enough to run first. Then we'll worry about what to do with his winnings."

Otis stopped rocking. "Does that mean—?"

"It does," Heddy said, making up her mind. Now that she had decided, there was no going back. "I think we just bought ourselves a racehorse."

Otis looked at her in disbelief for a moment, then he told the groom to take the horse back before he grabbed her and danced a little jig. "Whooeee! You ain't gonna be sorry, Heddy!" he crowed. "You'll see."

Slapping his hands away, Heddy straightened her dress. "Really, Otis, you're acting like a fool," she said, but there was a gleam in her eyes, and they both smiled as Otis wiped his brow.

"Boy, I'm glad that's settled," he said fervently. "Are you going to tell Paula?"

She'd already made that decision, too. They both knew how Paula felt about the racetrack. "No, I don't think so, just yet. Paula is so busy right now with the cookie store idea that maybe we'll just go along by ourselves for a time. What do you think?"

"I think that there's goin' to be fireworks when your Paula finds out," Otis said. "But you're the boss. Are you sure about this?"

"As sure as you are that the horse is going to run again," Heddy said.

"No regrets?" Otis said with a gleam in his eye.

"Just one," she said, smiling in return.

"Then let's go get him," Otis said, and led the way to the racing office where the transfer of ownership took place. By the time they walked out again, papers in hand, Heddy Bascomb and Otis Wingfield were the proud new owners of an aging, broken-down, also-ran Thoroughbred racehorse aptly named ... No Regrets.

And, grinning at each other like children, they had not a one.

CHAPTER TWO

AT THAT MOMENT, Paula was experiencing a multitude of regrets. She had never in her life been inside an investment bank, and when she had made the appointment to see John-Henry Hennessey, she had assumed his bank would be like any other: a friendly place with tellers behind counters and people chatting as they waited in line to deposit their money. She had never expected to walk into a vaultlike room with a high-domed ceiling and black-and-white tile in a checked pattern on the floor. For an awful moment, she thought she'd wandered into a cathedral by mistake. A marble staircase opposite, winding up to gloom above, reinforced that impression, and she looked round uncertainly. People sat at desks here and there, but a waist-length brass rail running the length of the big room separated her from them. No one looked up.

Even more unnerving was the smothering reverential silence. Unlike other offices, there was no ringing of telephones, or clicking of keyboards. Nonetheless, everyone seemed absorbed in what they were doing. Hoping to get someone's attention, Paula gently cleared her throat. No one seemed to notice. Now what?

Then she saw the reception desk almost hidden by a tall plant in a brass tub, and, with relief, she headed toward it. Surely the woman sitting there would be able to help.

Paula hadn't taken four quick steps before she realized that her high heels were making too much noise on that spotless tile floor. Every tap sounded like a firecracker going off, and she was sure she felt disapproving eyes on her back. Uncertain whether to slow down or tiptoe to deaden the noise, she decided just to get to the reception desk as quickly—and quietly—as possible.

The woman at the desk watched disapprovingly as Paula approached. She was wearing a severe brown suit that did little for her complexion, and very red lipstick that matched the color on her long nails. She kept a finger on the stack of mail she had been sorting, making Paula wonder if she should apologize for interrupting. A brass nameplate to the front of the desk indicated the woman's name was Miss Smithers.

"How may I help you?" Miss Smithers inquired prissily.

Her voice was a mere murmur, as though she didn't want to disturb any of the people at the desks across the way. Since no one was within twenty feet of them, Paula felt intimidated again until she reminded herself of the reason for her visit. She had an appointment, and she was not going to let Miss Smithers frighten her into being late. The receptionist's function, after all, was to receive visitors, and she, Paula, was one.

"I have an appointment with Mr. John-Henry Hennessey at eleven," she said, pleased that she sounded calm and composed, when inside she felt so shaky. She even managed a cool smile. "Would you please direct me to his office?"

"And you are . . . ?" the receptionist asked.

Despite her nervousness, Paula began to feel irritated. Who else would she be, unless Mr. Hennessey was in the habit of making appointments with two people at once?

She could see her name written down clearly in the book on the desk, and she resisted the impulse to point it out.

"My name is Paula Trent," she said, forcing another smile. "I'm sure if you call..."

Miss Smithers didn't have to call. Glancing languidly down at her book at last, she murmured, "Oh, yes. Miss Trent. If you'll—"

But just then, the huge grandfather clock on the wall behind the desk began booming the hour.

Bong...bong...bong...

Her nerves already strained, Paula jumped at the noise, but no one else seemed to pay any attention. In her jittery state, each clang sounded like a cannon going off, and she could feel her body tensing.

"I'm sorry—" she said, trying to speak above the noise without shouting "—but I can't hear you."

"I said—"

Bong...bong...bong...

This was impossible, Paula thought, exasperated. The contrast between the previous sepulchral silence and this clamor was too much. Didn't anyone else notice? Miss Smithers tried again, but even though she strained, Paula could hardly hear what she was saying.

"...just go through that way and take the—"

Bong...bong...bong...

"I'm sorry—" Paula repeated, glaring at the clock, willing it to be silent. She spread her hands in a helpless gesture.

Looking increasingly annoyed, the receptionist pointed this time. Following the direction of that crimson-tipped finger, Paula turned and saw an arch framing a small foyer. She hadn't noticed it before, but an ornate elevator was at the end. Obviously she was meant to take that, but take it where?

"Yes, I see," she said, turning back to the desk. "But—"

Bong . . .

She tried again. "But what—"

Bong . . .

And then, just when she thought she'd have to take a bat to that clock, blessed silence.

Into the quiet, Miss Smithers said calmly, "As I was about to say, please take the elevator to the fifth floor. Mr. Hennessey's office will be directly in front of you. His secretary will be waiting."

"Thank you," Paula said, with as much dignity as she could muster, and headed toward the foyer.

The elevator made her forget her annoyance over the clock. That sinking feeling she had been fighting from the moment she walked in hit her in full measure as she approached the scrolled and gilded door of the antique elevator. Hesitantly, wondering if she should be here at all, she reached out and pushed the button. When the doors slid open smoothly to reveal a paneled interior with crimson carpet on the floor, she was more sure than ever that she was making a big mistake. She didn't belong here. She belonged in a conventional bank, one with tellers and withdrawal slips and loan officers who had desks in plain view. She had no business in a place that had marble staircases and antique grandfather clocks and gilt-edged elevators. It took all her willpower to step inside and punch the right number.

With barely a bump, the elevator bore her swiftly up. She didn't have time to change her mind; she was still marveling at the handcarved paneling when the elevator stopped and the doors opened again. In front of her was a wide hallway carpeted in the same shade of crimson, and directly ahead was a door with a brass nameplate which read: John-Henry Hennessey, President. She swallowed. Obviously, she had arrived.

Wishing she had a mirror to see what damage the wind had done, she smoothed her hair with clammy hands. Then she straightened her skirt. She was just about to go in when she suddenly realized that she couldn't remember a word of the speech she had spent days perfecting. Oh, no, she thought in panic. How could she forget! The loan meant everything to her; she wanted it desperately and she'd planned down to the last detail what she was going to say. Now she couldn't remember anything!

"I don't know why you need to make a speech, love," Heddy had told her, when she had asked to practice it in front of her. "Just be yourself and say what you want right out. What's wrong with that?"

What was wrong was that it was too simple, too unsophisticated, too...unprofessional. She had to impress Mr. Hennessey; if she didn't, she wouldn't get the loan. So she had stayed awake night after night, writing and rewriting, until she was satisfied. Then she'd memorized it word for word and practiced it endlessly. It was so important, and now she had forgotten the whole thing!

Rubbing her hands together, praying that by some miracle it would come back to her, she realized she couldn't just stand out in the hall like a ninny. Every second she wasted here meant one less to convince the man inside that she intended to accomplish exactly what she said she would. She would make a success of her business; she knew it as sure as she was standing here.

"So go in and tell him," she muttered, and before she could change her mind, she reached out and opened the door.

A woman was sitting at a desk inside, but to Paula's relief, she seemed to be much more welcoming than the receptionist downstairs. Tall and blond and about fifty, she glanced up when Paula came in.

"Miss Trent?" she said. "I'm Mrs. Adams, Mr. Hennessey's secretary. Just a moment, and I'll tell him you're here. He's expecting you." She smiled. "You're right on time."

Because she was so nervous, Paula blurted, "I'm glad. I thought I was going to be late. The clock downstairs—"

The woman made a face. "Oh, that old thing. It's always fast no matter how many times we set it. Mr. Hennessey keeps saying he's going to get rid of it but he never does." She smiled again and shrugged. "Sentimental reasons, I guess."

Hoping that a man who kept a fast-running clock around for sentiment might look more kindly on someone who was trying to start her own business, Paula glanced around covertly while the secretary picked up the phone. A long couch and matching chairs upholstered in Dresden blue dominated the big room, and original oils hung on the dove-gray walls. The crimson carpet of the elevator and hallway was repeated in here, making everything seem elegant and sober. It was solemn and serious and definitely intimidating.

Thinking that it had certainly been that so far, Paula wondered belatedly why the bank's president had agreed to see her. The thought hadn't occurred to her until this awful moment, but once it had, she felt even more unnerved. She didn't know much about banking, but it seemed to her now that her request could have been—should have been—handled by someone other than the top man himself. Oh, what had she gotten herself into? She groaned inwardly, and was just wondering if she could make some quick excuse and leave, when the secretary put down the phone and smiled at her again.

"Right this way, please," the woman said, and stood to lead the way into another office.

It was too late to back out now. Her heart in her throat, Paula tried to swallow her panic as she followed the secretary, who opened a door.

"Miss Trent, Mr. Hennessey," the woman said, ushering her inside. Then she backed out and closed the door.

And just that quickly, Paula was left alone with the man who held the key to her future.

Now that she was here, John-Henry Hennessey seemed even more imposing than the rest of the bank had been. He was standing behind a huge desk that, despite its size, failed to dwarf the room. For what seemed an endless length of time, he just looked at her. With each passing second, Paula's urge to flee increased, and she was about to stammer something about having made a mistake when he seemed to realize he was staring. With a slight jerk of his head, he strode around the desk and held out his hand.

"Miss Trent," he said. "So pleased to meet you."

Now it was Paula's turn to stare. Despite her panic, she could see that his picture in the paper hadn't done him justice. He had looked almost stuffy in that photograph, the very image of the proper and serious investment banker. In person, he didn't seem like that at all. For one thing, he looked much younger—and even more good-looking. She was five-foot-six, but he seemed to tower over her, all broad shoulders and long legs and arresting face. As was proper for a banker, she supposed, he was wearing a three-piece suit in dark blue, with not a wrinkle in sight and every crease exactly in line. His black shoes shone, and he wasn't wearing a ring. Wondering why on earth she had noticed that, she tried to remember her manners, which seemed to have deserted her together with any semblance of composure.

"Thank you so much for seeing me, Mr. Hennessey," she managed, wondering why he was having such an impact on her.

"My pleasure," he said in a deep, pleasant voice. "May I take your coat?"

She had forgotten she was wearing one. Trying not to sound surprised, she said, "Why, yes, thank you."

Their hands touched just for an instant as he took the coat from her, and she glanced quickly up at him. Had she felt something, or was it only her increasingly feverish imagination? Annoyed with herself, she glanced away. She was being silly. It was clear she was just nervous. She never reacted this way to a man.

"Please," he said, gesturing to a beige couch that stood along the wall opposite the big desk. "Let's sit down, and you can tell me what I can do for you."

For an awful moment, she couldn't remember the purpose of her visit. It was his eyes, she thought, confused. She'd never seen eyes that color, such a deep blue they seemed nearly as black as his hair. The pale blue shirt he was wearing increased the effect, and the tie completed it, with stripes in the same hue. He hadn't stopped looking at her since she had come in, and she wondered what he was thinking. *Oh, why,* she thought bleakly, *did he have to be so good-looking?*

Somehow she managed to sit with good grace. It was time for her speech, but if she had felt blank out in the hallway, she was practically paralyzed in here. She felt so overwhelmed that she didn't even know how to begin. Her heart was pounding, and her mouth felt dry. She realized suddenly that what she felt wasn't due solely to nerves. She hadn't been so attracted to a man since...she couldn't remember the last time. Not even Randy had generated such an intense reaction. *You don't even know him,* she told herself, and tried to remember why she'd come.

"Would you like some coffee?" he asked.

She had been too preoccupied to realize that he'd gone to the desk, where he stood with his hand poised over the phone. "Why, yes, that would be nice," she replied. What she really needed, she thought, was a good stiff shot to restore her equilibrium. Shocked at the thought since she didn't ordinarily drink, she ordered herself to get it together before he came back to the couch.

"Now," he said, deliberately sitting down some distance from her. "What can I do for you?"

Now there was nothing to do but say it right out. "Mr. Hennessey," she said, "I came today because I plan to start a new business, and I need a loan."

"I see," he said, and paused. "Go on."

She had no choice. Hoping she wasn't going to make a fool of herself, she gritted her teeth and decided to get the worst over with first.

"I'd like to borrow—" she said, but suddenly, the amount spoken aloud sounded even more enormous and impossible than it had at home. Certain he was going to think the same thing, she continued quickly. "I've calculated everything down to the last dime, and I'm prepared to offer my house as collateral."

From what she had read about applying for a loan, she knew he would expect a statement of her worth, and she'd brought it along. Although she'd included everything she could possibly think of, she had cringed at the paltry amount of her assets. But then she had told herself that no column of numbers could factor in determination and capacity for hard work, both of which she had in abundance. She knew that, given the chance, she would succeed. All she had to do was convince Mr. Hennessey of that. Now, sitting in his office, it seemed a faint, foolish hope.

He still hadn't said anything, and she couldn't tell from his expression what he was thinking. Before she became too embarrassed to give him the outline she'd prepared, she reached for her purse. "I've brought a financial statement—" she began, and was interrupted by a soft knock outside.

"Excuse me," he said, and glanced the door. "Come in, Mrs. Adams."

The secretary entered with the coffee. As she set the tray down on the table in front of them, Paula couldn't help staring at the silver service, and delicate china cups. It was a far cry from the battered coffee machine and white stoneware mugs at the real estate office where she had last worked. She was still gazing in wonder when the secretary murmured, "Will that be all, Mr. Hennessey?"

"Yes, I think so," he said, and then reconsidered. "Unless—" He looked at Paula. "I think this might take a while. Perhaps we should continue our discussion over lunch. Would you mind if I had something brought in, or do you have another appointment?"

Paula wasn't sure whether the invitation was a good sign or not, but she knew she couldn't refuse. Thinking that she would sit here all afternoon if that's what it took to get her loan, she forced a smile. "No, I don't have another appointment. But I'm sure you're very busy. I wouldn't want to take up so much of your time."

"It's no problem," he said, and looked pleased as he turned to the secretary again. "Mrs. Adams, if you would...?"

The woman tried to hide her obvious surprise. "Certainly, Mr. Hennessey," she said. "But...er...what about Mr. Rasmussen?"

John-Henry looked as though he didn't remember who Mr. Rasmussen was. Then, with a wave of his hand, he said, "Oh, tell Charlie something...came up. He'll understand."

"Yes, sir," the secretary murmured. She glanced at Paula with a strange expression as she went out, making Paula realize that something out of the ordinary had just happened. Deciding she should say something, she leaned forward.

"I'm sorry," she said. "I didn't mean to upset your schedule."

"Oh, you didn't," he said with that smile that stirred something inside her again. "Now, where were we?"

Feeling nervous once more, Paula carefully put down the cup she'd taken. "We were talking about my loan."

"Yes," he said. "But first, tell me about your company."

A flush shot to Paula's cheeks. *Her company?* Didn't he mean her idea? Then she was annoyed with herself again. Oh, what did it matter? Telling him about the cookie store should have been first on the list; asking for a loan was supposed to come later, she realized. She was making a fool of herself, and all because she found John-Henry Hennessey far too attractive. A banker, she thought, should have white hair and wire-frame glasses and should keep looking sternly at his pocket watch because she was keeping him from much more important business. He had no right to be so handsome and physically overwhelming, and he certainly shouldn't have dark blue eyes that seemed to see right inside her.

"Well, I . . . I . . ." she stammered, and couldn't think how to go on. The cookie store idea that at home had seemed the answer to all her prayers seemed increasingly silly and childish now. Feeling more foolish by the second, she was tempted to get up and babble something about having changed her mind. Remembering how cool the receptionist had been, and how startled the secretary looked just now, she wondered why John-Henry Hennessey had agreed to see her. Had he thought it would be amusing? Had there been some ghastly mix-up? Maybe he'd thought she was someone else.

"Miss Trent?" John-Henry said.

He was looking at her with those eyes again, staring at her, making her feel even more nervous and confused than ever. Maybe she should just make an excuse and go, she thought—and then remembered Heddy.

She couldn't leave now, she thought determinedly. This was no time to give up. As Heddy herself had told her so often, they might not have much, but they had backbone, and neither of them was afraid to work. She could make a go of her idea; she knew she could. All she needed was a little help from John-Henry Hennessey to get started.

"I want to open a store that sells fresh-baked cookies," she announced, launching into it before she lost courage. "Now, I know that sound silly—"

She stopped when she saw his expression. "I'm sorry," he said, looking confused. "But I thought you said . . . *a* store."

"I did," she said. And then, with a feeling of dread, she asked, "Why?"

Looking perplexed and amused at the same time, he shook his head. "Forgive me. But I thought you represented a *chain* of stores."

She looked at him for a moment, not comprehending. Then she remembered something she had said when she first called for the appointment. She flushed bright red. Oh, why had she tried to be so clever? She had wanted the appointment so desperately that she had babbled something about a chain of stores when she was talking to the secretary, but she was sure she had said those were future plans. Hadn't she?

Now she was so flustered she didn't know what she'd said. All she knew was that she was making a terrible fool of herself in front of this man, and all because she had tried to impress him. Oh, why hadn't she just gone to a regular bank? If she had just been herself, she wouldn't be in danger—as she obviously was now—of falling flat on her face in an agony of embarrassment.

Wishing the floor would open up and swallow her, she got to her feet. "I'm sorry, Mr. Hennessey," she said painfully, hoping she could escape before it got any worse, "but there's been a mistake. I apologize for taking your time—"

He rose with her, in one lithe, athletic movement. Looking apologetic himself, he reached out quickly, blocking her escape. His eyes holding hers, he said, "There's been no mistake, just a simple misunderstanding. Please, sit down again."

She couldn't. "Oh, I—"

"Please, obviously the error was mine. I'd like to continue our discussion."

Because she could hardly push his arm aside and dash toward the door, she resumed her seat. But she knew her face was still red, and she had trouble meeting his eyes. "I'm sorry," she muttered. "I feel so . . . foolish."

"Then we both do. Why don't we start again. You were saying something about a cookie store?"

Only the thought of how much this meant to her and Heddy made Paula continue. Wondering if anyone in the world had ever felt as mortified as she did now, she said, "Yes, a cookie store—"

Once she got going again, however, it was easier. Encouraged by his calm and interested manner, as though he'd already forgotten the misunderstanding, she explained what she wanted to do, assuring him at one point, "I'm aware of the high failure rate for small businesses, Mr. Hennessey. But I don't intend to let that happen to mine. I know that success in what I want to do requires more than the ability to bake, but I'm not afraid of hard work. And I promise, you won't be sorry if you grant me a loan. I'll pay it back, on time, with fair interest."

"I believe you would," he said.

She didn't know what to make of that. Hoping after all she had gone through he wasn't going to give her a polite refusal, she said, "I've calculated all the expenses. The figures—"

He lifted a hand. "Wait. Why a cookie store?"

Deciding at this point she had nothing to lose, she said simply, "Because I make good cookies." Then, realizing how immodest that sounded, she added quickly, "And because, after researching it, I'm convinced it could be a lucrative business."

He gave her a shrewd look. "But there's something else."

"Yes, there is," she admitted. "I'm on my own—well, except for my grandmother, who is eighty-two years old. She's still well, and living by herself, but the time is coming when—'' She stopped, making a dismissive motion with her hand. He didn't need to know her family history. ''Well, that doesn't matter. The point is that I've already lost one job because the company I worked for folded, and I don't want to go through that again. I can depend on myself. I know I won't fail.''

''I see,'' he said again. She felt like screaming from sheer tension. Was that all he intended to say? It seemed not, for he gave her another curious look. ''Have you brought any samples?''

She hid her dismay. She hadn't thought of bringing any cookies with her; surely he didn't believe she was prepared to whip a tray out from under her coat and present them with a flourish! For an awful moment, she wasn't sure what to say. ''Well, no,'' she replied at last. ''But if that's necessary before you make your decision, I'd be glad to—''

''No, it's not necessary,'' he said, smiling. ''It's just that all this talk of cookies was making me hungry.'' The phone buzzed discreetly then, and he nodded. ''Ah. That should be lunch, I think. Just in time. I hope you're hungry, too.''

''Oh, yes,'' she said, even though her stomach was so tied in knots from this strange interview that she didn't think she could eat a thing.

The efficient Mrs. Adams entered the office, followed by two uniformed waiters pushing carts. Eyes wide at the splendor, Paula watched as they set the conference table at the other end of the room with linen, china and silverware. Finally they whisked the silver warming covers off the dishes with a flourish.

''Will there be anything else, Mr. Hennessey?'' one of the waiters asked, when all was ready.

"No, thank you. We'll manage," John-Henry said, and gestured politely for Paula to join him. When she did, he held her chair, while one of the waiters unfolded a starched linen napkin over her lap before pausing to ask which wine she'd prefer.

"Just . . . water, please," she said. She already felt dazed, and wine quickly went to her head. She needed to keep all her wits about her, for as gracious as the lunch invitation had been, John-Henry Hennessey still hadn't said he would give her a loan.

Paula was reluctant to continue her pitch over the salad or the perfectly poached Dover sole that followed, but John-Henry drew her out so adroitly over the meal that she was soon giving him all the details. She wanted to rent or lease store space, she told him, because her own kitchen was too small. Then she needed equipment: ovens and industrial mixing machines, and fittings like racks and counters. She'd researched it all thoroughly and had the figures memorized; not once did she falter over the details, or fail to answer any question to his complete satisfaction.

"Well, I must say," he said at one point, "you've certainly done your homework."

"It's important to me," she answered simply. "I know I can make a go of it."

Although he did not respond to that, she could see by his expression that he was beginning to think so, too. Or at least she hoped he was. After going through such trauma, she didn't know what she would do if he refused her.

But instead of commenting on her loan, he glanced at her plate. "You don't seem to be eating. Isn't the sole to your liking?" He smiled. "Perhaps you're one of those native Oklahomans who can't abide anything but beef. If that's so, I could have something else brought in.''

"No, no," she said quickly. The problem was that she had been too anxious to eat. "The meal is fine. In fact, it's the best I've ever eaten. Thank you so much.''

"It wasn't any trouble," he said with an engaging smile. Then, ''Are you sure you won't have some wine? I get impatient with people who rhapsodize about the merits of one vintage over the other, but this is an excellent chardonnay.''

It was one of the first personal things he'd said, and she felt herself smiling in return because she felt the same way about pretentiousness. Even so, she had to refuse the offer. With him sitting across from her, she was having a hard enough time keeping her mind on business; the last thing she needed was to get tipsy. It had happened to her before with only one glass, she remembered. As Randy had said so often, she just didn't have a head for alcohol. "I'm sure it is," she said regretfully. "But I'm afraid I...I don't care for wine.''

"Just cookies, eh?''

Because she was still feeling nervous, she thought he was poking fun at her. "No, not necessarily," she said, and then decided to go for it. "It's just that I make better cookies than I do wine.''

He laughed. "Touché. Tell me. Do you have a location in mind for the store?''

Her brief spurt of pluck vanished. "Well, not exactly," she was forced to admit. "I wanted to make sure I'd be able to afford it first.''

"Then you've solved at least one problem," he said.

At first she wasn't sure what he meant. Then, when realization dawned, she blurted, "You mean you're going to give me the loan?''

When he shook his head, she didn't know what to think.

"No," he said thoughtfully. "I don't think you asked for enough. From what you've told me, I believe you're going to need a bigger cushion, so I think we'll double it."

She gaped at him. "Double it! But—"

"Oh, same interest, of course," he said, as though it were of no consequence to him. "Same terms." Then he smiled. "You're so determined to succeed that I want to do my part to make sure you do."

She didn't know what to say. He hadn't even seen her financial statement—such as it was; he hadn't even tasted her cookies!

"I . . . I don't know how to thank you, Mr. Hennessey," she said finally, utterly dazed. She certainly never expected it to happen this way.

"You can thank me by making the store a success," he said, and then added, "And maybe one other thing . . ."

She was so grateful she would have granted him anything. "What?"

"Bring me a cookie once in a while."

Thinking that was the last thing she'd expected him to say, she laughed. Impulsively holding out her hand, she said, "Deal!"

His fingers held hers a moment longer than necessary—or maybe she was reluctant to let him go. She didn't know what it was; she just knew that in those few seconds when they stared at each other and she looked into those intent eyes, she couldn't help wondering what the future might hold.

"Deal," he murmured at last, and let her go.

JOHN-HENRY WAS STILL FEELING dazzled an hour later when his friend Charlie Rasmussen walked in wearing tennis whites. Charlie ran his father's company, Rasmussen and Roberts, a commercial construction firm. "Well, ol' buddy," Charlie said, throwing himself into a chair. "Tell me all about it."

John-Henry gave him a blank look. "All about what?"

"Why you canceled our tennis date, of course. Had to be something. Are you sick, or—" he grinned "—just feeling your age?"

John-Henry didn't think that was amusing. He and Charlie had known each other for a long time. Friends since college, they had been through a lot together, first when Charlie had lost his fiancée in a sailing accident two weeks before his wedding, then later, when John-Henry's wife Camilla died. Charlie was three inches shorter than he was, and thirty pounds heavier, but it suited him. And, while he wasn't as good-looking as John-Henry, he'd never had trouble attracting his own share of attention. Women seemed to find Charlie's grin endearing, but this afternoon it irritated John-Henry. His friend's remark reminded him of his birthday, and the party his mother had planned.

"Neither sick nor feeling my age," he replied. "I had an important appointment."

Charlie looked interested. "Did you finally snag Digitron Optic?"

Digitron Optic was one of the biggest optical companies in the country. When rumor started to spread that they were thinking of relocating their main offices, John-Henry immediately reviewed them for investment potential. Their move to Oklahoma City would stimulate growth and jobs, and he had contacted them personally.

But then, so had the presidents and executive officers of other institutions around the country. He had met with Digitron's CEO, George Copeland, at a fund-raiser the other night, but the company was playing it cagey. John-Henry had a feeling that things might work out, but it was still too early to say.

"No, it wasn't Digitron," John-Henry said, and then felt exasperated. He knew Charlie wouldn't let it go, so he decided to get it over with. "It was someone named Paula Trent."

"Paula Trent?" Charlie repeated. "I don't believe I've ever heard of her."

Despite himself, John-Henry smiled. "You will," he said.

That made Charlie even more curious. "What does she do?"

Remembering those flashing dark eyes, with their intriguing flecks of amber, he said, "She makes cookies."

"I beg your pardon? I thought you said she makes cookies."

"She does."

"And you gave her a loan."

"I did," John-Henry said, and then realized Charlie was looking at him strangely. He didn't know why, but that *was* amusing, and he started to laugh. When Charlie frowned, he laughed even harder. As incredible as it was, he hadn't felt this good in years.

HEDDY WASN'T AT HOME when Paula dropped over, bursting with the good news about getting her loan. Because she had to tell someone, she went to a friend's house close by. She and Marie had worked together at the real estate office, but when the company folded, Marie hadn't gone looking for another job. She and her husband had decided to start a family, and it seemed the perfect time for Marie to quit. She was now eight months pregnant and starting to waddle.

"You look wonderful!" Paula exclaimed, when her very pregnant friend opened the door.

"You look excited," Marie said, her eyes starting to sparkle. She always loved gossip, or, for that matter, any good story. Especially these days, when she had to spend so much time with her feet up, watching endless soap operas. Grabbing Paula's arm, she dragged her inside. "Come in and tell me all about it. Want a snack or something? I just made cookies. They're not as good as yours, of course, but they'll do in a pinch."

"No thanks," Paula said, sitting down at the kitchen table while Marie bustled around. "And you're a good cook, as you know very well. It's just that pretty soon I'm going to be in cookies up to my eyebrows."

Marie turned from the stove, where she'd been putting water on for tea. "You got the loan!"

Paula laughed happily, dizzily. She still couldn't believe it. "I did," she said. "Isn't it wonderful?"

"Oh, Paula, I'm so happy for you! What bank did you go to?"

"Hennessey."

The smile slipped a little from Marie's face. "What bank?"

Paula drew back. "Hennessey Bank," she repeated. "Why, what's the matter?"

Marie sat down at the table. "And they gave you the loan?"

"Yes," Paula said, beginning to feel anxious. Was there something she wasn't aware of? "What is it?"

Marie stared at her for a long moment, then she burst into laughter. "Oh, Paula, leave it to you!" she finally said between giggles. "Don't you know about Hennessey Bank?"

Paula didn't like to be laughed at, even by a good friend. Indignantly, she said, "Of course I know. Why do you think I went to them? They're an investment bank, aren't they? Well, I convinced them to invest in me. What's wrong with that?"

But Marie just laughed all the harder. Reaching for Paula's hand, she squeezed it delightedly. "Leave it to you!" she said again, through her laughter. "Do you know what they invest in?"

Beginning to feel irritated, Paula said, "Businesses. They invest in businesses! I saw it myself in the paper, and I don't see what's so funny!"

Marie's eyes were twinkling. "I take it you haven't seen the *Daily* today, then."

She hadn't had time to read the paper this morning; she'd been too busy preparing the brilliant speech she had forgotten even before she met John-Henry Hennessey. "No, I haven't," she said. "But I don't see—"

Still laughing, Marie went to fetch her copy. John-Henry had made the paper again, but this time in very good company. With a sinking feeling, Paula saw that handsome face she hadn't been able to get out of her mind since she'd left the bank. Right there, in black and white, was the man she had brazenly asked for a loan with which to start her cookie business. In the photo with Mr. Hennessey was someone named George Copeland, CEO for Digitron Optic, a multimillion-dollar industrial giant that was considering a move to Oklahoma City. The two men were smiling and shaking hands.

Her face flaming, Paula looked up and met her friend's sparkling eyes. Wondering if anyone had ever actually died of sheer embarrassment, she said faintly,

"The article I read just said that he was opening up the bank to new businesses." She swallowed. "I didn't realize..."

Marie giggled again. "You do now," she said.

CHAPTER THREE

THE FIRST THING Paula did when she received the papers confirming her loan was to open a business checking account—at her own bank. She hadn't thought of a name for her cookie store yet, but when the checks came, bearing her name along with the official Business Account printed on them, she was thrilled. The checkbook made it real; for the first time since she'd thought of the idea, she felt she was actually on her way.

The second thing she did was invite her grandmother to a jubilee dinner. Heddy had been in on the plan from the beginning; it was only right that they celebrate together.

"We're going to shoot the works tonight," she told her grandmother in the car on the way to the restaurant. "It's been a long time since we've had a treat, and if everything goes according to plan, it will be a long time until we get another." She laughed excitedly. "I intend to be very busy for the next couple of months!"

Even though Heddy was pleased for Paula, she still worried. "That's what I'm afraid of," she fretted. "If I know you, you're going to work yourself to death."

"No, I won't," Paula said. "I promise."

"I've heard that before. Now, listen to me, Paula Trent. I know how worried you are about money—"

"Not anymore!" Paula said blithely, and once inside the fancy restaurant, she grandly ordered Heddy a prime rib, a cut she loved but never ordered because it was too expensive.

"Oh, Paula! You shouldn't!" Heddy exclaimed, scandalized.

"Why not?" Paula said, impulsively squeezing her grandmother's hand. "You're worth it."

"And so are you," Heddy said, looking a little misty herself. Returning the squeeze, she sat back. "Now. Tell me all about your Mr. Hennessey."

"He's not *my* Mr. Hennessey!" Paula protested immediately, and felt herself blush.

"My, my," Heddy said, smiling. "What's all this about?"

Paula took a sip of water. She didn't want to talk about John-Henry Hennessey, she thought; her feelings about him were too confused. But if she didn't say something, Heddy would get that look, and that would be even worse. Quickly, she launched into an amusing—she hoped—tale about running the gauntlet of that crimson-lipped receptionist, about the clock she had wanted to take a bat to, about that amazing elevator with the carved paneling. Then, because she knew Heddy had never experienced anything like it, either, she told her about the lunch John-Henry had ordered in.

"But only because we weren't finished going over all the details," she assured her amazed grandmother. "Now don't go thinking it means any more than that."

But Heddy wasn't thinking about the two waiters trundling in those linen-covered carts. Her expression all innocence, she murmured, "My, my, I can't imagine. Do you suppose he treats all his clients that way?"

Paula had been wondering that herself. "Of course he does," she said. "He certainly didn't act as if it was anything out of the ordinary."

But his secretary had seemed surprised, she remembered, and felt a tingle. Maybe the gesture had been more significant than she let herself believe, she thought, and then became annoyed with herself. Why was she making such a big deal out of it? She had no reason to think she was anything special to a man like John-Henry Hennessey; until the morning of their appointment, they'd never even met.

But you'd like to see him again, wouldn't you?

The thought came out of nowhere, and she was still wrestling with it when Heddy inadvertently added to her confusion. "I don't know, Paula," Heddy said. "I'll bet he doesn't do that for everyone. You must have impressed him."

Because she found herself wondering how much, Paula decided it was time to change the subject. "I certainly hope so," she said. "After all, the purpose was to make him agree to give me my loan."

"And that's another thing," Heddy said. "Did you see Mr. Hennessey's picture in the paper the other day?"

Paula didn't think she would ever forget that awful moment at Marie's, when her friend showed her the picture in the paper. She should have known that John-Henry Hennesey customarily dealt with clients like Digitron Optical. But if she had known that she wouldn't have had the courage even to walk into the bank, much less ask for a loan.

"Yes, I saw it," she said, remembering yet another mortifying incident. Her cheeks burning, she recalled the misunderstanding that had afforded her an audience with The Hennessey's president in the first place. What a mixup! she thought. After seeing that article in the paper, she realized that John-Henry would never have agreed to see her if he hadn't been under the impression that she represented an entire chain of food stores. She was glad now that everything had turned out so well, but she still felt mortified every time she thought about it.

Heddy was still pondering the subject. "Well, all I can say, Paula," she said, "is that he must surely have been impressed with you and your idea, to grant you a loan just like that. You simply walked in, pretty as you please, and walked out with the money in your hand. Think of that!"

Paula *had* thought of that. In fact, now that Heddy had brought it up, she might as well admit to herself that, ever since she'd seen that article in the paper, she'd thought of little else. Why had Mr. Hennessey loaned her the money? she wondered. She'd gone in with no background and no experience and only a half-baked idea about opening a cookie store. Even after he realized what had happened, John-Henry had not only granted her the loan, but doubled what she had asked for. What should she think of that?

"Paula, dear, you aren't eating," Heddy said. "Don't you like your Dover sole?"

Reminded that someone else had asked her that same question recently, Paula looked down at her plate. She'd ordered the fish because the one at lunch the other day had been so delicious, but this meal wasn't like that other at all, and she pushed the plate away. Had it been the food itself, or the company, that had been so delightful? she wondered. Normally she didn't care for fish at all.

Now she had lost her zest. For some reason, the celebration she'd planned so enthusiastically for tonight had just fallen flat. But because she didn't want to spoil Heddy's good time, she said, "It's fine. I guess I'm more excited than I realized about everything that's happened."

"It has been a turn, hasn't it?" Heddy agreed, finishing the last of her prime rib. Even at her age, she hadn't lost her appetite. Setting her fork down with a satisfied sigh, she said, "So. You still haven't told me what you thought of Mr. Hennessey."

Paula had no intention of telling her too insightful grandmother anything about John-Henry Hennessey. "There's nothing to tell," she said, and determinedly changed the subject. "Do you want dessert?"

Heddy looked surprised. "We just finished our meal. Can we wait a few minutes, or are we in a hurry?"

"No, of course we're not in a hurry," Paula said, annoyed with herself again. "I just thought you'd like to look over the dessert menu. Would you like coffee instead?"

Something gleamed in Heddy's eyes. "Instead of talking about Mr. Hennessey?" she asked, and then shrugged. "Coffee would be fine. What would you like to talk about, then?"

Avoiding her grandmother's eyes, Paula signaled the waiter. Still embarrassed because she'd been a little too obvious, she said, "Let's talk about what you've been doing lately."

"Me?"

"Yes, you. I swear, Grandma, you're never home anymore. Where do you go? What do you do?" Now that she was on a safe subject, Paula could look stern. "You're not going to the track again, are you?"

"The track!" Heddy did her best to look indignant. "Why would I go there? Besides, it's been too cold, or haven't you noticed?"

Paula was not going to let her get away with that. She knew how fond Heddy was of the ponies, and cold weather or not, Remington Park was open nearly all year round. Even when racing wasn't scheduled, the track never shut down completely. Training went on almost all the time, and Paula knew from experience that her grandmother's round little form was a familiar one on the "backside," where the shedrows were. She had found Heddy there many a time when she couldn't find her anywhere else, and even though she felt she had talked herself blue, she knew she hadn't convinced Heddy to stay away.

"I *like* the horses," Heddy would say. "There's no harm in that, is there?"

Paula couldn't argue that point. She'd finally had to accept that the one good thing about it was that Heddy didn't gamble. She rarely spent money on the races; it was enough, Heddy always declared, that she got to watch.

But Paula still didn't like the idea of her little grandma wandering around the racetrack. The people there lived a rough life, and she'd seen for herself how insular that world was, and what kind of people it sometimes attracted. She worried about Heddy; the track wasn't a good place for her.

"Then where have you been lately?" Paula asked, after the coffee had come and they'd ordered a chocolate torte to share for dessert. "It seems that every time I go by your house, or try to call, you're never home." She looked up suddenly. "Don't tell me you've finally decided to drop by that new senior citizen's club I told you about!"

"Senior citizens..." Heddy muttered, as though she'd never heard of the place. Then she brightened and said enthusiastically, "Yes, that's it, but how did you guess? I have been spending a lot of time down at the Center. I've even met several new people."

Paula looked skeptical. Was Heddy just a little too enthusiastic? Deciding not to be so suspicious, she said, "Well, I'm glad. I knew that if you gave it a chance, you'd make some friends."

"Oh, yes, you were right, dear," Heddy said, digging into the torte that had just been served. "My, my, this is delicious. Not as good as one of your cookies, mind, but..." She pushed the plate toward Paula. "That reminds me. Have you decided what you're going to call your store?"

"No, not yet," Paula said, taking a taste of the torte. "This is good, isn't it? Now that I have the loan, I'm going to start looking for a location, and then for the equipment. After that, I've got to convert all my recipes to volume...oh, there's so many things to do." Impulsively she reached across the table and took Heddy's hand again. Her dark eyes with their intriguing amber flecks held her grandmother's face. "I'm going to make the store a success, Grandma," she said. "When I'm through, neither of us are ever going to have to worry about money again. That's why I'm so pleased that you've made new friends. I'm going to be very busy, especially over the next few weeks, and I'm glad you'll have something to do."

"Oh, I'll have something to do, all right, don't worry about me," Heddy said, dropping her eyes. Trying not to look as guilty as she felt, she asked, "Now, do you want the rest of that torte, or can I have it?"

Laughing, Paula pushed the plate toward her. "Here," she said fondly. "It's all yours."

But before Heddy complied, she looked up worriedly. "Promise me one thing, Paula—"

"What's that?"

"That you won't work too hard. I know how stubborn you can be, but no amount of money is worth your health and well-being. We'll get along even if the worst happens. We always have, haven't we?"

Touched, Paula reached out and grasped her grandmother's hand again. "Yes, we have, Grandma," she said softly. "But the worst isn't going to happen. Things are going to be different now. I know it, I can feel it."

TWO WEEKS LATER, Paula wasn't sure what she felt, other than exhaustion. She'd realized she'd been wildly optimistic in thinking she could get the new business off the ground in a month; at the rate she was going, it would take her six times as long.

The first difficulty she encountered was the real estate agent. Carefully she explained what she wanted, and then dutifully followed him around for days, looking at everything from plush new office buildings to vast echoing warehouses where she could hear the scurrying of rats. Finally she decided she hadn't made herself clear enough.

"What I want is a *small* shop," she repeated for what had to be the hundredth time. "It's a new business, and I'm only going to make cookies."

"I understand, I understand," the man said, obviously determined to earn a large commission. He took her to a vacant car wash. With optimism he said, "Maybe you could convert it?"

She gave up at that point, retreating to the newspaper's classified section where she met with even less success. On her own, she hunted down a cobweb-infested office that looked like it hadn't been used in years, then another store that had numerous electric outlets pulled halfway out of the battered walls. In a third place she judged had once been a small market, sagging shelves and freezer cases lay scattered over a cold concrete floor.

Beginning to wonder if she was ever going to find the right place, she stopped wearily at a coffee shop one afternoon after another unsuccessful morning. She wasn't hungry, but she desperately needed a cup of tea. She was staring blankly at the new shopping mall across the street, wondering what she was going to do, when the waitress brought her tea.

"That mall is some place, isn't it?" the girl said, following Paula's glance. "Have you been over there yet?"

Paula shook her head. She hadn't had time to do anything lately but make endless rounds of unsuitable real estate. "No, do they have many good shops?" She wasn't really interested, but it was something to say.

"I'll say!" the waitress exclaimed, her eyes lighting up. "When it's done, it's going to be the biggest shopping center in Oklahoma City—maybe the entire state."

Paula doubted that, but she smiled politely. Then she realized what the girl had said, and asked, "It's not finished yet?"

"Oh, no. There's lots of empty spaces where shops are supposed to be. They got boards and everything up to keep people out." The girl shook her head dolefully. "'Course, who'd be interested, anyway? I just wished they'd've put in a Macy's, you know? Then we could have some of those clothes you see in magazines right close to home. Wouldn't that be somethin'?"

Paula agreed that it would be, but her mind was somewhere else. The shopping center had taken on a new significance, and she quickly finished her tea. Suddenly energized, she left the coffee shop and crossed to the mall. It took her some time, but she finally found the manager's office tucked away in an alcove. The man inside, who introduced himself as Albert Galvin, beamed when she explained what she wanted, and immediately offered to take her on a personal tour.

"You're just in time," he said. "We have one unit—" she had already noticed he called them units instead of store or shop spaces "—available. It's still in the first stages of construction, of course, but before we rent, we finish the walls, hook up the power, that type of thing. We don't do much more because those details depend on who wants what when they rent, don't they? Now, what kind of store did you have in mind, Miss Trent?"

"A cookie shop."

"A cookie shop?" he echoed, stopping so abruptly that she nearly ran into him.

They were walking through the mall, which was already crowded with shoppers, some loaded down with packages, others who had obviously come just to look. Paula had to admit it was a sight: even though some stores still remained dark, the places that were open were doing a brisk trade, big grand-opening banners still festooned across the windows. The entire plaza, in fact, seemed to be bustling with activity and blazing with light, and as she looked around, she immediately saw all sorts of possibilities.

Trying not to betray her eagerness, she said, "Yes, a cookie shop. I intend to bake and sell fresh cookies." She hesitated, crossing her fingers behind her back. She'd already decided the mall was perfect; she couldn't bear it if there was a reason she couldn't rent space. "Why, is there a problem with that?"

"A problem?" he repeated, and then shook his head. "No, no, of course not. In fact, it will be a nice change from the usual fast-food restaurants we already have in place. I guess I was just a little surprised."

"Why?"

"Well, if you'll pardon my saying so, you seemed much too attractive to be spending your time in a kitchen. As stylish as you are, I was sure you had a boutique in mind."

Stylish? Wondering if he was making a pass at her, Paula glanced down at herself. As always on these treks to find store space, she wasn't wearing anything special: today she was wearing a coat, a simple skirt and sweater and flat shoes. She didn't look anything like the woman who had gone to John-Henry Hennessey's office two weeks ago and asked for a loan. Then, she had worn her best dress.

He had looked at her appreciatively, she remembered, and felt flushed again, as she always did whenever she thought of John-Henry Hennessey. She'd gone over that interview so many times since. She suddenly realized that if someone were to come up to her right now and ask her to describe the shopping mall manager without looking at him again she'd draw a complete blank. But she could remember every detail about John-Henry—how blue his eyes were, how thick and black his hair. She even remembered the way he tilted his head toward her when she spoke, as though he didn't want to miss a word of what she was saying.

And then there was that smile, the one that spread slowly across his handsome face, lighting his eyes with a devilish look that made her realize there was more to John-Henry Hennessey than she'd first supposed....

Abruptly she realized that Albert Galvin was giving her an expectant look. Blushing, she willed away her memories of John-Henry. She'd thought about him too often these past weeks; sometimes she wondered if the real reason she was in such a rush to find store space was so she'd have an excuse to make another appointment with him to report on her progress.

"Thank you for those kind words, Mr. Galvin," she said, trying to remember just what he said. Something about a boutique, she recalled, just in time. "But cookies are my interest, I'm afraid. Now do you think we might take a look at that last . . . er . . . unit?"

Galvin beamed again. "Certainly, certainly. But I warn you, it's just unfinished space right now. Not too impressive, I'm afraid."

It wasn't impressive at all. But it was at the very end of the plaza, and even though it was tucked under a beam, it did have a back door to the outside, affording easy access. The rest of the mall was locked up at night, with a security guard patrolling, so the shopkeepers on the ground floor had an advantage; they could slip in and out when they pleased, instead of waiting to be let in the front door.

"I know it's not in the best location, but it *is* almost four hundred square feet," he told her proudly, holding up the tarp that blocked the entrance from the rest of the mall.

Inside, Paula peered into gloom. Long and narrow, the rectangular room looked murky with no lights and the plastering unfinished. Dust was everywhere; a stream of motes disturbed by her entrance swam in a shaft of light that came in from outside. The place definitey did not look promising.

Then she was annoyed with herself. Had she expected everything to be ready, the ovens and counters and lights in place? Galvin had told her she was to provide those things, and if she was to do that, she had better decide quickly. This particular space seemed to be the only possibility in the entire city and unless she wanted to sell cookies door-to-door, or set up a stand in front of the Capitol building, she'd better commit herself to this place before someone else signed the lease.

"I think this will do nicely," she said, and then tried not to gasp when she found out how high the rent was.

"And you'll have to sign a lease, too," Galvin said, obviously not noticing her distress—or pretending not to. "Will that be satisfactory?"

She was still in shock over the rent, but she couldn't let the place go, not now. "A lease?" she said faintly. "Oh, of course."

Beaming again, he took her arm. "Then shall we go back to my office? I've got all the forms there."

It took less than ten minutes to sign her life away. By the time she finally got back to the car, Galvin's cheery, "Welcome to the plaza!" still ringing in her ears, she was so agitated she nearly dropped the keys. Collapsing on the front seat, she looked at the sheaf of papers clutched in her damp hand. Lease agreement, merchant's agreements, building code standards, standard building agreements. There were so many papers she wondered how she would ever get through all the fine print. She knew she should have read everything on the lease before she signed it, or at least taken it to a lawyer, but there hadn't been time. She'd been too afraid someone else would take the space to waste precious hours hunting up an attorney.

That was a situation she should rectify, she thought, starting the car. And she should probably look into hiring an accountant, as well. She didn't know anything about keeping business tax records, or even how to set up the books for the store. When she first thought up the idea of selling cookies for a living, it had seemed so simple. She hadn't realized, even with all the research she had done, just how much was involved in setting up a business.

But, she smiled, she finally had her location, and tomorrow she would start looking for equipment. Things were moving at last, and she was eager to begin. There was no doubt in her mind, no regrets. She was on her way, and she was going to be a success.

"DARLING," Henrietta Hennessey said, holding out her cup. "Would you please pour me some more coffee? Oh, and add just a dollop of brandy, if you wouldn't mind. There's a chill in the air tonight, don't you think?"

"There is indeed," John-Henry agreed with a smile as he took the cup from his mother's hand. Henrietta always asked for a single "dollop" of brandy, whether there was a chill in the air or not. It was her one luxury, her little vice, and she only allowed herself a single shot. It had been a ritual between them for years, long before John-Henry had moved into an apartment of his own, and sometimes he wondered who poured for her now that he wasn't here all the time.

Probably Henrietta herself, he thought with another fond smile. His mother disliked summoning servants to do what she could very well do herself; as she said, when the time came that she could no longer drive herself, or dress herself that would be the day she'd walk into the woods and never come out.

But she didn't mind asking her son to fetch her coffee and brandy on occasion, and she smiled up at him when he returned with her cup.

"Thank you, dear," she said. Now in her sixties, she was still an imposing woman, handsome rather than beautiful, with strong features John-Henry had inherited, along with her indomitable will. She had always been proud of her son, even in those "other days," as she thought of them, when she had despaired of him ever settling down.

Of course, she hadn't expected him to settle down so thoroughly, she mused, giving him a covert glance. Oh, the irony. She'd spent all that time when he was younger fretting about him, but surely there had to be some middle ground.

Remembering the call she had received the other day from one of the bank's officers, she wondered if the pendulum was at last starting to swing the other way. Despite herself, she had felt a twinge of alarm at the thought, but had quelled it until she found out for certain, herself. Jefferson Evers, the man who had called, had always been a prig, and in spite of the fact that she still held the title of chairman, or chairwoman, or chairperson, whatever it was these days, John-Henry ran the bank. That had been their understanding when he took over the president's chair, and she had no intention—or desire—to challenge that agreement at this late date.

But still, it didn't hurt to ask, and so she said carefully, "Why don't you sit down, darling, and tell me what's going on at the bank."

John-Henry had come for dinner, and as always on these occasions, they had both dressed. It was a habit begun long ago when Henrietta married Claude Hennessey, and in honor of his memory, they still upheld the formality. Tonight, Henrietta was wearing a pale mauve silk dress with a white fichu, an old-fashioned touch that somehow suited her perfectly. John-Henry was dressed in a dark suit with an appropriately sober tie. Obeying his mother's request, he selected a chair opposite the couch and said, "All right, which one called you?"

Henrietta stared at him for a moment, and then laughed. For one so formidable-looking, with her white hair piled high on her head, and her old-fashioned dress, her laughter sounded girlish, happy. But then, she was always happy, with her son.

"How did you know?" she asked.

But when John-Henry gave her his raised-eyebrow look, she smiled again and surrendered.

"Oh, all right, if you must know, it was Jefferson."

"And he's in a state about a small loan I granted several weeks ago, is that right?"

"Well, you know Jefferson."

"Yes," John-Henry said, not concealing his distaste. "What I don't know is how he found out. Not that it's a secret, but sometimes I wonder if he sneaks back into the bank every night to review everyone's files. Including mine."

Henrietta laughed again. "I wouldn't be surprised," she said, and gave him a look of her own. "You said it wasn't a secret?"

"Of course not. How ridiculous!"

"Then you can tell me what it's all about."

John-Henry looked exasperated. "It's not about anything," he insisted. "For heaven's sake, Mother, it was just a small loan. Hardly enough even for Jefferson to get into a lather about."

"Oh, yes, I quite agree," Henrietta said, taking a sip of her coffee. "Still, it was a departure from the usual policy, wasn't it?"

"Yes, it was," John-Henry agreed, abruptly getting to his feet and going over to the window. Pulling aside the heavy draperies, he stared into the night.

Behind him, Henrietta was silent, and he wanted to turn and tell her—what? He knew his mother well, and understood that she was wondering if his behavior somehow signaled a return to the "old ways," as she persisted in calling that time of his youth. She had suffered then, he couldn't deny it, and he wanted to reassure her now, but he didn't know how. He still wasn't sure what had happened in his office that day with Paula Trent; he couldn't say now why he had granted her that loan.

It wasn't the money, of course; in the greater scheme of things, an amount that small wouldn't affect the bank one way or the other. In fact, if he had been so inclined, he could have written her a personal check and not missed the money.

But that wasn't the point, and he knew it. The point was that The Hennessey did not usually deal with loans to small business ventures. Many other banks in town existed for that purpose. So, why had he agreed?

Remembering Paula Trent in his office that day—as he had done every day since—he decided it was because she had impressed him, not only with her audacity in approaching him in the first place, but with her obvious desire to make a success of her idea. She had done her research thoroughly. No matter what he had asked her, she'd had her facts in hand. She wasn't afraid of hard work, she had said, and he believed her. She obviously knew how easy it was for new small businesses to fail, for she had cited statistics. She hadn't been frightened by that; on the contrary, she was determined to succeed despite the odds. Was that what had convinced him?

Or had it been those dark eyes, he wondered, or that beautiful smile?

GAZING AT HER SON, Henrietta saw something in his face she hadn't seen for a long time. Did the expression she saw there indicate another swing of the pendulum? She closed her eyes, wondering if she was strong enough for that. She and John-Henry had come so far since those early days when all they'd had was each other and that little house on the other side of town, she thought with a pang. They had been through so much, from rags to riches, as the saying went, but was she prepared for still another change?

Then she looked at John-Henry again and told herself she had to be ready. Despite everything that had gone on before, he had not been happy for the past five years, and she realized suddenly that she had unconsciously been hoping for something to happen. She loved her son and she desperately wanted him to be happy.

"John-Henry?" she said softly.

It was time to leave, and John-Henry turned from the window, answering her earlier question. "I don't know why, Mother. I guess I thought it was about time we branched out a bit. The bank's been too stuffy lately, too out of touch, don't you think?"

The bank, my dear? Henrietta thought, and decided there was no point in telling him what she really thought, not so soon. Time will tell, she reflected, and smiled to herself.

"I do indeed, darling," she murmured, and presented her cheek for his goodbye kiss.

EARLIER, OUT AT the same shedrow behind the racetrack, Heddy and Otis shared a bag of cookies Paula had made. With Fernando's help, their horse had been made comfortable for the night. He now stood inside his box, all four legs wrapped in brightly colored stall bandages, contentedly munching from his pail of oats. Whistling under his breath, Otis gave the horse a last pat, and then joined Heddy on the bale of hay where she was sitting. Reaching inside the bag, she extracted a cookie and gave it to him.

"Well, what do you think, Heddy?" he asked, chewing with appreciation. Paula did make good cookies, he thought and winked at his partner. "Still no regrets?"

"Just one," Heddy said, her eyes on the horse. It had become a joke with them, and they smiled at each other. But when Otis helped himself to another cookie, Heddy's smile faded. She had something she needed to talk to him about, and now was as good a time as any.

"We've had No Regrets about two weeks, right, Otis?" she said, leading into it.

Otis thought. "Yes, that's right. 'Bout two weeks." He looked at the horse and grinned. "But he's comin' along, Heddy. He's comin' along."

"Yes, yes, I know," she said, although she hadn't really seen much improvement. To her eyes, the horse still favored that right hind. But if Otis said he was improving, then he was improving. As much as it hurt her pride to admit it, Otis had a better eye than she did. But then, she told herself, he should. He had earned his living training horses, while she just loved them.

But that was beside the point. As proud as she felt inside—so proud!—that she was part owner of a racehorse, she was a practical woman, and it was time to face practicalities. Otis's finances weren't in any better shape than her own; they both had only Social Security, and these days, oats cost the earth. And stabling. And just about everything else. Fernando's wages weren't much, but he had to be paid somehow, and more expenses would arise once the horse was ready for training. It was obvious that she and Otis couldn't handle all these themselves; they had to do something, but what?

Otis blithely assumed that something would come along, but Heddy wouldn't trust her entire future to the whims of fickle fate. The Lord might help those who helped themselves, she reflected, but only after they got off their behinds and went out and rustled up a little work.

Like Paula, she thought, and felt proud again. Paula hadn't waited for something to come along; she'd gone right out and grabbed it. Now she and Otis had to do the same. But how? And what?

"How's Paula doin' these days?" Otis asked, unconsciously echoing her thoughts. He'd heard all about the cookie store, and knew how proud Heddy was of her granddaughter. He also knew from Heddy how Paula would react if she found out too soon about No Regrets. He shook his head. He would never understand Paula's feelings about the track; he'd been around the backside nearly all his life, and it hadn't hurt him.

But he respected what he knew of Paula, and he was sure that, if they ever met, he'd like her. And besides, he thought, dipping again into the bag Heddy had brought, she sure made good cookies.

"Paula is doing just fine, Otis," Heddy said, momentarily diverted. "She told me that she found a location for the store, and now she's going to be out looking for equipment." She shook her head admiringly. "That girl sure has get-up-and-go, all right."

"Sort of reminds me of someone else I know," Otis said, with a wink. "Paula is a real pistol. I'll never forget how you told me that she just walked into that there Hennessey Bank, breezy as you please, and asked the president for a loan."

"That she did."

"Maybe we ought to do the same thing."

Otis had been joking, but Heddy suddenly looked at him as though he'd stumbled on the mother lode. "What did you say?"

He saw that gleam in her eyes and put up his hands. "Oh, now, Heddy, I was just flappin' my jaw. Let's just think about it, all right?"

But Heddy *was* thinking about it, and the more she thought, the more she decided that it could be the answer to all their problems. Paula had told her how nice John-Henry Hennessey was; hadn't he even sent out for lunch so they could sit there and talk? She'd thought at the time the man obviously had an eye for a good business proposition, and she suddenly decided that she had one for him.

"Heddy?" Otis said. "You're not thinking what I think you're thinking, are you? You're not going to go to that banker and ask for a loan, are you?"

"Of course not," Heddy said scornfully. Sliding off the bale of hay, she straightened her skirt and reached for her purse. "I'm going to do something much better."

Alarmed, Otis said, "What?"

Heddy had that gleam in her eye again. "Just leave everything to me," she said. And with Otis looking anxiously after her, she set off for home, looking for all the world like a little biddy bustling off to set the henhouse right.

CHAPTER FOUR

JOHN-HENRY HAD BEEN at his desk for three hours when he heard the commotion in the other office. He had received word from Digitron the night before that the company was looking for suitable premises in Oklahoma City for their main office, but as elated as he was over the coup, he still had other business to attend to.

The drop in oil prices that had begun in the early '80s had triggered an alarming number of bank failures all over the state. The great Penn Square Bank right here in Oklahoma City had closed its doors in July of 1982, a bleak day in Oklahoma's modern history, John-Henry knew. Even worse, a total of thirty-eight banks had failed in the four years that followed. The economic outlook became so grim that the state legislature had passed a bill allowing out-of-state banking organizations to acquire Oklahoma banks. John-Henry had to concede that the bill might help the state's banking system by bringing in new capital, but that didn't mean he liked the idea. When he had taken over at The Hennessey, he had felt it was the responsibility of the resident banking community to do everything in its power to improve Oklahoma's economy. He was convinced that if they all pulled together, they would not need outside help.

Amused at how fiercely protective he had become since returning home from all those travels abroad with Camilla—and how provincial his outlook was becoming—he smiled at himself and decided he didn't care. This was his home. He'd come a long way since those early days on the other side of town, he thought. He had vowed, even at that young age, to make enough money someday so that his mother would never have to cry again. In the end, Claude had rescued them from that life, but John-Henry hadn't forgotten those hard times. Sometimes he thought childhood memories affected the decisions he made for the bank, especially any that could help put Oklahoma back on its financial feet again. He had long ago determined that for the state to prosper, as it once had, it was vital to entice new businesses to move in—businesses other than out-of-state banks. His success with Digitron was just one of what he hoped would be a long string of companies coming to Oklahoma.

With that in mind, he had in front of him a prospectus on Milwaukee-Waukesha, a Wisconsin-based national tool company, as well as files on half a dozen other big firms, scattered around the country. He was totally absorbed in financial analyses and balance sheets when he heard his secretary's raised voice. Surprised, he glanced up. He couldn't remember Mrs. Adams ever raising her voice; something must be wrong.

He was halfway to his feet when his office door burst open. A small, round, white-haired woman stood on the threshold, indignantly clutching her purse, as though his secretary, who was quickly coming around her desk in pursuit, might snatch it from her grasp.

"Are you John-Henry Hennessey?" the little woman demanded.

John-Henry was so astonished, he just nodded. He had never seen her before; what could she possibly want with him?

"I'm sorry, Mr. Hennessey," his secretary gasped from the doorway. "I tried to tell her, but—"

His visitor gave Mrs. Adams a withering glance before turning back to him. "She tried to tell me I needed an appointment," she said, as though she'd never heard such a ridiculous thing in her life.

"Well, it is customary—" he started to say, but then broke off as the little woman straightened her hat and marched right in as though he hadn't said anything. Fascinated, he watched her sashay right up to his desk, where she leaned forward to scrutinize him.

"I told her that a man who was capable of running a bank was certainly able to decide for himself whom he wanted to see," she said, squinting up at him. "Was I right, or not?"

His secretary had followed the old lady into the room. "Mr. Hennessey—" she began.

Trying not to laugh, John-Henry said, "It's all right, Mrs. Adams."

His visitor turned toward the other woman. "You see?" she said, smiling graciously. "I told you it would be all right. My, my, such a fuss about nothing."

Mrs. Adams looked in his direction again, but John-Henry, his lips twitching in an effort not to smile, gestured that he would handle the situation. Looking a little grim, the secretary backed out and closed the door behind her.

Still trying not to laugh, John-Henry gestured his visitor to the chair in front of the desk. Further amused when she gave him a queenly nod before sitting down, he took his own place.

"I'm sorry," he said. "I don't believe I...er...I don't believe we've met."

Perching her purse on her lap, his visitor settled herself back. "No, we haven't," she said promptly, and held out a plump little hand. "My name is Heddy Bascomb."

Deciding that it really wasn't necessary to introduce himself, John-Henry solemnly stood and leaned over the desk to complete the handshake. "Pleased to meet you," he said, and sat down again, thinking it was true. Whoever she was, she was certainly a refreshing change from the people with whom he customarily dealt. He suddenly remembered he'd felt the same way about Paula Trent. Wondering why he should think of Paula just now, he glanced at Heddy again. Was it his imagination or was there a resemblance between Paula and his engaging little visitor? Annoyed with himself, he decided it must be coincidence. Lately, it seemed almost everything reminded him of Paula.

Heddy leaned forward. "I've come today because I have a proposition for you," she said. "One I know a businessman like you won't be able to resist."

Again he fought the impulse to laugh. A proposition for him? He wasn't sure what to say to that. "I . . . see," he said finally, hiding a smile.

"No, you don't," she said. "But you will. I've heard you're a fair man, and I know you recognize a good deal when you see one."

"And how do you know that?"

"I have my ways," she replied airily. "But I don't want to prejudice you, not just yet."

Intrigued, he sat back. Who was this little old lady? he wondered. She couldn't have wandered away from a home somewhere; she seemed far too sharp for that. Nor did she seem to be one of those sad, mistrustful old women who suddenly decided the money they had been stuffing into the mattress all these years would be safer in the bank.

But she couldn't be serious about having a proposition for him. What would she have that he would possibly want? Was she in the right place, or was she just confused, after all?

"Well, thank you for the compliment—" he began, and was hushed when Heddy waved an imperious hand.

"Oh, it's no compliment," she said. "I'm too old to waste time trying to butter people up—not that I ever found much use for false flattery anyway. No, I speak the truth as I see it, and as I said, I know you to be a fair man. I figured you'd at least give a listen to what I had to say."

Really intrigued now, he said, "Then I won't disappoint you. What is your proposition?"

For the first time, she seemed a little uncertain. Then her confidence returned in a rush. Leaning forward again, her eyes bright blue behind her glasses, she looked him straight in the eye and said, "I own a famous racehorse. And I'm prepared to give you half interest—under certain conditions, that is."

He nearly burst out laughing. But he realized in time that she was quite serious, and he couldn't offend her. He didn't want to hurt her feelings, but a racehorse?

"I...see," he said, trying to control himself. Even so, a chuckle escaped him, and he had to cover it with a cough. Clearing his throat, he said, "Perhaps you should tell me a little more."

"Gladly," she said, as though she'd expected him to ask for more details. "Now I know you're familiar with horses—"

That was a surprise. "How do you know that?"

Suddenly she seemed a little abashed. "I looked you up in the paper," she confessed. "You know, they have those things at the library, those...those micro... micro..."

"Microfiche?" he supplied, fascinated.

She nodded. "Yes. Well, they have all the back editions of the papers on them, did you know that? And when I told the librarian what I wanted, there you were, right in black and white." She lifted an eyebrow in a hoity-toity gesture. "The society pages, no less."

He frowned. "That was in my younger days," he said. "*Much* younger."

She gave him a conspiratorial smile. "You're not so fond of remembering those days, eh? Well, you cut a handsome figure, if I do say so myself."

"Thank you," he said, not sure if he ought to be flattered by the compliment. He hated to be reminded of that reckless time; just when he thought he had put it behind him, something like this would crop up, and he'd be faced with it all over again. Deciding to correct any misconceptions those often exaggerated—but not by much—society accounts might have given her, he said, "I'm afraid the papers only give part of the story—"

"Oh, you're trying to tell someone who's old enough to be your grandmother not to believe everything she reads, is that it?" she said, cackling. She gave him a sly glance. "Or are you trying to say you've had no experience with horses?"

She was too sharp for him; he conceded defeat by lifting his hand. "You've found me out," he said, smiling. "I admit I do have some experience with horses—but hunters and jumpers, not racehorses." He paused, gazing directly at her. "Besides, I've been told racing's a fool's game."

Her blue eyes snapped. "That's true," she said tartly. "But only if you're a fool to begin with." Then she squinted at him. "I'm not a fool, and I don't think you are, either. But are you saying the answer's no?"

He should have ended it right there, told her he was sorry, but he wasn't interested. But was that true? Despite himself, he had to admit he was intrigued by the idea.

Still, he had no business getting involved with her scheme, whatever it was. So many other matters claimed his attention that he just didn't have time for anything else.

But how much time would it take? he asked himself. After all, he hadn't even listened to her proposition; shouldn't he at least grant her the courtesy of hearing what she had to say?

"I'm not refusing—just yet," he began. "But I—"

"Good," she said briskly, anticipating him. "Now, I know you're a busy man, so I won't take much more of your time." She smiled sunnily at him just then, making him realize that she must have been a beautiful woman when she was younger. But why did she remind him of someone—and who was it?

Before he could decide, she became serious again, wagging her finger at him for emphasis. "Now, my partner and I have worked out all the details," she said, "and here's what we propose. We'll give you half interest in No Regrets—"

"No regrets?"

"The horse, the horse. That's his name."

"Oh, I see," he said, hiding another smile. "Well. No Regrets. And do you have any?"

She didn't appreciate his attempt at a joke. "No, we don't," she said crisply. "And you won't, either, if you come into partnership with us."

"And why should I do that?"

"Because Otis—that's my partner—and I are offering you a good deal. The horse can run, Mr. Hennessey," she said, and then added reluctantly, "Well, he will once he's well. But Otis says—"

John-Henry held up a hand. Obviously they'd come to the crux of the matter. "Might I inquire," he said delicately, "just what is wrong with the horse?"

She bristled. "Did I say anything was wrong with him?"

"You said, once he's well. Presumably that means he isn't quite . . . fit . . . at the moment."

Her cheeks turned slightly pink. "Boy, you don't miss a trick, do you?" she muttered, and sat up a little straighter. Looking him in the eye, she said, "I'll be honest with you, Mr. Hennessey. At the moment, I have to confess that the horse is . . . is a tad lame. But it's only temporary, I assure you," she added hastily. "Otis says that once that suspensory ligament heals, and the gravel pops, No Regrets will be as good as new."

John-Henry sat back. Ah, so now they had a horse with not one, but two, health problems, he thought. Did he really want to get into this?

As though Heddy had read his mind, she said, "I know how it sounds, Mr. Hennessey, but before you decide, why don't you come out and look at the horse. Talk to Otis—or the veterinarian."

"Well, I—"

Heddy leaned forward. Her eyes suddenly looked a little bleak behind her glasses, and her mouth trembled just slightly when she said, "We're not trying to put anything over on you, Mr. Hennessey—honest. It's just—"

She stopped. After a moment, she collected herself. He was touched. He could see how much this meant to her, but she wouldn't allow herself to beg, and he respected that. He waited until she became her brisk self again.

"This is the deal, Mr. Hennessey," she said. "Otis and I are prepared to give you a fifty percent interest in the horse, and half of all his future earnings if, in return, you pay all expenses." She sat back, her spine ramrod straight. "You can't ask for a better deal than that."

At that moment, seeing her fierce courage, the pride that reminded him so poignantly of someone else who had come to his office a few weeks ago, John-Henry knew he was doomed to buy into a racehorse that would probably never run successfully again, no matter how much tender loving care it received. But as he had so painfully learned in the past, there were more important things than returns on investments. How could he refuse this determined old woman when it meant so little to him, and obviously so very much to her?

Coming to the decision that had been inevitable all along, he realized that to accept her proposal too quickly would make her suspicious and hurt her pride. So he pretended to consider.

"I'm not worried about the gravel," he said. "But how bad is that ligament?"

Heddy looked at him a moment, then she threw back her head and laughed like a girl, in sheer delight. "I knew it, I knew it!" she crowed. "You're a horseman, as well as a shrewd businessman! Oh, my granddaughter was right!"

"Your granddaughter?" he said.

But Heddy didn't respond to that for the moment, eager to answer his question about No Regrets. "Otis doesn't think the ligament is the problem at all," she said. "It's that little bit of sand right up there inside the hoof. Once that pops, the horse'll be as good as new."

That said, she snapped open her purse and produced a slightly grubby piece of paper, which she placed on his desk. "That's the contract Otis and I drew up," she said proudly, smoothing out the crumpled edge with a loving touch, brushing at a smudge of dirt before she looked up and saw John-Henry's expression. "Oh, I know it's not one of them fancy documents all those expensive lawyers write out, but it's legal all the same, and when it comes to legalities, it doesn't matter whether they're written out on a hay bale or a desk, does it? The agreement is what matters, isn't that right?"

"It is, indeed," John-Henry said solemnly, hiding another smile. He couldn't help laughing inside at the thought of what some of his bank officers would say if they saw such a document.

"Otis and I have already signed," Heddy pointed out, obviously anxious for him to put his signature below theirs, before he changed his mind.

"Then I guess it's up to me," he said, and started to reach for a pen. He paused. It didn't really matter to him, but knowing she'd be suspicious if he didn't ask, he said thoughtfully, "Maybe before I rush into this partnership, we should discuss how much all this is going to cost."

"I knew you were going to ask that," Heddy said with satisfaction. She reached into her purse again and pulled out another grimy document. When she handed it across to him, John-Henry saw that it contained a minutely itemized list of every possible expense. Surprised, he saw one line with something about a bag of cookies.

"Cookies?" he asked.

Heddy turned pink again. "Oh, that," she said. "I tried to tell that old fool Otis that animals shouldn't have sweets, but he discovered that No Regrets just loves my granddaughter's cookies. Now he's talkin' about using them as a training aid, and he insisted we list them as an expense. It doesn't mean nothin'."

"Your granddaughter makes cookies?" he said.

Heddy looked at him in surprise. "Why, sure she does. You know that. You gave her the loan to start her cookie business."

"Paula Trent is your granddaughter?" he exclaimed, so startled he nearly dropped the pen with which he had just signed his name. Now he knew why Heddy seemed so familiar. Even though there had to be at least fifty years between Heddy and Paula, the family resemblance was there; all he'd had to do was look.

"Well, of course," Heddy said, and then looked embarrassed. "Didn't I mention that?"

He started to laugh. "No," he said. "You didn't."

"Oh," she said meekly. "I was sure I had."

Now he was really amused. "Is that why you were so sure I'd agree to your proposition?"

"I wasn't sure at all!" she protested, and then saw his skeptical look. "Well, I wasn't positive," she amended. "And it really didn't have anything to do with that. It was more your name that convinced me."

"My name?"

"Why, yes. With a namesake like yours, you'd have to be interested in racing."

"A namesake like mine..." he repeated, and when comprehension dawned, he laughed again. It had been a long time since he'd followed racing, but now he remembered. "You don't mean that racehorse, John Henry!" he said. "You're comparing me to him?"

"John Henry was Horse of the Year three times, Mr. Hennessey," Heddy said severely, as she stood. "*Three times.* And one of those was when he was eleven years old! Even as a gelding, he was unbeatable, unstoppable. And when they tried to retire him, he was so unhappy at home they had to bring him back. There was a horse born to run, Mr. Hennessey—born to win. A champion, through and through. I don't think you can be in any better company than that!"

Properly put in his place, he said, "You're absolutely right. I hadn't thought of it quite like that, I confess."

She gave him a brisk nod, as though he should have. "Well, then."

He went with her to the door. "Now that I'm a partner, do you think it's possible for me to visit No Regrets?" he asked. "I admit, I'm curious about a cookie-loving racehorse. What does...your granddaughter think of that? It would make a good advertisement."

Heddy turned quickly to him. "Oh, Paula doesn't know about No Regrets," she said swiftly.

He was surprised. "She doesn't? Why, is it a secret?"

"No, no, it's a surprise," Heddy said, her cheeks growing pinker by the second. "Paula doesn't...I mean, she's not really interested in horses, and she...she's been so busy with the cookie store that I...that I didn't want to bother her. I've been saving it for a surprise, you understand, don't you?"

No, he didn't. "Well, I—"

"Promise me you won't say anything if you see her," she said anxiously. "I'd hate to have the surprise ruined, don't you see?"

He hesitated. Was there something more here than she was disclosing? "But you are going to tell her, aren't you?"

"Yes, yes, of course," she said, not looking him directly in the eye. "We'll tell her when the time is right and she . . . she's not so busy." She looked up at him again. "Promise now. Paula loves surprises, and we wouldn't want to spoil this one, would we?"

Thinking that it was definitely going to be an eye-opener to Paula to find out her grandmother owned a racehorse, John-Henry gave his promise. He didn't see what harm it would do, and by then he was more interested in other things, anyway.

"How is Paula?" he asked casually.

Heddy was relieved to be off the subject of surprises. "Oh, she's fine. In fact, she's already got a store location in that new mall. You know, the one that's just a few blocks from here?"

"So close," he said thoughtfully, and then jerked himself back. "That's a good location, I think."

Heddy gave him an inscrutable look. "Yes it is, isn't it?"

John-Henry wasn't sure he liked that look. As he had learned, even in this brief encounter, Paula's grandmother saw quite a lot with those bright blue eyes. Quickly he said, "When do you think she'll be ready to open the store?"

"Oh, my, I couldn't say. There's so much more to do, she tells me. Since getting the space, she's been spending every waking minute trying to find the right equipment, and that's just the beginning." She paused, then looked up innocently. "Hasn't she called to tell you about her progress?"

"Oh, no, and I didn't expect her to," he said. "But I couldn't help wondering."

"Naturally."

"After all, it takes great effort and dedication to start up a new business."

"Yes, it does."

"When I granted her the loan, I didn't ask for a progress report."

"No, of course not."

"But when you see her again, you...you might suggest casually that she let me know how things are going."

"I'll do that," she said.

Deciding it was time to end the strange little duet they were playing, he said, "I try to keep track of all my clients. It's good business."

She was suddenly serious. "I know Paula is grateful for your help, and Otis and I are, too. Please come to visit No Regrets." She glanced around, then looked back at him with a smile. "We might not have a fancy office like this one, but the coffeepot is always on—" the smile became mischievous "—and we usually have a cookie or two lying around."

After she had gone, John-Henry went to the window and stared out. Heddy had thanked him for his help, but he felt he was the one who should be thankful. Without effort, it seemed—without even realizing it—Heddy Bascomb and her granddaughter were already making a difference in his life. Wondering why that was, he sat down at his desk again and pulled his work toward him. But as he stared at the papers he'd spread out, he wasn't concentrating on financial analyses or projections of future stock. Instead, he was thinking of a racehorse that liked cookies...and of the young woman who made them.

THE YOUNG WOMAN who made the cookies was at that moment up to her elbows in dirt, grease, cobwebs and dust in a barn loft outside the city of Tulsa. Piled high in every direction were abandoned and forgotten pieces of equipment of every description; the loft was so full that she felt as though she'd stumbled into the elephant graveyard of machines by mistake. Sighing, she wiped her forearm across her forehead and plunged down another aisle. She'd read about the restaurant equipment sale in the paper and had come with hopes of finding an oven or two for the store. From the looks of things, however, this stuff—stoves and counters and pots and and pans and heaven knew what else—had been old around the turn of the century. Wasn't she ever going to find an oven?

Then she spotted one—or what looked like one. It was shoved into a dark corner of the loft, piled high with some kind of rope the width of her wrist, a mound of chain with links that resembled sausages, and what looked like vacuum tubes from an old-fashioned radio. She wouldn't have seen it at all if a shaft of sunlight hadn't pierced the holes in the roof just then, spotlighting that area amid dancing dust notes. The stove didn't look all that promising, but she climbed over yet another pile of junk that had fallen into the makeshift aisle, pushed aside a stack of yellowed, curled newspapers almost as tall as she was, and was just reaching for her prize when the papers toppled and rained down all over her.

A cloud of dust immediately rose, and she started to sneeze. But now that she had found something that at least resembled a stove, nothing was going to deter her, so she put one hand to her mouth, kicked the newspapers aside, and practically flung herself over what was left of the pile.

Now the stove was right there in front of her, but how would she ever get it out? She reached out and gave the chain links an experimental pull. There was an ominous rattling that should have warned her, but she was tired and frustrated from clambering around up here by herself, and she didn't want to leave empty-handed after coming so far. She'd been searching for a stove for weeks now, and this was the most promising one she'd seen.

"So...go to it," she muttered to herself, and started tugging.

Nothing happened, so she tugged harder, putting all her weight into it. This time she was rewarded by a horrible screeching sound as the metal stove bottom slid an inch or two along the scarred wooden floor. Grimacing at the awful noise, she bit her lip and pulled with all her might.

The stove handle came off so suddenly she didn't have time to catch her balance. Flying backward, she hit something hard, bounced off, and fell onto the pile of newspapers. Grunting with surprise, she tried to get up, but her foot slid on the slippery stack, and her feet went out from under her again. Arms flailing, she slid a few feet along the floor, and finally came to rest, incredibly, against the stove, still holding the handle.

"Well, I'll be..." she panted, staring at her hand.

"Excuse me," a voice said. "Do you need some help?"

She'd thought she was alone. Startled, she tried to get to her feet, but the treacherous newspapers were still underfoot, and she nearly hit the deck again before a hand reached out and steadied her.

"Thanks," she gasped, looking into a pair of brown eyes under a short, almost military haircut.

"My pleasure," the young man said, and grinned. "The name's Rodney Quinn."

"Paula Trent."

"I take it you're trying to get to that stove?"

Paula glared at the oven. "I was," she said, gingerly rubbing her hip. "But I'm starting to think it's not worth it."

He gave the stove a cursory glance. "It's not," he said. "It's just a piece of junk."

She looked at him. "Do you know about stoves?"

He shrugged. "Sorta. Ever since I got out of the army a couple of months ago, I've been goin' around to these here sales and things—" He grinned again "—pickin' up junk and turnin' 'em into bargains." Glancing around the loft, he sighed. "But pickins' are gettin' scarce, even for me. Looks like I'm gonna have to find me another job, real quick."

"What did you do in the army?" she asked.

He grinned. "I was a baker, if you can believe that. Now *those* are stoves! Once you got a handle on them, you can cook just about anythin'. The funny part is I kinda miss that, but who's gonna give me a job with that kind of army experience? I would've been better off driving a truck."

"Oh, I don't know," Paula said, unable to believe her good luck. "If you're serious about a job, I might know of something."

"You do? Oh, boy, I been lookin' for a long time, and I don't much care what it is. If you know of something, I'm your man."

AND IT TURNED OUT that he was. In the two weeks that followed, Paula saw more of the state of Oklahoma than she'd ever seen in her life; she learned more about stoves and industrial baking than she'd ever thought possible. With Rodney setting a frantic pace, they went to restaurant liquidations, bankruptcy auctions, even an estate sale or two. By the end of that hectic period, with Rodney's crooked grin a fixture in her life, Paula not only had her equipment, but a friend and a valued employee as well. She had hired Rodney to help her buy what she needed, but when that task was done, he decided to stay on. She couldn't have let him go; she would have paid him anything. He had become her right hand.

But as dear as Rodney was to her, his was not the face that haunted her late at night when she finally went home and stumbled into bed, alone. Despite her best intentions, and her vow not to think of him, she couldn't forget John-Henry Hennessey. And when she slept, she dreamed of him.

CHAPTER FIVE

PAULA DIDN'T HAVE MUCH TIME to dream about John-Henry during the busy days that followed. She had been more fortunate than she knew to discover Rodney; when she found out he was handy with tools and willing to do some carpentry work, they began to build the store interior together.

Even though she had prepared herself for hard work, and certainly wasn't afraid of getting her hands dirty, one fourteen-hour-day seemed to flow endlessly into another. Sometimes she thought that if she had to pick up the hammer one more time, or measure one more board, she was going to scream. The night she and Rodney stayed late to finish installing the stoves, she was starting to see double from sheer exhaustion. To make matters worse, she hadn't even started to convert her cookie recipes. All this work, she thought, and she couldn't even bake a test batch yet!

"We're never going to be ready!" she complained wearily to Rodney when they finally got the last of the three big, side-by-side ovens in place. The days were slipping by, faster and faster, but as hard as they both worked, the grand opening seemed just as far away to her as it ever had been.

"Aw, you're just anxious, that's all," Rodney said. He patted one of the gleaming aluminum doors that she had spent hours rubbing with polish, then grinned in her direction. "Pretty soon, you're gonna be sick of these ovens. Take it from me. I've got experience."

"I wish I could say the same thing," she said, looking around. To her weary eyes, the store didn't look much different right now than it had when she signed the lease. Loose boards and piles of sawdust littered the floor, and junk seemed to be everywhere. Rodney's tools, as well as those she'd brought from home, were scattered all over. Adding to the clutter were the sacks and cups and wrappers from all the awful fast-food and deli lunches and dinners they'd shared.

She still felt guilty about that. In the beginning, she tried bringing food from home because she felt she owed Rodney some decent meals while he was helping out. Because she couldn't add cooking to the fourteen-hour shifts she was doing in the store, she finally agreed to his suggestion that they buy their food from other shops in the mall. A junk-food junkie, he quickly found the burger place a couple of doors down, and when he located a deli around the corner that served good salads, she couldn't argue. Meals were taken care of, then, but she insisted on paying for everything, even though very often she was too tired to eat what he brought for her.

At least with Rodney around, nothing went to waste, she thought. As fatigued as she was, she could still marvel at the vast amounts of food he could eat at one sitting, often finishing both his portion and hers. How he stayed so lean was beyond her, and she often teased him that, since he never gained weight, he could be her chief cookie tester.

"It'd be a pleasure," he'd grin at her, helping himself to a second hamburger, or another bag of french fries. "But for the real expert, you should ask my sister, Mary

Lou, back in Arkansas. Now there's a girl who knows how to eat!"

"And skinny as a rail, just like you, right?"

"All us Quinns are like sticks. It's in the genes, or somethin'," he'd say, and eye whatever was left on her plate. "Say, are you gonna finish that sandwich? It'd be a pity to let it go to waste."

Feeling as though she was wasting time just standing here tonight, Paula glanced around again. While Rodney finished the stove installation, she had worked on the front counter, but she didn't seem to be making much progress. She sighed. This "unit" had seemed so tiny when she first rented it; how could such a small space take so much time and effort?

Rodney heard her sigh and looked over his shoulder. "Don't worry," he said, polishing their fingerprints off the stove. "It'll all come together."

She was almost too discouraged at this point to believe him. "Do you really think so? When?"

He grinned. "Well, not tonight, that's for sure. You know what I think? I think we should just lock up and go on home. You're lookin' a little pale around the gills, and this'll all be here tomorrow."

"That's what I'm afraid of," she said, and shook her head. "No, you go. I'll just stay for a while and...and clean up."

He looked pointedly around at the litter that surrounded them. "When it's just startin' to look broke in?"

He could always make her laugh. "Well, then, since you've got the ovens all hooked up," she conceded, "maybe I'll just stay a while and do some temperature checks, how about that?"

"You work too hard, you know that?"

"So do you. In case you hadn't noticed, you're here as much as I am."

"Yeah, but that's different."

"Why?"

"Because I'm a man," he said, preparing to jump out of her reach. "And men can work harder than women."

"Oh?" she said, hands on her hips, her eyes dangerous. "Who says?"

"Everybody knows it," he said, teasing her. "Just read any magazine."

"I don't have time to read magazines, I'm too busy working," she retorted saucily, and glanced at the clock. It was already after eight, and they had started at six that morning. "You go along now, before I change my mind."

Still he hesitated. "I don't like leaving you here."

"Nobody's going to kidnap me. I'll be fine. And I don't intend to stay that long."

"You sure?"

"Positive. Now go."

"At least let me bring you something to eat."

She made a face. "No, thanks. Your idea of a good meal is a double cheeseburger with extra fries. If I see another french fry, I'm going to start counting them in my sleep!"

"But you haven't eaten dinner."

She hadn't eaten lunch, either, but she wasn't about to tell him that. In the short time they'd known each other, he'd become very protective, sometimes behaving as if he were an older brother. She appreciated that at times, but not tonight.

"I'll get something on the way home," she said, pushing him gently but firmly toward the front door. The mall was still open, and he preferred to go out that way. He preferred her to leave that way as well; he didn't like her going out into the dark parking lot at the back of the mall alone. "Now, go. I'll see you tomorrow."

He still didn't like the idea of leaving her by herself, but he knew her well enough now to obey that tone. Muttering something about wearing herself out before they even got started, he left, closing the paper-covered door carefully behind him.

As soon as he was gone, Paula felt her weariness descend like a smothering blanket. When she had company, she could forget how exhausted she was, but when she was alone, there was nothing to distract her. Maybe she should take Rodney's advice and go home, she thought, and was tempted for just an instant. Then she shook her head. Even with Rodney's help, the preparation was taking much longer than she had anticipated, and she had to keep going. Now that they had electricity, she could at least test the ovens while she finished working on the shelves in the back. If she worked an hour or so longer, she wouldn't feel so guilty about going home before midnight.

Despite her weariness, she felt a little thrill when she unwrapped the gauges she'd bought. They were used to calibrate the stove temperatures, and as she placed one inside each of the three ovens, she smiled. Every small step brought her closer to her goal. Once the temperatures were standardized, she could begin experimenting with her recipes.

Suddenly feeling less weary, she retrieved her hammer and heavy carpenter's belt. Hooking the belt around her slender waist, she clambered over some boards that were piled in her way and headed toward the back of the store. She and Rodney had erected a wall to separate the processing area from what would be the sales counter, and she was just reaching for one of the shelves they'd cut earlier when she heard the door open. Sure that Rodney had brought her back a hamburger after all, she didn't turn around, but called out, "Okay, if you insist on dinner, we're going out to a nice place. I'm tired of takeout from that greasy spoon!"

The rejoinder was swift in coming. "In that case," a voice said, "how about the Waterford?"

The dining room at the Waterford Hotel was one of the most exclusive restaurants in Oklahoma City. But that wasn't what startled her so badly that she dropped the hammer, which narrowly missed hitting her toes. She recognized that voice, and it didn't belong to Rodney. Whirling around, she looked right into the amused eyes of John-Henry Hennessey.

"Or," he said, smiling, "if you don't like the Waterford, we can try the Eagles Nest atop the Tower. Or any other place you prefer. It's your choice."

Her choice at the moment was to sink right through the floor. *What is he doing here?* she wondered frantically, and blinked, as though she could make him go away.

But he didn't go away. He was still standing there when she opened her eyes again, and she thought immediately of how she must look—her hair in tangles, her cheeks smudged with dirt, all covered in sawdust and her blouse untucked. Because she was so embarrassed, she became irritated. What was the matter with him? she wondered. Did he think he could just . . . drop in?

Apparently he thought just that. "I didn't mean to startle you," he said, picking up the hammer she'd dropped. He held it out, and she looked blankly at it, as though wondering what it was. Then she snatched it back.

"Well, you did," she said, and then realized how rude she sounded. Embarrassed, she shook her head. "I'm sorry, I guess I'm just a little tired. I didn't mean to snap at you like that."

"It's all right. Maybe I should have called first."

She looked around at all the clutter. "I'm glad you didn't try. The phone isn't hooked up yet, but I'm not sure I could have found it even if it was. As you can see, I'm not exactly ready for business yet."

"But coming along," he said. "I can see that."

"You don't have to be polite. I know it's a mess now." She looked down at the hammer she was clutching in a death-grip. With an effort, she loosened her fingers. "I...I didn't mean what I said earlier. I thought you were someone else."

"That's too bad. Does that mean you don't want to go out to dinner with me?"

He had to be joking. She couldn't go out dressed as she was, even if she wanted to. Which she did not. "No, I'm sorry," she said, not looking at him. "I can't."

He didn't seem offended by her abrupt refusal, merely disappointed. "I'm sorry."

"Yes, well..." Abruptly, she remembered she hadn't checked on the ovens. It seemed as good an excuse as any to extricate herself from this awkward coversation. "Excuse me," she said.

He followed, gingerly stepping over some of the clutter. "It seems a lot of work," he commented. "Maybe you need some help."

She didn't know why she felt so defensive; maybe because he had put her on guard with his remark about dinner. "I do have help."

He glanced meaningfully at the heavy carpenter's belt around her waist. "Not enough, apparently. There's no need for you to do these things yourself, is there?"

The big leather belt suddenly felt as though it weighed a ton, and she wanted to snatch it off and hide it behind her back. But because her pride wouldn't let her touch it, she said defiantly, "I don't mind. Why do you?"

She regretted the words the instant they were out. Why was she being so awful to him? she asked herself. She didn't have an answer. She only knew she was tired, and had circles under her eyes, and hadn't eaten, and . . . and didn't look at all the way she wanted him to see her. If, she thought, she wanted him to see her at all. Which she didn't. She might think about John-Henry Hennessey, but that didn't mean she wanted to get involved with him, even if such a thing was possible. Which it was not.

"I'm sorry," he said, a little stiffly. "I didn't mean to interfere."

Now she felt even worse. It was obvious she had hurt his feelings, and for what purpose? Why had he come here anyway? she wondered, and once again, said something she hadn't intended. "You think I'm going about this all wrong, don't you?"

"I didn't say that."

Some demon made her continue. "You didn't have to. I can see it in your face."

"The only thing you see in my face is admiration for all your hard work," he said. "Now, if we have to, why don't we continue this discussion over dinner? Don't you think we'd be a lot more comfortable?"

She doubted she'd ever feel comfortable with this man. She had felt completely disoriented ever since he'd walked in, and her feelings of confusion were growing by the minute. What was wrong with her? Why was she being so abrasive and rude? That wasn't like her; she must be more tired than she realized.

And he was more attractive than she remembered, she thought, and felt exasperated with herself again. What if he was good-looking? What difference did it make? They had nothing in common; he even had a better haircut than she did. There he stood, in his custom-made three-piece suit with the custom-made shoes and imported silk tie, while she was trying to ignore the carpenter's belt around her waist, and resist the temptation to brush the sawdust off her jeans. If anything dramatized the difference between them, she thought irritably, it was that haircut and this stupid belt.

"Or," he said, when she didn't answer, "if you've already eaten, we could just go out for coffee."

"I can't," she said stubbornly. "I'm not finished here."

"Then I'll help until you are."

Horrified at the thought that he might do just that, she exclaimed, "No, that's impossible!"

"Why?"

She was so discombobulated that she began fumbling with the carpenter's belt. "Here, let me help you with that," he said, and before she could protest, he had reached around for the buckle.

"No, I can get it," she protested quickly, and reached behind her at the same time he did.

Without warning, they were practically in an embrace, John-Henry's arms encircling her, she leaning forward as she tried to locate the buckle before he did. Their hands met, and she looked up. They were so close she caught a whiff of his after-shave—a spicy, provocative scent that should have been at odds with his polished appearance, but didn't seem out of place at all. He was so much taller than she was that he seemed physically overpowering—or perhaps she only felt his physical presence so strongly. From four inches away, she felt the warmth of his body—a heat that ignited a response in her own. Appalled by the flood of feeling that swept over her at his nearness, she jerked back.

"I...I can get it," she muttered, dropping her eyes from his face. She fumbled with the catch. Just when she thought she'd have to wrench the belt apart with her bare hands, the buckle gave, and she dropped the belt with relief. It fell to the floor with a clang of tools and nails and measuring tape, and she kicked it away. Now that she had extricated herself from one awkward situation, she had to deal with another.

But before she could think of something to say, John-Henry bent down and looked into her face. "When was the last time you had anything to eat?"

She didn't want to talk about that; she had something more important to say. "I don't remember. Now, please, Mr. Hennessey—"

"John-Henry, please."

"Mr. Hennessey," she repeated firmly, "I know you're being kind, and I appreciate that. But I really don't want to go out for coffee. There's so much to do, and I just don't have—"

"Then I will help," he said, and to her horror, started taking off his coat.

"What are you doing?" she cried. "You can't do that!"

He stopped with his arms still in his sleeves. "Why not?"

"Why not? Why not?" She vehemently shook her head. "No, you can't...I mean, I won't let you... No, it just isn't right!"

He shrugged back into his coat. "Then let's go."

"No, I told you—no coffee."

"Then we'll find some place close for dinner. You're pale as a ghost. You obviously need something to eat."

"What I need is to finish up here!"

"All right, then we'll order in and keep working," he said, and glanced around as he started taking off his coat again. "What do you want me to do first?"

Oh, this was impossible! she thought wildly. "Why are you doing this to me?" she cried. "Do you act this way with all your clients?"

That stopped him. "No," he said slowly, looking a little surprised himself. "I don't." Then he smiled at her. "But that doesn't mean I'm going to let you off the hook."

She saw that he meant what he said. He wasn't going to let her out of this, and so she gave in, but ungraciously. "All right," she said. "But I don't want to go any place fancy. I'm not dressed for it."

His expression changed. Softly, he said, "You look just fine to me."

What could she say after that? Five minutes later, after washing her hands and brushing off as much of the sawdust as possible, she settled into his shiny black Jaguar. Touching the butter-soft leather seat, she sighed at such luxury, and thought: *Some day...*

"Where would you like to go?" he asked, starting the car. The engine caught with an eager, rumbling purr.

She told him she didn't care—the nearest hamburger place was fine with her; she just wanted to get it over with. He took her to one of the new Mexican food restaurants in the city, only a few blocks from the mall. At that time of night, "happy hour" was long over, and the bar was empty; the place was quiet, with only a few patrons lingering over coffee and dessert. The hostess seated them in a booth far from the door, and came back with a bowl of tortilla chips and salsa.

"Your waitress will be right with you," she said, giving John-Henry a lingering smile that he didn't notice until she asked if they cared for anything to drink.

"Um . . . Paula?" he said.

A drink was the last thing she needed, Paula thought. She was so tired now that even a whiff could put her right to sleep. "No, thank you. You go ahead."

But he shook his head at the hostess, and after she'd reluctantly gone away, Paula said, "You didn't have to forego a drink on my account."

He shrugged. "It doesn't matter. I've had more than my share at times."

She didn't know how to respond to that, so she took a tortilla chip from the bowl. It was homemade, crisp, with just a hint of salt, and when she reached for another, she realized how hungry she was. Suddenly ravenous, she was helping herself to the salsa when she realized he was staring at her. "Here," she said, pushing the bowl toward him. "These are good. Have some."

Absent-mindedly, he took one. But when he continued to gaze at her, she became so unnerved that she suddenly demanded, "Why are you staring at me like that?"

"Was I staring? I'm sorry," he said, and reached for one of the menus the hostess had left behind. "What would you like for dinner?"

Paula took the menu he handed her, but she didn't read it. "Mr. Hennessey," she said, "why did you come to the store tonight?"

Slowly, he put down the menu. "Please call me John-Henry," he said. "Or John. Or even . . . no, don't call me Henry. But otherwise, I'll have to call you Mrs. Trent, and that makes things very formal. Would you prefer that?"

"I'd prefer to know why you came to the store," she said. "Was it because you weren't sure there would be a store?"

He looked startled. "Why do you say that?"

"Well, you don't know me, after all. Maybe I borrowed that money and then...just ran off with it. Maybe you came to see for yourself that I—"

To her annoyance, he burst out laughing. "If I'd thought for one second that you were a con artist, I'd have had you thrown out of the bank!"

"I don't see what's so funny," she said, piqued. She hated being laughed at. "I could have been pulling a scam. You had no way of knowing."

Seeing that she was annoyed, he tried very hard not to laugh. "I knew," he said.

"How?"

"Let me tell you something, Mrs. Trent," he said, smiling despite himself. "Don't ever get involved in a high-stakes poker game. You just don't have the face for it."

She straightened. "What's wrong with my face?"

He suddenly looked serious. "Not a thing," he said, and without warning, reached for her hand. "I think it's the most expressive face in the world."

She hardly heard what he said. Keenly aware of his fingers over hers, she wanted to snatch her hand out from under his, but she couldn't seem to move. Suddenly, achingly, she realized she wanted to do more than hold his hand. Instantly, she dropped her eyes. She could feel her cheeks flush.

Was this all it took? Paula wondered. His hand over hers? She had never felt such an intense reaction to a man, not even to Randy in their courting days, when they were young and hot-blooded.

But she was older now, more mature. She was supposed to be able to control her feelings, not abandon herself to them as she had back then. Was it because she had been without a man for so long? she wondered, and then knew that didn't even enter into it. She had seen men look at her since Randy left; she knew that all she had to do was strike up a conversation, or smile in a certain way, and she wouldn't be alone. She had never felt the slightest inclination to do such a thing... until now.

Slowly, she looked up into John-Henry's face—and knew instantly that he felt the same way she did. She could feel his desire for her even in the simple touch of his hand over hers; she could see it in his eyes, in the sudden jump of a muscle along his jaw. He was as tense as she was, and as his fingers closed down convulsively over hers, she glanced at their joined hands.

I'm not ready for this, she thought, suddenly afraid. *I don't know if I'll ever be.*

And then someone said, "Sorry I took so long. You two ready now?"

Blinking, Paula looked up at the girl who seemed to have appeared out of thin air. She was standing there with notepad and pen in hand looking expectantly at them, and for a dazed second or two, Paula couldn't imagine what she wanted. Then she realized the girl was their waitress—and that she, Paula, had not even glanced at the menu. Helplessly, she looked across the table at John-Henry, who looked just as baffled as she felt.

"I'll have whatever you're having," she said to him, too disoriented to make a decision. What had happened just now?

John-Henry didn't seem to know, either. But he was clearly more adept at recovery than she was—or at least, he seemed to be as he gave the waitress their order. She went off with a flounce of her petticoated uniform skirt, promising to return "in a jiff" with their meal. Paula was sorry to see her go; absurdly, she'd felt…protected with someone else at the table. Without the girl's diversionary presence, she had to face John-Henry again, and she wasn't sure what to say. Had he really felt what she had, or was her fatigue making her imagination work overtime?

"Is it me," John-Henry said, pulling at his collar and glancing around the room, "or do you think it's warm in here?"

"It is a little warm," she agreed and reached quickly for her water glass.

Looking as though he wished he had ordered a drink after all, he reached for his glass, too. "Tell me about the store," he said.

Relieved that he'd brought up a safe subject, Paula immediately said, "Well, as you saw tonight, there isn't much to talk about yet."

"But you have plans."

"Indeed I do. But I told you all about that when I applied for my loan."

He leaned forward. "Tell me again."

Even that slight movement made him seem far too close, and she unconsciously sat back. Swallowing, she said, "Well, as soon as Rodney and I get the store interior set up—"

"Rodney?"

"Rodney Quinn," she said. "Oh, he's been an absolute jewel. I don't know what I would have done if we hadn't met—" Forgetting herself in the memory, she laughed. "I'd probably still be up in that dusty old warehouse of a barn, trying to get that stove out!"

As confused as he looked at the turn in the conversation, John-Henry didn't ask about the stove. He seemed far more interested in the "jewel" she'd found.

"This...Rodney person," he said. "Have you known him long?"

"Rodney? Oh, just—" she started to say, and then paused. Was he really asking if she and Rodney were...involved? Feeling a tingle at the thought, she admonished herself not to be ridiculous and said, "No, not long." But she couldn't prevent a casual, "Why?"

He sat back. "No reason. I was just making conversation."

Unreasonably, she was disappointed. Then she was annoyed with herself. What had she expected—that he would erupt in a fit of jealousy because she was seeing another man? Telling herself that his response served her right, she said, "Rodney used to be a baker in the army. We met when I was shopping for a stove, and when he told me about his experience and background, I hired him to help out in the store."

"You don't have to explain."

"I know. But I wanted to. Rodney has been such a big help, and I'm very grateful to him." Without realizing it, she sighed heavily. "Time seems to go so fast. I have to get the store set up, so I can start revising my recipes, but it's taking so much longer than I anticipated, and every delay—" She stopped abruptly when she realized how she sounded. "I'm sorry," she said. "I guess I'm more tired than I realized. You're not interested in the problems I'm having setting up the store."

"But I am," John-Henry said. "It means a lot to you, I know. I could tell that the day you walked into my office."

"It does mean a lot to me," she said, intense again. "It means everything!"

"Why?"

Sometime during the conversation, the waitress had come with their plates. Paula pushed hers aside. She didn't know why, but she had to make him understand. "If it was only for me, it wouldn't matter so much. But I've got to think about my grandmother, too. Did I tell you about my grandmother?" she said, not noticing his reaction. She smiled fondly. "Her name is Heddy, and she's just about the most wonderful person in the world. She's the only family I have left, and I feel so responsible for her. If something happened—" She shuddered, just thinking of it, and looked at him again. "That's why I'm so anxious about getting the store going. I want to have a cushion, just in case something happens. Not that I expect it to," she added quickly. "Grandma is eighty-two years old this year, but so far, you wouldn't know it. She has more energy than I do."

"Yes—" John-Henry murmured.

"I beg your pardon?"

"Oh, er…I mean, I can imagine," he said hastily. "Go on, please. You were telling me about—what is her name? Heddy?"

"Yes, Heddy Bascomb. Anyway, as I was saying, she's the only family I have left, and I owe her so much. She's always been there for me, especially when Danny was killed—"

"Danny?"

"My brother," she said, her voice catching a little. Even though it had been twelve years since the accident, sometimes it seemed as though she had heard the news about it only yesterday. "He was my older brother—by a year," she went on. "He was killed the night he was celebrating his twenty-first birthday, driving to a party some friends were giving him. A man who'd had too much to drink broadsided the car. He was killed instantly." Despite herself, bitterness crept into her tone. "The other driver walked away without a scratch."

John-Henry didn't say anything for a moment. Then, sounding as though he truly meant it, he said, "I'm sorry."

"So was I," she said, forcing the memories away. "I still am. Danny wasn't just my brother, he was one of my best friends."

"How lucky you were, even for such a short time," John-Henry said. "I never had a brother—or a sister, for that matter."

She was glad to change the subject. "Ah, an only child."

"Yes, but not by choice, really. My mother would have liked more children, she says, but the man she married was much older than she was—" his expression softened again with a fond smile "—and Claude always said that I was the equivalent of a pack of wild horses as it was."

Unable to imagine John-Henry as an unruly child, Paula laughed. "He must have been exaggerating."

"Not by much," he said ruefully. "I wasn't always the staid banker, you know."

That piqued her curiosity. "You weren't?"

"Good grief, no," he said, looking amused. Then he sobered, and his eyes took on a faraway look for a moment. "In fact, my early childhood was completely different from how I grew up," he said. "Until my mother married Claude, things were always...tight at home." He shook his head slightly, as though reluctant to continue, and smiled. "But we weren't talking about me, were we? We were discussing you."

Put on the spot again, Paula shifted in her seat. "Oh, but your history sounds much more interesting than mine," she protested.

When he saw how uncomfortble she was, he said, "All right, then, how about neutral ground? Tell me about the store. You were saying how anxious you were to get started. Do you have a date targeted for the opening?"

Despite the fact that she longed to hear more, to learn everything she could about such an intriguing man, she was immediately distracted by business problems. "I did have," she said, and became glum again. "But the way it looks, I'm going to have to push it forward."

"A few weeks won't make much difference, will it?" he asked. It was the wrong thing to say.

"Yes, it will!" she said glaring at him. "It *will* make a difference!"

"Why?"

She had thought about that, almost endlessly, wondering why she felt so…so driven. It wasn't only Heddy, it was something else, she had realized, and said, almost wonderingly, "I never thought of myself as ambitious, but I now know I am. I'm in a position to make my dream come true, and nothing is going to stop me. I'm going to be a success, and I'm not just saying that because you loaned me that money. I know I'm going to succeed. I can feel it."

"Then you will," he said. "But—"

"But what?"

He shook his head. "You don't want my advice."

"Yes, I do," she said, leaning forward intently. "Tell me."

Still he hesitated. Then, finally, he said, "I've seen people get too caught up in dreams of success, Paula. Don't let your ambition change who you are, or drive you further than you want to go."

"That won't happen to me," she said positively.

"I hope not," he replied, and gestured for the check.

Paula thought about that conversation on the way home, after John-Henry had dropped her back at the parking lot to pick up her car. The evening had ended on a quiet note, both of them preoccupied with their thoughts. As she watched the black Jaguar glide smoothly away before she climbed into her Volkswagen, she wondered, for the first time, just how far she would go to achieve her ambition. The thought was a sobering one, for she realized suddenly that she had no answer.

JOHN-HENRY WAS PENSIVE himself as he drove back to his apartment. Much later, in fact, long after the clock struck three, he was still sitting in his study, thinking about Paula and nursing a brandy he'd poured in the hope that it would make him sleep. He'd never met anyone like Paula—so open, so honest, so direct. He had been fascinated by the expressiveness of that beautiful face, by the fluctuations of those dark eyes. One minute they flashed with inner fire, the next—when she'd been talking about her brother—they'd looked so bruised that he'd wanted to gather her in his arms and make everything right in her world again.

"This is ridiculous," he muttered to himself, and shifted in his chair. But the new position didn't help, for an instant later, he was remembering something else she'd said, and smiling despite himself.

Then he thought of Heddy and frowned. He'd nearly given himself away when Paula had started talking about her grandmother. Why in hell had he ever made that foolish promise not to reveal that he and Heddy knew each other? It was alredy complicating things, and he'd seen Paula only once outside the office.

His expression became even more thoughtful as he set his brandy glass aside. Everything was about to change, he decided. Promises to feisty old ladies notwithstanding, he wasn't about to step aside where Paula was concerned. Now that he had found her, he wasn't going to let her go. He'd done juggling acts before; he could do it again.

And as far as Paula herself was concerned, well, he had plans for her. She could be as stubborn as she liked, but this business of working herself to death was going to stop. She would probably mount all kinds of objections, but it wasn't going to change his mind. He was going to help her whether she wanted him to or not.

Realizing he had a meeting with some executives from Milwaukee-Wakesha in five hours, he decided he'd done all he could do for the moment. Whistling under his breath at the thought of how pleased he was sure Paula would be with his plan, he turned out the study light.

CHAPTER SIX

PAULA WAS HARD AT WORK the next morning when company arrived. She was hanging shelves in the back of the store when she thought she heard someone in front, but after the embarrassing incident with John-Henry the night before, she had learned her lesson. Setting aside the board she was holding, she peered around the corner. Two men were standing in the doorway, looking around; they wore carpenter's belts and carried lunch buckets. Thinking they had made a mistake and come to the wrong store, she came out, dusting her hands.

"Can I help you?" she asked.

The tall, skinny one spoke first. He was wearing a baseball cap, heavy work boots, and under his open jacket a faded T-shirt emblazoned with the Oklahoma Land Run logo, commemorating the state centennial. "Are you Paula Trent?" he asked.

"Yes, I am," she said.

The shorter man grinned. He was dressed like his partner, except his T-shirt was plain white. "Then we're here to help you," he said, and glanced around. "Looks like you could use it, too."

"Wait a minute," she said, as they started peeling off their jackets. "I don't understand. I think there's been some mistake."

"No mistake," the tall man said. "Not if you're Paula Trent. We were hired to help you finish fitting out the store." He looked around for a place to put his lunch bucket, then set it on the floor. "Uh . . . do you have any blueprints, or—" he grinned to show he was just teasing "—are we just wingin' it?"

We aren't just winging it, Paula thought, mildly exasperated despite the man's smile. Did he think she was a complete idiot? She and Rodney had made a diagram, of sorts; it was on a table, buried under sawdust and a scattering of nails she'd dropped while trying to measure something. Before she realized what she was doing, she gestured. "The plans are over there—but wait," she said, when they both turned in the direction she'd indicated. "I'm sorry, but I don't know who you are. I'm sure there's been a mix-up."

The tall one tipped his baseball cap. "Sorry, ma'am. My name's Verl, and this here's Emmett. I guess we should have introduced ourselves."

"Yes, well, I'm pleased to meet you, but as I said, there's been some mistake. You're obviously here to work, but I didn't hire any workmen."

"Oh, sure, we know that," Emmett put in. "You wasn't the one who hired us. We got a call this mornin' from our boss, saying that Mr. Hennessey wanted us to come over and help you finish up the place, and that's what we're here to do." He grinned. "Now do you mind if we get started? The day's a-wastin', and it looks like we got plenty to do."

Nonplussed at the mention of the Hennessey name, Paula watched them walk over to the table where she'd put the plans. But as they started to unroll the papers, she rushed over. "When you said Mr. Hennessey," she said, "did you mean John-Henry Hennessey?"

Verl nodded. "Yes, ma'am, we do. He's the one who called the boss, Charlie Rasmussen, you know him?

Well, Mr. Rasmussen said that Mr. Hennessey said that we was supposed to do whatever you wanted us to do."

"I see," Paula said. The more she thought about it, the more annoyed she became. She had told John-Henry she could manage; she thought she had made that very clear. Did he think that just because they'd gone to dinner, he could take over? If she had wanted carpenters, she would have hired them herself.

Realizing that the two men were looking curiously at her, she forced a smile. It wasn't their fault, she realized, and decided right then to confront the man who was to blame. "Why don't you gentlemen take a coffee break until I get this straightened out?" she said sweetly. "It won't take long, I promise you."

And with that, she tucked in the tails of her blouse, dusted off her jeans, grabbed her coat and marched out. Behind her, Verl and Emmett looked at each other, sighed, and reached for the flasks of coffee they'd brought.

"Well," Verl muttered, pouring himself a cup and settling in for a long wait. "Better him than me. From the look in that little lady's eyes just now, I'll bet he's gonna get an earful!"

THE CLOSER SHE GOT to John-Henry's office, the more indignant Paula became. By the time she pulled up in front of the bank, she didn't stop to think that she wasn't exactly dressed for a visit to The Hennessey; she was too preoccupied with what she was going to say to John-Henry. He couldn't take over like this, even if he had loaned her the money. She was capable of organizing her own store, and the reason she hadn't hired extra help was that she was being careful with finances. She had calculated down to the last cent, and her budget didn't include carpenters. Buying quality ingredients for her cookies was more important to her than whether the shelves were perfectly planed, and she intended to tell him so in no uncertain terms.

The same supercilious receptionist was sitting at the desk when Paula entered the bank, but today she was wearing a lime-green suit that clashed horribly with her bright red lipstick. She looked up primly as Paula came striding in, but Paula didn't have time for games this morning; ignoring the woman's startled expression, she headed directly toward the elevator.

"Just a minute!" Miss Smithers called in alarm. "You can't—"

But Paula was already stepping inside the waiting car. Before the elevator doors closed, she glimpsed the receptionist half rising from her desk, and then reaching quickly for the phone. Pressing the button for the fifth floor, Paula hoped the woman wasn't summoning security.

Well, let them try to stop me, she thought as she was borne swiftly upward. She had a few things to say to Mr. John-Henry Hennessey.

JOHN-HENRY WAS AT HIS DESK, when he heard voices in the outer office. Oh, no, he thought, amused. Not again. He was just wondering if he was about to meet yet another lively female member of the Trent-Bascomb clan when his secretary opened the door. Looking resigned, Mrs. Adams said, "Ms. Trent to see you, Mr. Hennessey. I'm afraid she insists."

Because Paula was standing behind the secretary, he couldn't see her face. If he had, he would have been warned. Instead, thinking that Paula had come to thank him for sending her the carpentry help, he began to smile in anticipation. "Well, show her in," he said.

Paula had obviously not come to thank him. When the secretary withdrew and Paula marched in, John-Henry could see from her stormy expression that he was in trouble.

"I'd like to talk to you," she said.

"Well, of course," he said, wondering what had gone wrong now. He had told Charlie to send two good workers; he'd thought Paula would be so pleased. "Why don't we sit down?"

When she looked like that, her eyes flashing, her color high, he forgot, for an instant, that she was angry with him. All he could think of was how desirable she was. Thinking that what he really wanted to do was take her in his arms and kiss her, he forced himself to smile. His smile soon faded.

"I'd rather stand, if you don't mind," Paula said. "I came to talk to you about those two men you sent over to the store this morning."

He still didn't know what was going on. "I see that you're not pleased," he said.

"No, I'm not."

"Well, if they weren't satisfactory, we can find someone else."

She looked at him as though he were missing some obvious point. "I don't want to find someone else, John-Henry. I want to do it myself!"

Beginning to realize he had blundered into very murky water here, he said, "Yes, I know you said that, but I thought a little help—"

"I don't want your help," she interrupted. "Don't you understand? You loaned me some money, and I'm grateful. But please, don't tell me how to spend it."

He stiffened. "That wasn't my intention at all."

"Then why did you call someone to send those men over? Didn't you think I was moving fast enough? Did you want to hurry things along so that you'd get your money back? If I'd wanted carpenters, John-Henry, I would have hired them myself!"

He could feel himself getting angry at her unreasonable accusations. With an effort, he managed to remain calm. "I don't think you understand, Paula—" he started to say.

Those dark eyes flashed again. "Oh, I understand, all right! You think I'm incompetent!"

"For your information, incompetence would be the last word I'd use to describe you!"

"Then why—"

Exasperated, he said, "I wanted to help. Is that so wrong? If I offended you, I'm sorry. I was only trying to—"

"Don't!" she said, holding up her hand. "Don't try to do anything for me! You loaned me the money, that's enough. It doesn't entitle you to take over and expect...expect to run my life!"

All right, he'd had it. His quick temper had always been a trial in the past; that was one reason he'd controlled himself so scrupulously these past five years. His anger was the cause of Camilla's taking that final, tragic drive. They'd had a terrible argument, shouting at each other until she'd finally stormed off, screeching down the wet driveway, tires smoking as the Ferrari took a curve. She had driven off like that before, when they had quarreled, which, toward the end, was often enough. But the difference was, that night she hadn't come back.

John-Henry pushed that memory away; with Paula standing angrily in front of him, Camilla was the last person he wanted to think about. Tersely, he said, "Is that what you think? That I gave you that loan because I expected something from you in return?"

"What else am I to think? Do you go out of your way for your other clients? Hire people for them, stop around to see if you can help? Somehow, I don't think companies like Digitron Optic receive such personal attention, and Mr. Hennessey, *I* don't want it, either. If you want your money back, just say so. Otherwise, let me run my business my way!"

And with that, she whirled around and started for the door. He caught up to her before she reached it, taking her arm and turning her to face him again. "Oh, no, you don't," he started to say, as she stumbled against him. "You're not—"

But he forgot what he was going to say when she instinctively clutched him to regain her balance. He put his arm out to steady her, and suddenly both arms were around her and he was holding her close. It happened so quickly that she didn't have time to struggle, and he was caught unaware when a bolt of desire shot through him. Startled, he jerked back. No woman had ever evoked such an intense and instantaneous reaction in him, not even Camilla.

"Paula . . ." he said, and looked down wonderingly.

She seemed to feel it, too. Color rose to her cheeks, and her dark eyes flared with some emotion he didn't dare put a name to.

"This isn't—" she started to say and faltered into silence as he continued to gaze at her.

John-Henry couldn't take his eyes away from Paula's face. No woman had ever looked so desirable and sensuous as she did at that moment, her mouth slightly open, the lower lip trembling a little. Gazing down, he could feel every fiber of his body urging him to seize the moment, to kiss her, to pull her against him with even more urgency. He could feel his muscles quiver with the effort to hold himself back, and the thought flashed through his mind: *What would it hurt?*

But it was too soon...or too late; he didn't know which. He only knew that if he didn't let her go, he wouldn't be able to control himself. He ached with desire and passion. Every nerve on edge, he forced himself to release her and step back.

"I'm sorry," he muttered. "I shouldn't have done that. It wasn't..."

He didn't know what he was trying to say; he felt confused and disoriented, not at all the composed banker he had convinced himself to become. In a flash, he realized the image he'd so carefully cultivated was all a sham, a house of cards easily blown down by a breath from this woman he hardly knew. The unwelcome thought came to him that he hadn't changed after all; he'd just added layers of respectability, hoping to smother the man he had been. Obviously, he had failed, if a single encounter such as this could throw him right back again. Hadn't he learned anything?

Looking a little dazed herself, Paula moved unsteadily away. "I..." she started to say, and then put a helpless hand to her throat. "I shouldn't have come," she finished weakly. "I'm sorry."

He tried to pull himself together. "No, I'm the one who's sorry," he said. "I shouldn't have interfered."

She had to force herself to meet his eyes. "No, I shouldn't have been so quick to...to judge."

Somehow he managed to say, "I'll cancel the order for the carpenters, if you like. But I would much rather you accepted their services as my contribution to your success. Not that I don't think you can manage on your own," he added quickly. "But since I'm instituting a new program to help small businesses, I'd like to consider this an . . . experiment. Could we do that?"

What could she say to that? If she refused, she could be jeopardizing the chances of someone else who might really need the extra help. "Well, I guess, under those conditions, I really can't object, can I?" she said reluctantly, and then realized how ungracious she sounded. "Thank you," she added. "You're very generous, John-Henry."

Not as generous as I'd like to be, he thought.

AFTER SHE HAD GONE, he went to the window and waited until he saw her head to her little car. He had so much, he thought, more than he could possibly want or use, while Paula was struggling to get along. If only she would allow him to help her, he mused—and then abandoned that line of thought. She didn't want what he had to offer; she had made it clear she didn't need his help. The only reason she had accepted his offer just now was because she was thinking of those who would come after her, who might really need such assistance.

Depressed and deep in thought, he sat down again at the desk after he watched the Volkswagen drive off. His head in his hands, he wondered how much worse he could feel. Everything he did for Paula seemed to go wrong; he wasn't used to this feeling of failure.

Oh, yes, he was, he thought, lifting his head. If he had ever failed at anything, it had been his marriage. His expression turned sad as he thought of his beautiful, disdainful, willful wife. He had thought Camilla loved him; he had certainly loved her. She was so wild, so headstrong. He hadn't realized until it was too late how cruel and selfish she was. Sometimes, during those hurricane years of their marriage, he'd thought she hadn't a scrap of feeling for anyone but herself.

Why had he loved her? he wondered. He had asked himself that question too many times to count. Was it her beauty, her allure, her charm that attracted him? Or was it only that he'd wanted to possess such a beautiful creature?

His head in his hands again, John-Henry despised himself. He didn't like to think of that period in his life when he had obviously been as shallow and unfeeling as Camilla. To this day, he didn't know what had possessed him; he'd been on a collision course with disaster, and that's exactly what had happened.

But Paula isn't like Camilla, he thought, and wondered if he was falling in love with her. He couldn't be, he told himself bleakly. After Camilla, he had vowed never to love again. Love had turned him into something he didn't want to be; it had controlled him, and made him do and say things he never intended. Camilla had been partially responsible, to be sure; she had taunted him with her beauty, with her hint of affairs, with her favors offered and then withheld. But he was responsible, too, in that sham of a marriage; if he hadn't been so reluctant to admit he'd made a mistake, he would have ended it long before that fatal car crash. He had been prepared to live without love—until Paula came into his life.

And what was he prepared for now? Could he trust his feelings for Paula?

It was too soon to think about it, he told himself. He and Paula hardly knew each other; they were both preoccupied with other things. Maybe he should just take it slowly, one step at a time. Then, if something developed, he could decide what to do. Yes, that seemed the sensible approach, a decision the banker, John-Henry Hennessey, would make. He had things under control now, and he took a deep breath. It was time to get back to work.

He started with the files he'd been working on before Paula had come in. He had been totaling assets for a particular company, but after he had added the same column of figures four times and had come up with four different answers, he impatiently shoved the papers away. He'd obviously lost his concentration; it was time to move on to something else. But everything on his desk annoyed or irritated him, and finally he gave up and put all the files into a drawer. Then he took his coat and went out to speak to his secretary.

"I'm going out, Mrs. Adams," he announced. Then, on impulse, he did something he'd never done before. "And I won't be back today."

His secretary looked surprised. "Yes, sir," she said, and then asked tentatively, "Does that mean you want me to cancel your appointment with Mr. Cavendish?"

He had forgotten about that. He was supposed to meet with Jerold Cavendish, an electronics company executive, later this afternoon. He had been trying to set up a time convenient for both of them for weeks now, and he hesitated. But because the last thing he wanted to talk about today were diodes, cathodes and transistors, he said, "Yes, cancel it."

Mrs. Adams looked astonished again. This was so unlike her employer that she gave him a concerned look. "Are you . . . are you ill, Mr. Hennessey?"

Maybe that was it, he thought. He was coming down with something. "I might have a . . . a cold coming on," he said, although he was rarely sick, and couldn't remember the last time he'd been hit by a virus. "I'm sure I'll be all right by morning. Why don't you take the rest of the day off yourself? Miss Smithers can field any calls downstairs, and we'll get an early start tomorrow."

Looking pleased at the unexpected bonus, Mrs. Adams immediately began shutting down the word processor. "Well, I do have some errands I can run," she said. "Thank you, Mr. Hennessey, I'll do that."

Nodding, John-Henry shrugged into his topcoat and headed out. But once he'd started the Jaguar, he didn't feel like going back to his apartment, so he headed onto the Interstate 44. Before long, the exit for Martin Luther King Boulevard came up, and on impulse he turned off toward Remington Park. He hadn't been to the track in years, but suddenly he remembered he had half a racehorse stabled there. Despite his promise to Heddy, he hadn't visited yet, but as he parked the car and headed toward the guardhouse to explain who he was, he breathed in deeply and realized this was just what he needed. It had been a long time since he'd been around horses, and maybe a few minutes with such elemental creatures would clear his mind.

HEDDY WAS SITTING in the tack room by the portable heater, checking out the *Daily Racing Form* when Otis nudged her arm. Preoccupied with stakes and claimers and allowance races, she looked up impatiently. Otis had been going in and out all morning with one thing and another, and she was tired of being interrupted. "Now what?" she asked.

Otis pulled her toward the doorway. "Who's that?"

When Heddy saw who he meant, her eyes widened. The man walking along the shedrow should have looked out of place in his topcoat, suit and glossy shoes, but instead he looked as though he owned the entire park. Nimbly stepping over one of the numerous puddles decorating the aisle between shedrows, he glanced around, not noticing Heddy and Otis peeking from the doorway.

"Well, I do declare," Heddy said. "That's Mr. John-Henry Hennessey!"

Otis immediately looked alarmed. "What's he doing here? Do you think he's come to tell us the deal's off?"

"Don't be an old fool, Otis," Heddy said, although the thought had already flashed through her own mind. She decided to fix on something more pleasant instead. "Maybe he's come to see No Regrets. I told him to stop by whenever he wanted."

"Why'd you do that?"

"Because he's paying for the horse's upkeep, Otis," she said tartly. "Don't you think he deserves a look now and then?"

Otis cast a worried glance in the direction of the horse's stall. It was empty at the moment, Fernando having taken the big Thoroughbred for a slow walk around the perimeter of the training track. The horse wasn't ready to start training yet, let alone race, but his muscles had to be kept in shape. Both Heddy and Otis blessed Fernando's strong, young legs, and his never-ending patience. If Otis had told him to, Fernando would have walked that horse to Cleveland and back.

"But Heddy," Otis whispered. "No Regrets isn't here! What'll we tell Mr. Hennessey?"

"The truth, of course," Heddy said, and pulled her arm away from Otis's grasp. Putting a welcoming smile on her face, she came out of the tack room, dragging Otis behind her, just as John-Henry came up.

"Why, Mr. Hennessey," she said. "What a pleasant surprise."

"There you are," John-Henry said. "I was beginning to think I'd gotten the wrong directions. You're so far from the gate."

"Well, we're not exactly on the A-list around here," Heddy said wryly. "Those barns in front are for the big trainers, not one-horse operations like us."

John-Henry glanced thoughtfully back along the long shedrow. "We'll have to see about that," he murmured. "I don't like the idea of you being so far removed from everything."

"Oh, we're just fine back here," Otis said quickly. Deciding he should stop hiding behind Heddy's skirts, he stepped forward and held out his hand. "The name's Otis Wingfield, Mr. Hennessey. I've heard a lot about you."

John-Henry shook Otis's hand. "Call me John-Henry, please," he said with a smile. "Or J.H., whichever you prefer. John-Henry is a bit of a mouthful, as I've told my mother many a time."

Otis grinned in return. To Heddy, who was watching the exchange, it was obvious that these two were going to get on fine. "John-Henry is a good name to my way of thinking," he said. "You're in good company, you know."

"So I've been told," John-Henry said, looking amusedly at Heddy, who had pointed out his relationship with his more famous namesake that first day in the office. "So, where is this horse who's eating me out of house and home?"

Otis immediately looked anxious again. "I know the bills seem high, but we've itemized every one, and tried to keep down expenses as best we can."

Apologetically, John-Henry clapped the other man on the shoulder. "Don't worry, Mr. Wingfield, it was just a figure of speech. I have no complaint about either the bills, or the way you're taking care of the horse." He hesitated slightly. "I've been involved with horses before, and I know these things take time."

"I'm glad to hear that," Otis said, relieved. "Some owners don't understand that."

"Well, I do."

"In that case, call me Otis," Otis said with a grin. "That's what all my friends call me."

Just then, Fernando returned with their racehorse. As groom and horse approached, Heddy tried to view the animal as John-Henry would, seeing the big, gangly gelding for the first time. She remembered her introduction to the slab-sided, rawboned, pitiful-looking creature, and how she'd felt that nothing was going to improve his appearance, but even she had to admit that, after these past few weeks in Otis's care, No Regrets didn't look like the same animal at all. His mane and tail would never be long and luxurious, but at least his coat shone with daily rubdowns, and he'd lost that rough, unhealthy look. His eyes sparkled, and his ears pricked with interest. He looked every inch the proud racehorse.

Until, Heddy thought glumly, the horse took a step. Then the lameness, while not as obvious as it had been, was still evident. Anxiously, she looked at John-Henry for his reaction and saw that he had noticed it immediately, too. Eyes slightly narrowed, he watched as Fernando led the horse up. Quickly, Heddy glanced at Otis, who was watching John-Henry, too.

"He's still got a problem with that right hind, I see," John-Henry said matter-of-factly.

"It's coming along, it's coming along," Otis replied. "That suspensory ligament is going to take a little more time, but it's the gravel that's hard to predict." He squinted up at John-Henry. "Heddy told you about that?"

John-Henry nodded. "Yes, she mentioned it."

Otis nodded, too. Now that the horse was in front of them, Otis's manner had changed subtly, and he seemed to have gained both stature and confidence. Heddy gave him an admiring glance. This was the Otis she knew.

"Is he still carrying heat in that foot?" John-Henry asked.

Otis gave him an approving glance. That was a question only someone knowledgeable about horses would have asked. "Sometimes," he said.

"What does the horseshoer say?"

"What they all say—the good ones, that is," Otis said with a grin. "He could dig around in there, but it wouldn't do any good. It'll just have to pop all by itself, and there's no telling when it's going to do that."

"I agree," John-Henry said. "In that case, then, we'll just have to wait." Reaching out, he patted the horse's glossy neck. Immediately, No Regrets looked around, nudging his hand. John-Henry laughed, patting the horse's head, but the animal nudged him again. "What's he looking for?" he asked. "A carrot, sugar?"

Heddy's cheeks turned pink. She gave an I-told-you-so glance in Otis's direction. "He's looking for a cookie," she muttered.

"A cookie?" John-Henry said, and then remembered the notation on the bottom of the horse's bills. "Oh, yes, a cookie," he nodded, hiding his smile as he remembered Otis's unique training aid.

Now Otis was red. "I know I shouldn't have done it, but I gave him a cookie once, and the darn fool horse loves 'em," he said. "Now, every chance he gets, he's begging for one."

John-Henry turned back to pat the horse again. "Sorry, old boy," he said. "I didn't think. Next time, I'll bring you a whole bag." His eyes twinkling, he winked at Heddy. "Should I get a particular kind?"

Heddy looked even more embarrassed. "He only likes Paula's cookies," she said. "We've tried other kinds, but he won't eat them."

"I see," John-Henry said solemnly. "And does he have a favorite?"

Obviously deciding they couldn't look any more foolish than they already did, Heddy said, "Well, he prefers chocolate chip cookies, but he'll eat the oatmeal-raisin in a pinch."

John-Henry laughed. "What does Paula think of this?"

Otis and Heddy gave each other a quick glance. When John-Henry saw their expressions, he nodded. "I see," he said. "We're still keeping secrets."

"Only for a while," Heddy said hastily. "Once No Regrets starts racing, we'll tell her." Her eyes sparkled suddenly behind her glasses. "We'll have to, then, because we're going to share our winnings with her. That's what this is all about, don't you see? I know Paula will be a big success with her cookie store, but this way, she won't have to worry so much about me. I'll be able to take care of myself, and she won't feel so pressured about things. Instead of worrying about an old woman like me, she'll be able to concentrate on herself and her own future." She looked anxiously at John-Henry again. "You nderstand, don't you?"

John-Henry understood a great deal in that moment. "Yes, I do," he said, his tone serious. "And I think Paula's very lucky to have a grandmother like you."

Heddy flushed. "I'm the lucky one," she said. "Paula's a wonderful girl."

Something changed in John-Henry's expression. Just for an instant, there was a softening in his eyes, a tender expression that made him look even more good-looking than he already was. "Yes," he said. "She is." Coming back from wherever he had gone, he smiled at them again. "Well, I'll be on my way. It was nice meeting you, Otis. Keep up the good work."

"I will," Otis said. "Don't you worry about that."

"Will you come again?" Heddy asked.

John-Henry smiled down at her. "You couldn't keep me away."

"Good," Heddy said with satisfaction, and waved goodbye. But as soon as John-Henry's imposing form had disappeared down the shedrow, she turned to Otis. "No Regrets will win, won't he?"

Smiling, Otis put his arm around her plump shoulders. "No doubt about it, Heddy girl," he said. "Don't you worry about that. You trust me, don't you?"

"Oh, I do," Heddy said, and deep in thought, turned to look in the direction their visitor had gone. Smiling to herself, she murmured, "Now that that's settled, let's see what we can do about Paula and John-Henry."

"Now, Heddy—"

But Heddy just smiled and patted his arm. "You train the horse, Otis," she said. "And leave the rest to me."

CHAPTER SEVEN

ONCE AGAIN, to Paula's chagrin, John-Henry was right. His gesture in sending the carpenters to finish the store interior put her weeks ahead of schedule—time it turned out she desperately needed as she began the work of converting her cookie recipes to volume.

A perfectionist where her baking was concerned, she had decided from the beginning that she would use only high quality ingredients. Thus, it was an unpleasant surprise to discover that even though she had bought all the best flours and sugars and chocolates she could afford, nothing seemed to go right. She made good cookies—or thought she did—until she started spending night after night in the store trying to bake hundreds, when before she had only made dozens. To her increasing dismay, she kept making costly mistakes. If she changed one ingredient, the entire batch was far too sweet; if she altered another, the texture wasn't right.

When she had first conceived her cookie-making idea, she had contacted industry professionals who had warned her that she'd be crazy to use real butter instead of lard, and they had laughed at her naive decision to buy the best chocolate for her chocolate chip cookies.

"You'll go broke in a month," more than one had told her.

She hadn't believed it then, but now she was beginning to wonder if that prediction might come true. She was spending so much money just testing recipes that there were times when she despaired of having enough left over with which to open the store. But then, every time she thought of giving up, her stubborn streak came to her rescue. It *had* to come out right, she would tell herself, or she had no business opening up a cookie store in the first place. Determined to make the product as good as it could be, she stayed night after night, working alone long after even the devoted Rodney had gone home. There were times she was so tired she couldn't even see straight, much less trust her sense of taste; after a while, everything seemed to have the same flavor.

"I'll never get it!" she groaned to herself one night, after bagging yet another batch to give to a shelter. She couldn't just throw all this food out, and so she saved what she could for those less fortunate. Somehow, it didn't make her feel any better. If she was going to give something away, she wanted it to taste right.

Wearily, she was just starting to measure sugar and butter again for the next batch of oatmeal-chocolate chip cookies, when she heard someone tapping on the back door. She had been luckier than she had realized when she rented this space. Tucked away behind a wall, she could come and go as she pleased without having to bother security, but the two men who patrolled knew she often stayed late, and sometimes they came in to see if she was all right—or to see if she had a few extra cookies to help them through the long night. Sure that one of them had stopped by, she dusted off her hands on her towel apron and went to see who had knocked.

"Who is it?" she called through the door. Even with security on patrol she was still careful, and wouldn't open the door at night unless it was someone she knew.

"John-Henry."

She blinked. *What was he doing here?* she wondered, panicking, and glanced down at herself. As always, she was wearing jeans and a turtleneck, and she was covered with flour from head to foot. Oh, why did she have to look like a ragamuffin whenever he came around? she wondered in despair. Resignedly, she unlocked the bolt and opened the door.

"Hi," she said, holding onto the doorjamb and blocking the way. She wasn't sure of the reason, but she didn't think it would be a good idea to invite him in.

"Hi," he said. "I was just driving by, and I saw the lights here, so I thought I'd stop and see if you needed any help."

It occurred to her then that he looked different. Then she realized why. For once he wasn't wearing a suit. Instead, tonight he had donned jeans and a sportshirt with—of all things—a leather bomber jacket. The clothing changed his entire appearance; she knew she was staring, but she couldn't help it. Dressed that way, he didn't look like a banker at all, but younger and casual and... almost boyish. Even his hair looked different; windblown and curly, with a lock or two falling onto his forehead. With an effort, she jerked her eyes away and tried to remember what he'd said.

"That's very kind of you, but I—" she began, but just then the oven bell went off. One of the trays of cookies was ready to come out, and since she could hardly leave him standing here while she checked it, she invited him in. "Excuse me, but I have to go check that batch. Would you like to come in?"

"Thanks," he said, carefully closing the door behind him and making sure it was locked. He followed her through the storeroom into the cooking area, where he sniffed and said, "That smells good."

"I hope it tastes as good as it smells," she said, crossing her fingers as she took the cookie sheet out of the oven and put it on the counter. But then, as she transferred the cookies to the cooling rack, she gave them a professional glance and frowned. These weren't right, either.

"What's wrong?" John-Henry asked.

She felt like heaving the entire rack of cookies out the door. She'd worked so hard on this batch, and they looked like lifeless little lumps. "These," she said. "It looks like I'm going to have to toss them, too."

He looked shocked. "Throw them away, without even tasting them?"

"I can tell they aren't right."

"How?"

"How?" she repeated incredulously. "Do they look like the kind of cookies people are going to line up to buy? They're just *sitting* there!"

She felt like bursting into tears. She was tired; she felt as though she had been slaving over these hot stoves forever. It wasn't bad enough that she had done something wrong—again—now John-Henry was here to witness her failure. Beginning to think nothing would ever go right for her, she wondered why she had ever thought up such a crazy scheme. Why hadn't she decided to sell greeting cards, or plastic ware—something someone else made?

"They look just fine to me," John-Henry said.

She glared at him. "Don't you dare patronize me!"

"I'm not. I mean it. Do you mind if I have one?"

"Yes, I do," she said childishly. "I told you, I'm going to throw them away."

"Not until I taste one," he said. "I haven't had dinner, and I'm hungry."

"Well, you can't have these!" she declared, reaching for the rack to pull it out of the way.

It was too late. Grinning, he had already snatched a couple and popped them into his mouth. "Hey," he said, his voice muffled. "These are great!"

She glared at him again. "I told you—"

"No, I mean it," he said, reaching for some more. "I don't know what you're worried about, I've never tasted better."

"You're just saying that," she said, but she looked doubtful.

Chewing appreciatively, he shook his head. "No, it's true."

"Do you really mean that, or are you just trying not to hurt my feelings?" she asked, and then frowned again. "Because if you are, I swear—"

Grinning again, he grabbed another handful. "Would I be eating like this if they weren't good? Look, I've wolfed down half the tray already."

She looked down and saw that indeed he had. Still, she said uncertainly, "You said you were hungry."

"I was," he said, biting into another. He held it up to the light, as though it were a wine of rare vintage he was examining. Then he put the whole thing into his mouth and winked. Between chews, he said, "These are like potato chips. You can't eat just one. They're too tempting."

Pleased despite herself, she still scoffed, "These aren't like potato chips at all."

"No, these are sweet . . . sweet temptations."

"I didn't know you were so poetic," she said, and then broke off, staring at him in astonishment. "That's it!"

"What?"

"That's the name!" she said, getting excited. "I've been trying for weeks now to think of the right name for the store, and you've just come up with it! Sweet Temptations! It's perfect!"

He thought about it for a few seconds, then he nodded. "Yes, it is, isn't it?" he said, obviously pleased with himself. "That calls for a celebration. I think I'll have another cookie."

She was so delighted she shoved the entire rack at him. "Help yourself," she said, laughing. "You deserve it. Oh, I thought I was never going to come up with a name for the store, and you just pick one out of the blue! How can I ever thank you?"

"How about going out to dinner?"

Her elation vanished. "Now?"

"What better time? We'll have champagne, toast the name of the store. What do you say?"

Stalling for time, she said, "I say that you're going to make yourself sick. You've just had about a dozen and a half cookies. You can't possibly want to eat anything else."

"Have you had dinner?"

She'd had a sandwich about six hours ago, nothing since. "That's not the point," she said, backing away. "You don't have to—"

"I want to."

"But it isn't necessary," she said, and wondered why she didn't want to go out with him. Did she even know the reason? Yes, she did, she thought. John-Henry was way out of her league; it was as simple as that. Despite his casual attire tonight, she had never been able to forget how he looked at the bank—couldn't forget that he ran the bank. She didn't know where he lived, but just thinking of the car he drove reminded her that he took for granted a life-style she could only dream about.

So it wasn't right; it would never work, even if she wanted it to. And she didn't. With John-Henry, she would be totally out of her element. They had nothing in common, and despite his hints about not always having lived in such grand style, the fact was that he lived that way now. He might try, and she might try, but in the end the differences between them would be overwhelming. She'd be left with another big hurt, and for what? All she would have done was allow herself to be diverted for a time from her true goal, and she couldn't afford to do that. She wouldn't do that. She had promised herself that getting the business running would be her top priority, and she couldn't abandon all her dreams now just because…because John-Henry Hennessey had a nice smile.

"I know it's not necessary," John-Henry said just then, interrupting her frantic inner flow. He held her eyes. "That's all the more reason to do it, don't you think?"

Under the influence of that deep-blue gaze, she could feel herself weakening. What did it matter that he ran the bank? What did it matter that he drove a top-of-the-line luxury car? Right now he was here with her, and he'd come voluntarily. That said something, didn't it?

No! she told herself, and said aloud, "I can't. I really have to stay and finish." Then, because she could tell by his expression that he was going to try and change her mind, she added quickly, "But I'll take a rain check. I'll have more time once the store opens, and we can go out and celebrate then." She smiled, remembering how he had helped her tonight. "My treat—to repay you for giving me the name of the store."

With such a gracious refusal and the promise of an invitation in the future, John-Henry could hardly object. But his disappointment was clear when he said, "Am I only allowed one dinner, then? Why can't we go get something now—and then later, really celebrate?"

She was beginning to feel desperate again. What *was* it about him that made her feel so off balance inside? She was never this way with other people; why him?

"Because I have work to do," she said.

"I'll stay and help."

Despite her growing tension, she laughed. The picture of John-Henry Hennessey rolling up his sleeves and plunging his hands into flour and baking powder right here in her kitchen, was too amusing. "No, I don't think so," she said, leading the way toward the backdoor. She smiled impishly. "My recipes are secret ones, and for all I know, you could be an industrial spy."

Resigned to leaving, he smiled, too. "If I am, it's too late. I'm so deft, I pocketed some of the goods when you weren't looking. I planned to eat them on the way home, but maybe now I'll just sell them to the highest bidder."

She laughed again. "Just make sure they know where the store is so they'll come back for more."

"You won't have any trouble drawing crowds."

That sobered her. "I hope you're right."

"I know I am," he said, and without warning, took both her hands in his. "I won't let you forget about the celebration. I'll hold you to your promise."

With their fingers entwined, she longed just to step toward him, to have his arms go around her as they'd done once before, to experience the touch of his lips on hers. But she made herself say lightly, "You won't have to remind me. It's a date."

He, too, looked as though he wanted to do or say something more. Instead, he gave her hands a little squeeze before he dropped them and reached for the doorknob. His gaze lingering on her face for a moment longer, he said, "Call me if you need anything—anything at all." Then he was gone.

TWO WEEKS LATER, Paula opened the store—but not before she had had to face one crisis after another. Some days were so stressful that she had been tempted to call John-Henry, just for moral support. She had complained to Heddy instead, who was always sympathetic, but who couldn't really do anything about Paula's supply problems.

The first disaster came the day she found out that the company she had contracted to supply her raisins had folded. When the company's representative called her with the bad news, shortly after the night John-Henry had visited her store, she had panicked for five minutes, then started calling other suppliers. One after another the companies she contacted refused her, and by the fourth one, she was beginning to feel desperate. The recurring theme was that she was too small for them to bother with.

"Call me when you want to order ten thousand pounds or more," one nasty man said. "Until then, we're not interested."

She had come to the last name on her list. By then she was too desperate to worry about an image. "I'm a very small company," she told the man who answered, "and can't buy very much. But I would like to test your raisins—"

A salesman showed up that very afternoon, hauling in big plastic bags from the trunk of his car. His name was Albert, and he immediately asked if he could taste some of her cookies. Her heart in her throat, she set out a plate, and he took a bite of each kind.

"You're right, these could definitely be improved," he said, and then saw her crestfallen expression. "But don't worry. Let me tell you what's available, and what it will cost. I also know of a good-but-small chocolate company, if you're interested."

She most definitely was, and he stayed two hours, talking nonstop, while she took copious notes. When he was finally ready to leave, she said, "I don't know how to thank you, Albert."

Winking, he said, "Send me a new, improved batch, and make 'em so good, your next order of raisins will be a couple of hundred pounds."

She agreed with a laugh, and then spent the next two weeks at the store, baking up a storm. At the end of that time, she finally had some cookies she was proud of. Wrapping several different kinds in a gaily decorated package, she sent it to Albert by express mail, and received a call that very night.

"Never tasted better," he said. "When's your next order?"

Delighted, she laughed. "After the opening, I hope."

"When's that?"

"Next week," she said, crossing her fingers.

"Don't worry," he said. "You'll be great."

"Let's hope the cookies are even better," she said fervently, and promised to call as soon as possible.

She opened the store the next Monday. The day was overcast, but she was warm—and getting warmer, since the ovens had been going full blast four hours before she flung open the front doors for the first time. Terrified at the thought that she was actually going to be doing business, she had hardly slept the night before, and had arrived before dawn to start making the first batches of cookies. She had counted on Rodney's help, but when he dragged himself in with a temperature of one hundred and four and glazed eyes, she sent him home to bed, despite his insistence that he could work. Three hours later, she had made semisweet chocolate chip cookies with nuts, and semisweet chocolate chip cookies without nuts. She had a batch of oatmeal-raisin, and another of oatmeal with chocolate chips. Heddy had always liked the raisin-spice cookies, so she had those on hand, and since John-Henry had raved about her chocolate with chocolate chips, she had made that kind, too.

Although she'd planned to make several different kinds of brownies, as well, she didn't have time. At five minutes to nine, she was still arranging the trays behind the protective sheet of glass that separated the customer and the product—and glancing nervously at the clock when the health inspector came.

"Good day for opening," he said, looking around to make sure everything was as it should be.

"I hope so," she said, and offered him a cookie. The man had been here many times over the past few weeks, coaching her until she knew what the health department rules and regulations meant, making sure she knew about the various codes, helping her get the required approvals. She owed him a lot, and said so, but he just waved that aside. "It's my job," he said, and helped himself to another cookie. This morning, he nodded in final approval.

"The place sure looks nice," he said.

She looked around, too, trying to see it as her customers might. Because she'd read that "hot" colors stimulated appetites, she had decided to use touches of red against the white of the floor and walls. The front of the store opened directly into the mall so there were no windows for the red curtains she'd planned. But the red trim on the counters and shelves provided a splash of color that contrasted well with the green plants she had carefully placed around—airy asparagus ferns that helped to camouflage the cash register, which she hoped would soon be ringing its head off.

It does look nice, she thought in satisfaction, and suddenly wished John-Henry was coming. But when he had called earlier in the week to ask when the great day would be, she had asked him not to come, thinking she would be too busy to pay much attention to him. Now she was sorry. She wanted him to see the store finally finished, the cookies in place, everything in readiness for the hordes of customers she anticipated. She knew nothing would keep Heddy away, and as she said goodbye to the health inspector, who again wished her luck, her grandmother arrived wearing her best dress.

"Well, I do declare, Paula, you've done a splendid job. Everything looks just wonderful," Heddy said, glancing around. She spied the trays of cookies, each with its own descriptive sign in front of the tray and peered closer. "And you've made so many cookies! What time did you get here this morning?—" she frowned maternally "—or did you spend the night again?"

"Oh, Grandma," Paula laughed. "I've never spent the night here. And I came at six." Smiling, she reached for one of the trays. "Here, have one on me. I made your favorite. I thought it would be good luck."

"You won't need luck, my dear," Heddy said, giving her a kiss on the cheek. "You're going to be a success, I just know it. Now, are you sure you don't want me to stay and help? I'll be glad to, you know that."

But Paula had already refused the offer once. She didn't want Heddy standing on her feet so long, so she had said that Rodney would be here, and together they would manage. Now, with Rodney home sick, she could have used the help, but still, she shook her head.

"No, thanks, Grandma, I'll be just fine. But I'll call you tonight to let you know how things went. Are you going to the Center today? Would you like some cookies to take along?"

"The Center..." Heddy seemed a little disconcerted for a moment, then she quickly shook her head. "No, those folks don't need any of your cookies—not today, sweetheart. You've worked too hard. Save 'em to sell this time. But we'll take a rain check, is that all right?"

After Heddy had gone, Paula realized that mention of a rain check had reminded her of John-Henry. Wishing again that she hadn't told him not to come, she gave the store a last quick inspection, and then, her heart pounding madly with fright and excitement and anticipation, she opened the store's doors with high hopes and a grand flourish. It was exactly nine o'clock.

An hour passed, during which Paula could feel herself getting more and more tense. As the mall filled up, people would stop and look, ask how much the cookies cost, seemingly oblivious to the big sign she had put up, nod, smile—and walk away.

"They're not buying because it's so early," she muttered to herself. It was stupid of her, opening at nine. Who wanted to eat cookies then?

Two hours later, at eleven, she still hadn't made one single sale, and could no longer convince herself that it was too early for people to buy sweets. Feeling increasingly desperate, she wondered why the signs she had plastered all over the mall weren't working, or if anyone had seen the ads she had put in the paper, announcing the store's grand opening. Why weren't the people who *had* stopped in buying anything? What was wrong? *What was wrong?*

By noon, she hadn't sold a single cookie, and was nearly in tears. She was a failure before she even started. If this kept up, she'd close the store, take the first bus out of town, and never be seen again. Oh, what was she going to do?

And then someone came in. A little boy who wasn't looking for cookies, but who had lost his mother. He was very young, and very scared, and when Paula called security, she gave him a cookie.

"Here," she said. "This will make you feel better until your mommy comes."

Looking up at her with huge brown eyes, he handed it back with a grubby hand and a politely whispered, "Thank you very much, lady, but my mama won't let me eat sweets."

She couldn't even *give* cookies away! Desperate now to do anything, she suddenly had an idea. If she couldn't sell any cookies, she could certainly give away a taste. Maybe people didn't want to buy until they tested her product, she thought, and quickly filled a tray with samples. Then, holding the tray, she took a deep breath and stepped out into the walkway in front of the store.

"Here, try a sample," she said to passersby, offering the tray.

Forcing herself to hold a fatuous smile, she held out the tray again and again to whomever came by. Some took a sample, some shied away as though the cookies were suspect for some reason. Even though she felt like a fool, she made herself carry on.

"These cookie samples are from Sweet Temptations, right behind me. Please try one; they're free."

And finally, "Would you like to taste a sample of cookies from Sweet Temptations? Today is our grand opening, and we're offering a special today. A baker's dozen . . . thirteen for the price of twelve . . ."

Three hours later, hoarse and feeling as though her face was going to crack from the effort of trying to keep up her smile, she had only twenty-two dollars in the cash drawer, and dozens of cookies left. One of her ideas when she had planned the store—so long ago now!—was to give away what few bits might be left at the end of the day. That plan seemed the height of arrogance now, as did another of her brainstorms: starting fresh every day. No day-old cookies for Sweet Temptations! she'd thought haughtily, never dreaming she would have to throw out, or give away so many. What was she going to do?

Resigned to continuing this humiliating display until she could close the store and slink home, she was just setting out new samples on her tray when someone came in. She looked up eagerly, and then blanched when she saw who it was. *Oh, no,* she wailed internally, *what is he doing here?*

JOHN-HENRY KNEW the instant he walked through the door to Sweet Temptations that he'd made a terrible mistake. Even though he had promised Paula he'd stay away on the first day of her grand opening, by three o'clock, he was so distracted at the office that he had to come and see how things were going. One look at her expression, and he knew.

In a flash, he realized that it would be disastrous to betray what he was thinking by even a flicker of an eyelash. Somehow he managed a smile. "Hi," he said cheerily.

She looked back. "Hi."

He thought the best approach was to ignore the look on her face. "I know I promised to stay away, but I couldn't just ignore your grand opening day. I hope you're not angry."

Instead, Paula looked ready to cry, which made him feel helpless and then angry himself. What was the matter with all those people out there? he wondered. Why hadn't they mobbed the place? Didn't they know what they were missing?

Paula was too proud to betray her distress. Trying to smile, she said, "The only thing that might help is that you buy all these cookies." She looked at her counters, where trays of cookies waited for customers, and forced herself to add, "As you can see, I'm not doing a roaring trade."

He didn't trust himself to come anywhere near her. She looked so unhappy that he wanted to take her in his arms and promise her that he'd buy the entire store. But as fiercely protective as he felt, he knew she wouldn't appreciate his offer, far from it, so he said awkwardly, "Opening days are notoriously tough."

"Tough?" Paula said, looking down at the tray of cookies she was holding. "If I'd known this..." She stopped, flushing a little as she looked at him again. "I shouldn't be saying this to you, should I? You'll be wanting to call in my loan."

The loan was the last thing on his mind; he hadn't thought about it since he had signed the authorization. He wouldn't even have gone to that trouble if he hadn't sensed how proud she was. Trusting her on instinct, he would have been happy to give her a personal check. No, he didn't care about the money; what he cared about was Paula, and suddenly he had an idea.

"All new businesses get off to a slow start," he said. "You just have to be patient."

"For how long?" Paula said. "I'm beginning to think patience is as expensive as pride."

"But more rewarding," he said. "You'll see."

"Do you think it'll be before I go broke?"

My brave Paula! he thought. She was trying to make jokes even in the face of disaster. "Oh, I think things will turn around," he said casually, and then reached into his pocket for his wallet. "Now, then, I came in to buy some cookies. Would you mind wrapping up a dozen of each for me?"

Despite her obvious misery, she smiled. "You've already proved what a cookie monster you are, but really, John-Henry, you can't possibly eat that many."

"Don't be too sure," he said with a smile. "I've got a long afternoon ahead of me at the office."

It was the wrong thing to say. The smile slipping from her face, she said bleakly, "So do I."

JOHN-HENRY DROVE back to the bank. Carrying bags of cookies, he dashed inside. The elevator to his office never seemed so creakingly slow, and he practically pried the doors apart with his bare hands when it finally arrived at his floor. Mrs. Adams looked up in surprise when he burst in, his arms filled with so many bags, but he ignored her startled reaction.

"Come with me," he said, and headed into his office, where he deposited the bags on his desk. The secretary followed obediently, carrying her pencil and pad.

"Yes, Mr. Hennessey?"

He paused a moment, organizing his thoughts. Then he said, "Issue a...a request to all departments—immediately. There's a cookie store in the new mall called Sweet Temptations. I want everyone to take a break—staggered, of course, so they don't all stampede in at once—and go there and buy some cookies. I don't care how many—one or a dozen. But I want everyone in this bank to bring back a sample. They'll be reimbursed."

Halfway through this little speech, Mrs. Adams's pencil faltered, and then stopped altogether. She looked at him in undisguised amazement.

"Yes, what is it?" he asked impatiently. He knew he hadn't lost her; the woman took dictation at two hundred words a minute.

"Cookies, sir?" she said.

"From Sweet Temptations," he repeated, looking her directly in the eye.

She dropped her gaze. But he was sure he saw a smile hovering at the corners of her mouth when she said demurely, "Yes, sir. I'll get on this right away."

"Thank you," he said. "I'd appreciate that."

But then, as she rose to leave, he had another thought. "And make sure everyone realizes that this is a request, not an order."

Again that hovering little smile. "Yes, sir," she said as she went out. "I understand."

"Good," he muttered as the door shut behind her. Then, feeling pleased with himself, he reached behind him and took out a handful of cookies from one of the bags he'd brought. Biting into one, he nodded in satisfaction.

PAULA WAS OVERWHELMED when droves of people started arriving late that afternoon. By then, she had nearly given up hope of racking up anything but total failure for her opening day. Instead, she had to run back and forth, selling all the cookies she'd made earlier, and whipping up several more batches between customers to keep up with the demand. For two hours, the store was mobbed, and as the crowd grew in front, other shoppers stopped to see what was going on, and those people bought cookies, too. By closing time, Paula felt she'd been through a whirlwind; every muscle in her body ached, but when she looked at the stuffed cash drawer, she whooped with delight. She didn't know what had happened, but she couldn't wait to tell Heddy: she was a success!

Giddy from weariness and delight, she was just putting the last of the trays away when she had the feeling that she wasn't alone. Whirling around, she saw John-Henry leaning casually against the door frame. In her excitement, she had forgotten to lock the front door. Great, she thought. She'd have to watch that.

"I told you things would work out," he said with a smile. "Now will you go out to dinner with me to celebrate?"

Despite her weariness, she picked up something in his eyes, and she looked at him suspiciously. "How did *you* know things worked out?"

Pointing at the empty spaces behind the counter, he pushed away from his casual pose by the door. "It's obvious, isn't it?"

"I could have put the cookies away," she countered.

"But you didn't."

She hesitated, but she was too happy to argue about it. "No, I didn't. In fact, I sold every one." She looked at him again, unable to rid herself of that strange feeling. "Are you sure you didn't have anything to do with this?"

"Me?" He seemed genuinely surprised. "You know how many cookies I bought. *I* certainly wasn't responsible for your selling out tonight."

But she still wasn't convinced, and didn't know why. Maybe it was the twinkle in his eye; maybe it was because she was dead on her feet. She had hardly slept a wink last night, and she had been a bundle of nerves since she arrived. Her emotions had swung like a pendulum throughout the entire day—from high hopes to the depths of despair, and then to exhilaration at her success, so that now all she felt was wrung out.

"I can't go out," she said. "I'd love to, really I would, but I have to be back here tomorrow morning at six to start baking."

He looked both dismayed and disappointed. "But don't you have Rodney to help out?"

"He's sick, and I don't know how long he'll be laid up," she said, but she wasn't really thinking of Rodney. Now that she knew she was going to be a success, she could feel her enthusiasm sweeping over her again. She was starting to think, to plan—and what plans she had! Excited again despite her weariness, she looked at John-Henry, wanting him to share it, too. "Now that I know my standard cookies will sell, I'm free to experiment with some other ideas I've had. I don't know if I told you, but eventually I want to develop about a dozen kinds of cookies. I haven't had time to work on them yet, but I will! Tomorrow I plan to start testing peanut butter cookies. They're not as easy to make as it sounds, you know. The quality of peanut butter has to be just right— not too much—"

She stopped suddenly on a laugh. "Your eyes are glazing over, I can see."

"No, no, I'm interested," he protested. But it was obvious that dinner—unless it was in the form of cookies—was out of the question, and he wondered if he had unwittingly created a monster. Maybe he shouldn't have been so eager to help.

Realizing how disappointed he was, she came around the counter and put a hand on his arm. Buoyed by her success, she said, "But we still have that rain check, don't we?"

He looked down at her. But instead of answering, he pulled her to him and gave her a quick kiss. It was no more than a brush of his lips against hers, but her entire body vibrated with the intense reaction it generated. Gasping, she looked dazedly at him when he pulled back.

"Now before you get any ideas," he said huskily, gazing down into her eyes, "that was congratulations on your success."

"I . . . of course . . ." Paula stammered.

Looking as though he wanted to say something else, John-Henry touched her face. "I'll hold you to that rain check," he said, and then he left.

She stood there for a long while after John-Henry had gone, her lips tingling from that quick kiss, her body longing for more than that hasty embrace. She was still bemused when she was tidying up, and despite herself, she kept glancing at the door, hoping he'd come back. Then, annoyed with herself, she turned out the lights.

The next morning, she was back in front of the oven at six sharp. Congratulatory kisses notwithstanding, she told herself firmly, she still had cookies to mix.

CHAPTER EIGHT

JOHN-HENRY WAS SITTING at his desk, staring into space, when his mother walked in. Surprised to see her, he immediately got to his feet. "Hello, Mother. What are you doing here?"

Dressed in a dusty-pink silk-and-linen suit, with pearls, gloves, and a fashionable hat, Henrietta seemed amused at the question. "Today is Tuesday, is it not? I believe we had a luncheon date, John-Henry, before the board meeting this afternoon. Don't tell me you forgot."

"Of course not," he said quickly, although to be truthful, both appointments had completely slipped his mind. As he reached quickly for his suit jacket hanging over the back of his chair, he pretended not to notice his mother's raised eyebrow. Contrary to his usual custom, he had been working in his shirtsleeves; normally he was much more formal in the office, but, as in so many things lately, he had loosened up. Trying not to think why that was, he slipped into his jacket and came around the desk. He knew he looked guilty.

"You did forget, didn't you?" Henrietta said, giving his lapel a maternal pat.

"No, I—" he started to say, and then gave it up. "I'm sorry, Mother. I've had too much on my mind lately."

"Yes," she agreed mildly. "So I've heard."

"And what is that supposed to mean?"

"Why don't we discuss it over lunch?" she said imperturbably, and led the way out.

They took Henrietta's Cadillac instead of his Jaguar because she felt more comfortable in the larger car. But after they had been seated at a table in the elegant Park Avenue Room, John-Henry said resignedly, "All right. Who was it this time—Jefferson, or someone else?"

Obviously suppressing a smile, Henrietta removed her gloves. "Apparently you've managed to get the entire board in an uproar, darling," she said, and gave him a look. "Were you going to tell me about it, or were you going to surprise me at the meeting this afternoon?"

John-Henry sighed. He should have known this was going to happen when he decided to implement that new small business program to help people like Paula get a start. "How did you find out?" he asked. "The board doesn't meet until this afternoon."

"There's always the telephone, dear. I'm afraid the instrument has been ringing off the hook lately. I do think every member of the board has called to discuss your...er...new policy." She paused. "Except you, that is."

"If I'd known what a ruckus this was going to cause, I would have warned you," he said. "But since it's just a small experimental program, I didn't think there was any point in bothering you with the details."

"Perhaps you could give me a hint or two now?"

"As the bank's chair, you mean."

"No, as your mother."

"First tell me what you've heard."

"Only that you've been making some rather erratic decisions the past few weeks."

"Erratic!" Irritated, he sat back. "Was it erratic to entice Digitron Optic, or to bag Allied Tool?"

"Of course not, darling," she said calmly. "But we're not talking about that, are we?"

"No," he agreed grimly. "We're not." Then he sat forward again. "But I just don't see why my decision to set aside a certain small portion of investment capital for small business expansion should be a cause for concern. Aren't we in the business of encouraging new businesses? For heaven's sake, what does Jefferson and his little entourage think we're doing at the bank?"

"Well, you have to admit, darling, that it is a departure from the way The Hennessey has done business in the past."

"The state was in better economic shape then!" he retorted.

Henrietta gave him a look. "You don't have to be angry with me, darling. I'm on your side, remember?"

"Sorry," he said, and gave her a brief smile before his grim expression returned. "It's just that sometimes I don't have much patience with men like Jefferson Evers who can't see beyond the ends of their noses—or past the bottom line of a profit/loss sheet."

"I know that, darling. But you knew your decision to defer interest on these small business loans would alarm our more conservative officers. I'm afraid some of them view the idea as... revolutionary. Not to mention a disastrous precedent. Suppose a national company—Digitron Optic, for example—asked for the same consideration. There's a concern about where you're going to draw the line."

"I don't see why there's cause for concern. A company like Digitron has assets. Small businesses just getting started don't. It's as simple as that."

"I'm afraid some of our officers don't see it that way."

"And what about you?"

"I agree that we need to stimulate the economy. And I agree that one way to do it is to support the smaller private sector. But you have to admit that this is all new to the board. After all, The Hennessey has never granted simple loans; we leave that to other banks."

"Not when Claude first founded The Hennessey," John-Henry reminded her. "In his time, the individual proprietorship received just as much consideration as the giant corporation."

Henrietta's expression softened as she thought of her husband. "Yes, you're right, of course," she said, and then ruefully shook her head. "But that was years ago, and circumstances are different now."

"Circumstances are what we make of them."

"That's true," she agreed, and touched his arm briefly. "I'm with you, darling," she said, smiling. "And, after all, you can always vindicate yourself by pointing to your first success."

"What's that?"

"Sweet Temptations, of course."

Sometimes he thought she would never cease to amaze him. "How did you know about that?" he asked, and then held up a hand. "Never mind. Your network is legion around here. Everybody knows you have ears to the ground throughout the entire state."

"Well, I did hear about certain invoices for... carpenters," she said mildly.

"It was a goodwill gesture, that's all," he said, exasperated at the thought that such an insignificant detail had been noted, and reported. He shook his head angrily. "I swear, doesn't Jefferson have anything better to do than to run to you with the least little thing? I've half a mind to fire him the instant I get back to the office!"

"I'd rather you invited Paula Trent to tea on Saturday," Henrietta said calmly.

That took the wind out of his sails. "I beg your pardon?"

"I said that I'd like to invite Miss Trent to tea on Saturday," Henrietta repeated. "Now, I'll be sending her a written invitation, of course, but I thought you might like to ask her personally in my place."

He didn't know what to say. "How do you know about Paula Trent?" he asked suspiciously.

"I don't. But since you seem so... involved with her, I thought I might like to meet her."

"I'm not involved with Paula!"

"Then you have some objection to my inviting her to tea?"

Aggravated, he said, "Of course not. Don't be silly. I just don't understand your sudden interest in someone you've never met."

"But darling, she is one of our investments, is she not? And I would like to meet the young woman who is causing all this fuss."

"With Jefferson, you mean."

"No, darling," Henrietta said, amused. "With you."

THAT NIGHT when Paula looked at the calendar, she couldn't believe that Sweet Temptations had been open only a month. Already it seemed like a lifetime. Business was booming, and she had established a routine: up at six, at the store by seven, or earlier, to start the first batches of cookies for the morning, then a short lull, during which she usually ate a sandwich while working on the books, or ordering more supplies, or going over inventory, before starting the big mixers again for the afternoon run.

Rodney was working full-time, and business was so good they could hardly keep up with the demand. Already she'd had to hire a high school girl to help out in the afternoons; with a constant stream of customers, Rodney found he needed more help in front, and she had quickly learned that she couldn't run back and forth between the counter and the oven.

It was all coming together, she thought with a happy sigh. Now she could almost smile at the memories of those first rocky hours on opening day, instead of reliving them in nightmares. All that worry, she thought, for nothing. Business had become so good that even with the new help, she still didn't have time to develop new products during the day, as she had planned, but had to continue staying after the store had closed, to work on recipes.

Not that she was complaining, she thought hastily. Word had spread, and different clubs and organizations had started calling her about supplying cookies for their meetings. She rarely found time to fill those orders during the day and had to stay after closing to get them done, so she had to stay late, anyway.

"Let me help," Rodney had said, just the other day. "I don't mind staying—honest. And you're working too hard. When was the last time you had any time off?"

"You sound like my grandmother," she'd said, but fondly. She was grateful for the offer, but had to refuse it all the same. Rodney worked hard during the day; he needed his time off more than she did. After all, the business was hers to tend; she couldn't expect her employees to devote all their spare time to the store. Besides, she didn't want Rodney to get burned out and maybe quit. She didn't know what she would do without him; he'd been such a big help already that she couldn't imagine trying to run Sweet Temptations without him.

But that meant that she was all alone again tonight, faced with a big order from the Women's Auxiliary that had to be delivered tomorrow. She was thankful for the business, delighted that her reputation was spreading. Only the other day she had received an order from Tulsa, and one from as far away as Sallisaw. Ordinarily, she would have been pleased, but not tonight. Today had been a long one; all the merchants in the mall had gotten together to promote a sidewalk sale that had brought in more people than usual. Even with the three of them: herself and Rodney, and Lisa, their high school help, they hadn't been able to keep up with the demand. She felt as though she had been churning out cookies by the thousands all day, and now she had to fire up the stoves again.

But not just yet, she told herself wearily, as she sat by the big butcher-block table, drinking a cold cup of tea. She didn't even have the energy to get up and fetch more hot water. Rodney was right, she thought. She was working too hard. Her entire body ached, and right now she thought she'd gag if she saw one more chocolate chip.

Fortunately, she didn't have to. The ladies had ordered oatmeal-raisin, and plain spice, so with a sigh, she put aside her teacup and dragged herself up. If she started right now, she might be able to finish by ten...or eleven. Trying not to think longingly about how wonderful a hot bath would feel right now, she set to work.

Fifteen minutes later, having already creamed the butter and eggs and sugar and vanilla, she was just adding the flour mix when the big Hobart mixer made a very strange noise.

"What...?" she muttered, setting aside the flour. Thinking that the beaters had become too clogged, she turned off the mixer and used the spatula to scrape dough away from the blades. Tentatively, she turned the mixer on again. To her relief, it sounded just fine.

Picking up the flour mix again, she had just added the entire bag when the Hobart sputtered. The sound was even more ominous than before, and she was looking at the machine in consternation when right before her eyes, it went out of control. To her horror, the motor started racing, the beaters spun madly, and the entire machine jiggled and jittered, sending up clouds of flour dust into her face.

Blinded, coughing and choking, she put one hand over her mouth and nose and groped with the other for the turn-off switch. By this time the motor was emitting a terrifying, high-pitched whine. Sure the mixer was going to explode, she forgot about the turn-off switch and dived across the table to jerk the plug out of the wall. Cord in hand, flour dust obscuring everything, she covered her head just as the mixer mercifully wound down with a shriek.

Was she safe? She was so shaken at this point that she thought the Hobart might suddenly turn itself on, like something out of a horror movie. Cautiously, she looked up from under her protecting arm. Everything was quiet. The flour was slowly settling, covering everything with a white film. There was utter silence.

Paula hauled herself to her feet. She'd banged her elbow on her wild dive for the outlet, and she rubbed it as she approached the counter warily. Now what?

Biting her lip, she examined the mixer. Obviously she was going to have to start over, but first she had to clean the machine completely. Slowly, she surveyed the damage. Everything was covered with white dust, and when she realized she'd have to wipe off all the counters, as well, she felt like weeping. It was already after nine, and it would be hours now before she'd finish—if she could finish at all. She still didn't know if the Hobart would start, but she couldn't find that out until she cleaned up the mess.

"Why is this happening?" she muttered, and tried to release the beaters from the mixer head so she could take the bowl out. The catch refused to work. Angrily, she pulled again. It wouldn't budge.

"Let go!" she cried, and gave the bowl a mighty heave.

This time she won. Before her horrified eyes, the entire mixer jumped off the table, right toward her. It was a valuable machine, and she grabbed for it with both hands. The weight threw her off balance and sent her crashing to the floor.

That was the last straw. Landing hard, she burst into enraged tears. She was tired, and covered with flour, and her mixer had come off the stand, and she didn't know if she could fix it, and she still had eighteen dozen cookies to make before morning. It was all too much. With a little voice inside her telling her not to give in to her urge to throw the mixer as far as she could, she closed her eyes and cried in a fury, "Damn this mixer and every cookie ever made straight to hell!"

"I see this might be a bad time to visit," a voice behind her said.

Spinning around from her awkward position on the floor, Paula saw John-Henry standing in the doorway. Had she forgotten to lock the back door again? Rodney had warned her about that a dozen times or more; lately, she'd been so preoccupied that she didn't remember to keep the catch on. Anyone could enter, he had said, and he was right. Now look who had just walked in.

"What are you doing here?" she cried. "And why do you always have to sneak up on me like that?"

"I didn't 'sneak' up on you," John-Henry said mildly. "The door was open—"

She was still incensed. Why did he always have to see her when she looked like a wreck? Coated with flour, her hair standing on end, she probably looked like a demented spook. That thought made her even more irate.

"And so you just walked in?" she cried.

"No," he said calmly. "I knocked. But you were making so much noise—"

That reminded her of the mixer, and she glared balefully at him as she tried to get to her feet, struggling to hold on to the Hobart. It was heavy, and she couldn't get a grip on it.

He reached out. "Here, let me help."

"No! I've got it!" she cried, and promptly let the stupid thing fall to the floor with a crash. As though it had been his fault, she turned on him. "Now see what you've done!"

"Sorry," he murmured, and picked it up as though it weighed no more than a piece of paper. It was dripping batter, and he held it away from him. "Where do you want it?"

She didn't know whether to scream or burst into tears again. He was absolutely calm, while she felt like flying into a million pieces. She wanted to snatch the mixer away from him, but she had learned her lesson. The thing was too heavy for her, and, tight-lipped, she pointed to the table. "Right there," she said, hating it, and him, and the entire situation. How could this have happened? Why had he come? Wishing he would just go, she added unthinkingly, "Not that it will do much good. The stupid thing is broken."

"Would you like me to fix it?"

"You?" she said incredulously, and glanced pointedly at his sharply creased slacks, and immaculate white shirt with the sleeves rolled up to the elbows. She hadn't noticed before, but his arms were so tanned. How did he manage that, she wondered, when he spent his days inside an office?

Looking amused at her disbelief, he shrugged. "Well, I could try. Do you have a towel or something, so I can clean it up?"

She wasn't going to let him near the damn mixer. All she wanted was for him to leave. Glaring at him, she said angrily, "I'll fix it myself."

He seemed about to say something else, but then backed up a step, his hands up. "Okay, I was just trying to help."

"I don't need your help," she said testily, and reached for a towel.

"I can see that," he said. "I'm sorry. I didn't mean to offend you."

"Well, you did," she muttered. The crash must have loosened the release catch; it functioned this time when she tried it. Oh, swell, she thought. *Now* it works.

Setting the mixing bowl aside, she wiped the body of the mixer and looked at it. Now what? She cleaned the powerful beaters, then holding her breath, she examined them carefully. To her relief, the blades weren't bent, so she could use them—if she could get the mixer itself to work. She reached for the little toolbox she kept under the counter, and extracted a screwdriver from it.

"I wouldn't use that just yet if I were you," John-Henry advised.

Although she had intended using the screwdriver on every screw she could find in the hope that she could fix the mixer, she immediately banged the tool down onto the table. "I wasn't going to!" she said in exasperation. "I was just getting it ready in case I had to!"

"Okay, okay," he said. "I didn't mean to make you angry."

"I'm not angry!" she cried, and furiously pushed past him, reaching for the cord to insert the plug into the wall socket again. Straightening, the plug still in her hand, she looked at him. "Why are you here, anyway? Did you come to laugh, or did you have a purpose for this visit?"

"I'm not laughing," he said seriously, although he had to hide a smile as she irritably pushed floury hair out of her eyes. "And I did have a purpose. I've tried calling you at home for two days, but never could get an answer. My mother would like to invite you to tea on the fifteenth."

She couldn't believe she had heard right. "What?"

He looked slightly embarrassed. "I know it sounds old-fashioned, but my mother is that way. She said she sent you a note, but since she hasn't had a reply, she asked me to pass along the invitation. Didn't you get it in the mail?"

It was her turn to look embarrassed. She was always so tired when she was finally able to drag herself home at night, that days would pass before she glanced through her mail. A pile of it had been collecting on the kitchen table this past week, but she hadn't had the energy to sort through it. Nothing ever came for her but bills, anyway.

"I don't know," she said, avoiding his eyes. "I haven't . . . looked lately."

"Then that explains it," he said, and hesitated. "Will you come?"

The invitation had been so unexpected that she felt flustered. "Oh, well, I—" she started to say, and without thinking, reached down to plug the mixer in again.

"Oh, I wouldn't do that—" John-Henry began.

He was too late. She'd forgotten to turn the switch off, and before he could finish the sentence, the Hobart erupted into pulverizing life. There was an earsplitting shrieking noise, and before Paula's horrified eyes, the machine started a macabre dance across the table. She and John-Henry leaped for it at the same time.

"I got it—"

"No, let me—"

He got there first. Slashing at the switch, he jerked the cord from the wall at the same time. But as the shrieking sound was cut off in mid-shrill, Paula's already taut nerves snapped. Bursting into tears, she cried, "Oh, this is too much! Now I'll never finish that order!"

Instantly, John-Henry put the machine on the table. Reaching for her, he pulled her against him. "It's all right," he soothed, smoothing away her hair. "It's all right."

She was at the end of her rope. "No, it's not!" she cried, weeping against his immaculate shirtfront. "I've got dozens of cookies to make, and I'll never get them done by hand! Never!"

"Don't cry," John-Henry said. "I'll fix the machine."

Her mouth trembling, she blinked back tears and looked up at him, suddenly realizing what a compromising position she was in. With him holding her so close, she couldn't think. She knew she should push him away, but she just couldn't. She hadn't felt this safe and secure and comforted, for longer than she could remember. Oh, how she longed just to give up and let him handle things, she thought. She was so tired. So tired.

"No one can fix that machine," she said.

"I can," he said, and held her even closer. Before she knew what was happening, he had kissed her lightly on the lips.

She was caught so off guard by the gesture, by his nearness, by that kiss, that she hardly knew what she was saying. "You...can?"

"I can," he said, smiling into her eyes. "Didn't I tell you I wasn't always a banker?"

Then he kissed her again.

This kiss was not like the first brush of his lips. Now there was nothing tender, or gentle, or hesitant about the way his mouth came down on hers. He pulled her so tightly against him, she felt his burgeoning erection. The sensation caused a tumult of emotions to sweep through her, and without realizing, she put her arms around his neck and pressed her hips into him. Moaning, he responded by kissing her more deeply. When his tongue probed her mouth, she felt helpless against her mounting desire. A terrible longing to join with him was spreading throughout her entire body, and she felt a warmth deep inside that she knew would soon become a fire, unless she found the will to put a stop to it right now.

"No, I can't!" she gasped, and pulled away with every ounce of willpower she possessed.

John-Henry looked at her blankly, as though he didn't know what had happened. She was still within the circle of his arms, and it was all she could do not to wind her fingers into his hair and draw his face down to hers for one last kiss. But she knew what would happen if she did, and so she put her hands against his chest and pushed him away instead.

"I'm sorry," she muttered, feeling as though a storm had passed, leaving her exhausted. From a safe distance of two feet she forced herself to look at him. "I . . . shouldn't have allowed . . . that to happen."

John-Henry looked bemused. "Why not?"

She didn't know what to say. The silence stretched on, and she knew she had to answer somehow. Trying not to think that no other had ever aroused her to such a pitch by a mere kiss, she said shakily, "John-Henry, I have to tell you that I don't have time for a relationship, not now, or even in the near future. I have to make a success of my cookie store, and that's going to take all my energy. It isn't fair to pretend otherwise, and I . . . I never should have allowed things to get out of hand."

"And that's what you think they are—out of hand?"

"I don't know what I think," she said miserably. "It's just that I have so many responsibilities, so many—"

His expression made her break off. Softly, he said, "You have responsibilities to yourself, Paula. Can you deny there is something between us?"

"No, that would be a lie," she said, forcing herself to admit it. "I do feel something, John-Henry. Maybe I feel too much. But I can't give in to that feeling."

"Is it because your husband left you?"

She had nearly forgotten Randy. "How did you find out about that?" she asked, and then shook her head. "Never mind, it doesn't matter. No, it doesn't have anything to do with Randy, except for the fact that when he walked out on me, I realized just how . . . how vulnerable Grandma and I were. I told you about my grandmother, and how I feel about her—"

"Yes," he said, with a strange tone in his voice. "You did. But Paula—"

She wanted to make him understand. "I feel so responsible for her, John-Henry," she said. "She's eighty-two years old, and there's only her and me. If something happened to her, and I couldn't take care of her, I don't know what I'd do. She means everything to me. There's nothing I wouldn't do for her."

"Including sacrificing your own happiness?" he asked. "Do you think Heddy...er...your grandmother wants that?"

Tears filled Paula's eyes again. "Don't do this to me, John-Henry," she said. "It isn't fair."

A demon seemed to have possessed him. "You're the one who's not being fair, Paula," he said. "Don't you see? I could help you—"

When she stiffened, he knew he'd made a mistake. "You already *have* helped me," she said. "I can't ask for any more."

"I didn't mean it that way," he said quickly. "I meant—"

"Why are you doing this to me?" she cried. "Is it because you've never been denied anything in your entire life? I've told you I don't have time to get involved!"

"I can wait."

"I don't want you to wait!"

"That's not your decision."

Suddenly she became angry. "It's not yours, either!" she shouted. "Oh, you'll never understand! You have no idea what it means to worry about money, about where your next meal is coming from, or if you're going to have a roof over your head because you can't pay the mortgage!"

Without warning, a vision of a little boy playing in a dirt yard choked with weeds flashed into his mind. It was summer, and he wasn't wearing his only pair of shoes because he was supposed to save them for school in the fall. For toys, he had an old tin can and some smooth stones he'd found by the creek. He had used them to create a fortress for an imaginary playmate who, once behind the little stone walls, would always be safe.

"That's not true," he said quietly, forcing the images away. "I've told you, I grew up in a privileged environment, but it wasn't always that way. When I was very young, my mother had to scrape for every penny. In fact, she—"

She looked at him with scorn. "So you've told me. But that didn't last long, did it? After your mother married that Claude, I'll bet that the only time you felt poverty-stricken was when there were six horses in the stables instead of a full dozen!"

An image of a gangly Thoroughbred racehorse flashed into his mind just then, but he didn't want to talk about horses. "If you're saying these things in an effort to drive me away," he said, "it won't work. I'll wait, Paula. I've got lots of time."

And before she could respond to that, he picked up the screwdriver from the table and started to repair the big Hobart mixer.

"You don't have to do that!" she said sharply, just wanting him to go.

"It's done," he replied, and switched the machine on. It began to whir powerfully, just as it was supposed to, and she felt like a fool.

"You fixed it," she said, stating the obvious, and avoiding his eyes. "Thank you."

"You can thank me by coming to tea on Saturday," he said.

"I can't."

"I see. Then will you make your apologies to my mother, or shall I?"

She was about to say she'd do it when something in his tone made her pause. Was he challenging her in some subtle way? Her chin lifted, and she said rashly, "Neither. Tomorrow I'll call and tell her I accept."

"Fine, then," he said. "I'll see you on the fifteenth."

He left before she could ask him what he thought was so damned funny. Right before he went out the door, she was sure she saw him smile. Muttering to herself, she turned back to the mixer. Whether or not she regretted her hasty decision, she still had cookies to make before tomorrow.

CHAPTER NINE

THE IDEA OF GOING TO TEA with John-Henry's mother terrified Paula so, she tried to put all thought of it out of her mind until the fateful day. That wasn't so difficult; her days—and nights—continued to be so busy she hardly had time to think about anything but the store.

What continually amazed and delighted her was that now that she was rolling, she couldn't seem to make a mistake with the cookies. After much testing, she introduced two new varieties—peanut butter, and chocolate with white-chocolate chips. Both were instant hits, selling out quickly every day, with customers clamoring for more. In time, they were as popular as her stock recipes, and so she added them to her inventory.

Buoyed by these triumphs, she decided it was time to put another of her ideas into practice. Hoping to draw the breakfast crowd into the store, she'd been thinking of adding muffins to her line. Now that the cookies were selling so well, she felt she could afford to try the muffins. After more nights and early mornings spent testing, she introduced three kinds: lemon-poppyseed, bran, and banana-nut. All were an instant success. Soon, customers who came in for cookies for their afternoon work breaks stopped by in the morning for muffins to take to work. Thrilled that the idea had taken off so well, she started giving away an extra muffin for every dozen a customer bought, wrapping it separately so the buyer could eat it on the way to work. The idea was such a success that she made it standard practice for the cookie sales, too. Rodney warned her at first that she was giving so much away that she would go broke, but it had quite the opposite effect. Word spread about her "baker's dozen," and soon it seemed that the more she gave away, the more she sold.

She was working on yet another idea—little waxed paper baggies that clipped on to belts or purses, leaving a customer's hands free to carry other things, when she realized it was Saturday, the day of the tea party.

Fortunately, Heddy was there to give her moral support when she rushed home at eleven to get ready. She had hoped to find time, on an afternoon or an evening, to go shopping for something new to wear, but even though she was surrounded by stores at the mall, it seemed she never had a spare minute to get away. Now she was sorry. Boy, was she sorry!

"I don't have a thing to wear!" she wailed, after frantically searching through her closet. She knew every article there intimately, but she went through them all anyway, on the chance that she had miraculously forgotten about a new linen suit, or a flowing tea-length dress in tissue faille. Pulling her head out of the closet, her stricken expression told all as she looked at Heddy. "What am I going to do?"

"Wear that lovely peach-colored dress," Heddy suggested. "It's a wonderful color on you, and shows off your figure."

Paula looked horrified. "I don't want to show off my figure! And that dress is ten years old if it's a day!"

"They won't know that," Heddy said, and then saw Paula's petrified expression. "All right, then, if you don't like the dress, why not a skirt and sweater?"

If possible, Paula looked even more appalled. "Grandma, I don't think—"

"Or," Heddy said, reaching for the carryall she'd brought with her, "why not this?"

Paula watched uncomprehendingly as Heddy pulled out a tissue-wrapped package and handed it to her. "What's that?"

"Open it and see," Heddy said.

Puzzled, Paula pulled away the wrapping, and gasped. She was holding a dress in her hands, a garment made of such delicate and silky fabric that it nearly slipped off her lap when she looked from it to Heddy. "Grandma—"

"Don't say it," Heddy said. "I knew you wouldn't make time to go shopping, and this is an important day for you. I wanted you to have something nice."

"Nice!" A lump in her throat, Paula looked down at the dress Heddy had given her. She couldn't remember ever having something so lovely, and she leaped up to give Heddy a hug and a grateful kiss. "Thanks, Grandma, but you shouldn't have. I know how expensive it must—"

Heddy raised her hand. "Don't say it. What's money for, if we can't occasionally spend it on someone we love?"

Paula started to say something more, then bit her lip. Maybe her grandmother was right, she thought, and gave Heddy another quick hug. "Thanks, Grandma," she whispered. "It's perfect. I don't know how to thank you."

"You can thank me by having a good time," Heddy said. "Now, go and try it on. We'll both feel pretty silly if it doesn't fit, won't we?"

But the dress was perfect. Heddy was in the living room, scrutinizing Henrietta Hennessey's elegant invitation, when Paula emerged from the bedroom. As soon as she saw her granddaughter, her eyes lit up.

"You look beautiful!" she exclaimed. "I *knew* that color would be wonderful on you."

Secretly, Paula had to agree. When she'd slipped the dress on and turned to look at herself in the mirror, even she had been taken aback. With her hair freshly washed and set in a soft style, and makeup applied in a way she never used for the store, the feminine woman staring back at her was unfamiliar for a moment. The deep rose of the dress brought out the amber flecks in her dark eyes and gave her skin a glow. To complete the picture, she added an antique brooch that had been her mother's. For courage, she hoped, and touched it now for good luck.

"Well, I guess I'm ready," she said.

"You certainly are," Heddy agreed, and glanced at the clock. "It's almost time to go, too."

Instantly Paula felt terrified again. Why had she agreed to this? she groaned inwardly. She knew she was going to feel completely out of place, and what would John-Henry's mother think, when she drove up in her ancient little Volkswagen?

"Oh, Grandma," she said, rubbing her hands together. "I don't think I should go. What am I going to say to someone like Mrs. Hennessey? You saw the invitation she sent me. I've never seen anything like it, but it has to be parchment, doesn't it? And embossed! And did you see her writing? It's so elegant, just like she must be."

Heddy looked down at the ivory-colored invitation she'd put back on the coffee table. "So she has good stationery," she said with a shrug.

"Oh, Grandma, that's not the point!" Paula cried. "I just know I'm going to make a complete fool of myself!"

"Nonsense," Heddy said briskly. "You'll be just fine. All you have to do is remember to be yourself."

"Myself!"

"Or, failing that, take your cue from the great actresses in the past," Heddy said, warming to her favorite tale. She struck a pose. "Like Hedy Lamarr, who was named after me. You can't get any more sophisticated or elegant than that."

"Oh, Grandma, that story isn't true, and you know it!" Paula said, but she smiled, and with the smile, her moment of panic passed. Able to feel relatively calm again, she said, "Oh, I almost forgot. Before I go, I've got something for you, too."

"Me? Oh, Paula—"

"Oh, it's nothing on the order of the dress," Paula said, leading the way into the kitchen. She took out a waxed paper bag and held it out. "I didn't like the idea of you taking only those broken cookies from the store down to your friends at the seniors center, so I made some extra for you to take—perfect ones, just like those at the shop."

Heddy seemed taken aback. "Oh, Paula, that isn't necessary. My...my friends down at the Center don't care if the cookies are broken or not. It's the taste that counts."

"I know," Paula said, pressing the big bag into Heddy's hands. "But all the same, I'm the cookie maker, and *my* grandmother deserves nothing but the best!" She smiled. "Besides, you never know where new customers will come from. Who knows, these may start a whole new trend!"

"They already have," Heddy muttered.

"What?"

"Never mind," her grandmother said hastily, and gave her a quick kiss. "Thank you, darling. I know everyone at the . . . at the Center will appreciate these."

"Then that's all I can ask," Paula said, and glanced at the clock. She couldn't delay any longer; she had to leave now or she would be late. "Well," she said. "Wish me luck."

"You won't need any," Heddy said, and waved her goodbye.

HEDDY WAITED until Paula's beige Volkswagen turned the corner before she fetched her purse, locked the door behind her, and set off for the bus stop. With each step, the bag of cookies Paula gave her seemed to get heavier, and she wanted to stash it under a bush and leave it behind. Out of sight, out of mind, she thought, and sighed as she took a firmer grip on the bag. She couldn't waste good food, especially cookies Paula had made just for her.

That thought made her feel even worse. She hated keeping secrets. She should have just told Paula the truth, and let the chips fall where they may. The cookies she had been taking all along weren't for her friends at the Center, but for Otis and No Regrets, and she should have just come right out and said so.

She had intended to . . . yes, she had. But she knew how nervous Paula was about this invitation to tea, and she couldn't upset her any further—not on the great day. But my, hadn't she looked beautiful in that dress? It had been worth eating soup for dinner all this time. The money she'd saved had enabled her to give Paula confidence.

Heddy's spirits fell again. She knew the dress wasn't going to make up for not telling Paula the truth. Then Heddy started to feel annoyed with Otis. In a way, it was all his fault. He had told her *months* ago that the horse would soon be well; he kept promising that the stupid gravel was going to pop any day now. So far, she hadn't seen much evidence that the horse was any sounder than he'd been when they first signed the papers. Otis was confident—or so he said, but she was beginning to wonder.

Well, today when she got to the track, she'd sit that old fool down right there in the tack room and give him a piece of her mind. He might have all the time in the world, but she had to know when the horse was going to get better; it was too much of a strain keeping all this from Paula. If she had to go on keeping secrets, she was going to start having palpitations, and then where would they be? Paula would find out anyway, and the situation would be a hundred times worse.

Heddy's annoyance carried her all the way to Remington Park. Getting off the bus with a grunt, she grimly clutched the bag of cookies, waved to the gate guard, and started toward the shedrow that had become almost as familiar to her as her little house around the block from Paula's. Because she'd spent so much time there, she could tell as soon as she came around the corner of the barn that something was different. At this time of day, No Regrets was either being patiently walked by the devoted Fernando, or he was in his stall, picking at the giant hay ball Otis hung outside for him every morning. He certainly should not be standing in the aisle, with Otis practically dancing around him. Heddy quickened her steps, sure something was wrong.

"What is it, what is it?" she asked anxiously, coming up to where the three stood.

Fernando turned with a big grin and pointed, but before Heddy could see what he was pointing at, Otis came around the rear of the horse, grabbed her, and proceeded to skip with her up and down the aisle. With everything jiggling from Otis's exuberance, it was a moment before she could catch her breath. When she did, she pushed him away.

"Otis, you old fool! What's the matter with you?" she cried.

Otis did a couple more fancy steps before bowing low before her. "You didn't think it would happen, Heddy girl," he said gleefully, his face creased in a big, wide smile. "But I knew, I knew I was right, and I was! Now, are you going to say you're sorry for doubting my ability?"

"What are you talking about?" she demanded, straightening her hat. She'd nearly dropped her purse, and the bag of cookies had taken a good shaking, too.

Grabbing her plump little arm, Otis practically dragged her over to where Fernando stood with No Regrets. Proudly, and with a great flourish, he pointed to the horse's right hind leg. Heddy squinted, but she couldn't see anything different.

"What...?"

"There!" Otis said. "Don't you see that little hole right by the hairline?"

Heddy squinted again. Maybe if she concentrated very hard...but no, she couldn't see a thing. "No, I don't see it," she said. "What—"

Otis couldn't control his delight any longer. Grabbing her around the waist, he whirled her in a little circle again. "No Regrets popped that gravel this morning,

Heddy darlin'!" he exulted. "He's sound as a dollar! We start trainin' tomorrow!"

Heddy was so astounded that she planted her size four shoes firmly on the ground. Otis, still with his arm around her, came to a stumbling halt, too. "Otis, are you sure?" she asked, not daring to believe it.

"As sure as I'm standin' here!" he replied, his grin nearly splitting his round face. "I've got a call in for the shoer, and we're *trackin'* come sunlight!"

Heddy could hardly believe it. She had come here prepared to give Otis what-for, and now she didn't have to. Laughing in sheer delight—and relief—she dug into the bag of cookies she'd brought. "In that case," she crowed, "it's cookies all around!"

They gave the first one to No Regrets. Only when the horse had cautiously nibbled it to crumbs did Heddy realize it was an oatmeal-raisin. Well, no wonder he took so long to eat it, she thought fondly, digging into the bag for another that the horse took more eagerly. He always *had* preferred the chocolate chip.

"WOULD YOU PREFER one lump or two?" Henrietta Hennessey asked, one hand gracefully holding the sugar tongs poised above the sugar bowl.

"No sugar, thank you," Paula said, and willed her hands not to shake as she took the cup her hostess passed across to her.

"John-Henry, I know you take yours black," Henrietta said, holding out a cup of tea to him. He was sitting with Paula on one of the burgundy and cream-striped Queen Anne sofas near the fireplace. His mother sat opposite on a matching chair. The silver service was on the low coffee table between them, and as he looked down, the brightly polished Georgian teapot reflected his face, distorting it just slightly, so that he looked a little wild-eyed.

Which was exactly how he felt, John-Henry thought, and didn't know why he should be so nervous. Paula seemed perfectly composed and relaxed as she sipped from her cup, but what had he expected—that she would make a complete fool of herself in front of his mother? But that's what he was doing, it seemed, wondering why he couldn't calm down. Maybe it was because he wanted the two most important women in his life to like each other, he thought, and then realized they seemed to be doing just fine on that score.

Paula had never looked lovelier. She was wearing a rose-colored dress of some silky material that rustled mysteriously when she moved. He couldn't keep his eyes off her face. He had always thought she was beautiful, but she seemed even more so today, her eyes large and luminous, the amber flecks brought out by the color of her dress.

And her hair was down, not in the ponytail she usually wore, or under that awful net. It seemed to float around her shoulders, begging to be touched, and unconsciously, his fingers tightened on his teacup.

"Biscuit, John-Henry?" his mother asked, bringing him back from wherever he had gone. Loathing the little scones Henrietta had ordered made to accompany the tea, he took some just to be polite, and then realized he'd missed part of the conversation. His mother was just congratulating Paula on her success, and Paula was looking embarrassed and pleased at the same time.

"I've heard that your cookie store is doing very well," Henrietta said with a smile, as she put the plate of scones down. "Congratulations. It's not an easy task starting a new business, but to be in such demand after such a short time is an achievement indeed.''

"Thank you, Mrs. Hennessey," Paula replied, with a quick glance in John-Henry's direction. "I've been very fortunate."

Henrietta glanced musingly around the beautiful room. "So have I," she murmured. Then she returned her glance to Paula. "But it's been my experience that it's what you do with good fortune that counts. Nothing, not even luck, can take the place of hard work."

"Being in the right place at the right time helps, too," Paula said, smiling. "I don't know how successful I would have been if I hadn't found that last space at the mall. I couldn't have asked for a better location."

"And I hear you've already expanded your operation. Muffins now, is it not?"

Paula seemed surprised. "How did you know that?"

Henrietta smiled. "Oh, I have my ways...especially when someone catches my interest."

John-Henry looked at his mother in astonishment. Henrietta was rarely so forthcoming, especially with someone she had just met. But then, he thought, his mother had seemed to like Paula right from the start. To his relief, the polite but aloof look she reserved for those who failed to meet her high standards was absent today, and a warm smile was in its place.

Realizing he should contribute something to the conversation, he set aside the dainty little teacup, and said, "Business must be good. I heard the other day that you'd hired someone new to help at the counter."

"Yes, I did," Paula said. "But who told you that?"

Deciding he might have betrayed himself more than he should, he tried a casual shrug. "I don't remember. I suppose it was someone at the bank."

Paula gave him a thoughtful look. "You know, it's the strangest thing, but I have quite a few customers who work at The Hennessey." She paused meaningfully. "Isn't that odd? I can't imagine how that happened. Can you?"

John-Henry saw Henrietta hiding her smile behind her teacup. So she had guessed, he thought, and said, "It's obvious, isn't it? Sweet Temptations has already made quite a reputation for itself. And well-deserved, I might add. Would you like some more tea?"

Paula held his gaze for what seemed an endless moment. Was it only his guilty knowledge, or did he imagine that knowing look in her dark eyes? He'd never told her about that memo ordering all his employees to buy cookies on her opening day, but he wouldn't be surprised if she hadn't figured it out anyway. Behind that lovely face was a quick mind—as he'd found out, the hard way.

"No, thank you," she said, and turned back to Henrietta, who had been watching the little scene closely. "But it was lovely. Thank you so much for inviting me."

Henrietta set aside her cup, too. "Would you like to see the house?"

Paula's eyes lit up. "Oh, I would! But wouldn't it be too much trouble?"

"Not at all," Henrietta said, rising. "Come this way. We'll start with the library."

John-Henry was so surprised that his mother had offered to give Paula a tour of the house that he didn't think to protest that *he* wanted a little of Paula's time, now that she was finally away from the store. Before he could recover from his astonishment, the two women were heading toward the curving staircase in the entry. As they went up the stairs, he could hear Paula saying something to which his mother responded with a low laugh. He shook his head in amazement. His mother was very protective about the house; she rarely offered to show it, even when pressed.

The Hennessey mansion, built during the Oklahoma Land Rush a hundred years ago, when the Oklahoma Territory was settled, had been in Claude's family for years. The house was considered a local landmark, and many people, some of whom had even been guests here, had almost begged Henrietta to display it. She rarely took anyone beyond the dining-room or living-room door. It was *her* house until she died, she claimed, and she didn't want strangers, no matter how well known or friendly, pawing through it until she was gone. The fact that she had spontaneously offered to show Paula around so astounded him again that he laughed. Well, well, he thought. He knew what had happened to him. But it seemed that his mother had fallen under Paula's spell, too.

He found out just how much when Paula was leaving, her eyes still sparkling from her tour, agreeing, on Henrietta's invitation, to return.

"I had a lovely time, Mrs. Hennessey," she said. "Tea was wonderful, and you have a beautiful home."

Henrietta clasped one of Paula's hands. "Then you must come often and enjoy it," she said fondly. "Whenever you have time."

"I don't know when that will be," Paula said regretfully. "As I mentioned, if I expand, I'm going to be busier than ever."

"Expand?" John-Henry said. This was the first he'd heard about it.

"Oh, it's just something I was discussing with your mother, John-Henry," Paula said. "Nothing is definite yet."

He certainly hoped not. It was hard enough prying Paula away from one store as it was, he thought. If he had two of them to contend with, things would be impossible. "I really think that's a good idea—" he started to say, but his mother put a restraining hand on his arm.

"Paula has to leave, dear," she said. "We can't take any more of her time."

"Oh, it's I who have taken yours, Mrs. Hennessey," Paula said, with a hasty glance in John-Henry's direction. "Thank you again," she said before John-Henry could get a word in edgewise. "I did so enjoy myself."

John-Henry decided he'd been shunted between the women's conversation long enough. "I'll walk you to your car," he said, as Paula turned to go down the front steps.

She looked over her shoulder. "Oh, that's not necessary."

"Yes, it is," he said firmly, and took her arm, trying not to notice his mother's expression as she gently shut the door.

Paula's car refused to start. The engine gave a halfhearted grumble when she turned the key, and nothing at all when she tried again. "Oh, no," she said. "What is it now? I just had it in to the shop!"

"I'll take a look," John-Henry said, trying to hide his elation. If something was wrong with the car, Paula would have to stay longer, and they might be able to have a conversation without his mother looking on. He loved Henrietta, but sometimes she could be trying.

"No, no, I'll just call a cab," Paula said, and looked around anxiously. "If I can use the phone, I'll have someone tow my car to the garage."

"I can run you home."

"Oh, no, I don't want to put you to the trouble."

"It's no trouble."

"No, really, John-Henry, a cab will be just fine."

He leaned against the car. "Why don't you want to be alone with me?"

"It isn't that."

"Then what?"

"Well—" Obviously grasping at straws, she glanced up at the imposing house. "What would your mother say?"

Laughing at the absurdity of needing his mother's permission for anything, he said fondly, "With the way she took to you? She'd probably give you her Cadillac to drive."

"I doubt that," Paula said, still looking at the big brick and glass mansion. Unconsciously, she sighed. "It's a beautiful house."

He glanced over his shoulder. "Oh, I don't know. It seems too big and ostentatious to me. I keep telling Mother she should turn it over to the historical society and move into a smaller place."

Paula looked horrified. "Oh, but that would awful! She loves that house!"

"It sounds like you do, too."

"Well, who wouldn't?" she asked. Then added, "Don't you live here, too?"

"God, no," he said with a shudder. "As I've told you, it's too big for me. I moved out years ago—long before Camilla—"

He stopped suddenly.

"Camilla?" she said.

"My wife," he answered briefly. "She died some time ago."

"Oh, yes," Paula said, her voice low. "I'm sorry."

"Yes, well. So was I," he said, but he wasn't thinking about Camilla at that moment; he was wondering how he was going to restrain himself from reaching out and gathering Paula into his arms. She looked so damned beautiful in this light, he thought. But then, to him, she looked beautiful in any light, under any conditions, even with her hair in a net and flour on her nose, as he had seen her so often at the store.

In an effort to distract himself, he shrugged. "It seems as if we've both lost someone, doesn't it?"

"Yes, but Randy walked out on me," she said. "It's not the same thing."

"No, I guess not," he agreed, and told himself not to think how warm and soft her lips had felt under his. Wondering how any man could leave Paula, he said, "Well, I guess I'd better get you home."

"Oh, no, I'm going to call a cab."

"Afraid not. My Victorian mother would draw and quarter me if I didn't show you properly to your door."

"But—"

"No protests," he said, wondering how he was going to get her home without pulling over somewhere and kissing her until they were both frenzied. Then he pulled himself together. Paula had made it quite clear that she wasn't ready for a relationship, and after the way he'd been vacillating, he wasn't sure he was, either. Paula had revived something in him that he thought he had buried with Camilla—a recklessness, a restlessness. He had seen the damage those feelings could do, and he had spent the past five years pounding them into respectability. He was

John-Henry Hennessey, banker, now; he had to remember that.

"But what about my car?" Paula brought him out of his reverie. "I can't just leave it here."

"I'll take care of it."

"I can't let you do that."

John-Henry couldn't help himself. Stepping closer, he took her arms—just that, although it was an effort not to draw her tightly against him—and looked down into those beautiful, expressive eyes.

"I said I'd take care of it," he said softly. "Don't you trust me?"

"Don't be ridiculous," she said. "Of course I trust you. It's just..." But her voice trailed away under his unwavering stare, and she finished faintly, "It's just that I...don't want to...to cause you any trouble..."

Don't you know you already have? he thought, and wondered if he could hold fast to his resolve. Already he could feel the edges crumbling; it had started the first day Paula had walked into his office and asked for a loan. Since then, among other things, he had acquired a half interest in a lame racehorse, formed a conspiracy with an eighty-two-year old woman against her granddaughter, and caused an uproar at the bank by radically departing from customary procedures. Now, was he falling in love, as well?

"It's no trouble," he said, and with supreme effort, released her to go fetch his car.

PAULA GOT UP EARLY the next morning. Despite the fact that it was Sunday, she had a lot to do. Then she remembered she didn't have a car.

Trust me, John-Henry had said. But even he couldn't create mircles. What mechanic would fix a car over the weekend?

Then she looked out the window. Her Volkswagen was sitting by the curb, and when she came out to the porch, she found the key taped to her front door. Taking it down, she stared at it wonderingly. Whoever had dropped it off had come and gone without her hearing anything. When had that happened? The sound of her ancient engine was so distinctive; she should have heard it coming a block away.

Wondering if she were dreaming, she walked down to where the car was parked. To her amazement, it had even been washed and waxed. Running a finger along the roof, she shook her head, and then unlocked the door. John-Henry might have been able to make the car all shiny on the outside, but even he couldn't do much with an engine that was too old and had too many miles. Sure that she would still have to pump the gas pedal and cajole the starter, she inserted the key and turned. When the engine sprang to life, purring like a kitten, tears sprang into Paula's eyes. If John-Henry could do something like this, with so little effort, what else might he do for her? Resting her forehead against the steering wheel, she closed her eyes. She felt so confused, so unhappy, so...she didn't know what she felt.

Trust me, John-Henry had said, but did she dare even try?

CHAPTER TEN

AFTER THE TEA with Henrietta Hennessey, and the embarrassing incident with her car, Paula tried to tell herself that she was too busy to think about John-Henry. It wasn't true. Even when she was working so hard at the store, waiting on customers, mixing endless batches of cookies, writing out checks for bills, or testing new recipes, he was on her mind. She thought about him constantly, and despised herself for it.

"We have nothing in common!" she'd mutter fiercely to herself in an effort to put him out of her thoughts.

But the differences were not always obvious. Despite the fact that their life-styles and backgrounds were miles apart, she never remembered those things when they were together. It was only afterward that they became an issue; when she was with John-Henry, nothing else seemed to matter. She'd never known anyone like him. He certainly wasn't like Randy, who couldn't have cared less about what she thought or wanted or did; no matter what she said, John-Henry seemed interested.

And he did things for her, she thought, like repairing her mixer, or having her car fixed. Randy had never volunteered to mend anything; if something got done around the house when he was there, it was because he finally got tired of her constant nagging—or was shamed into it because she started doing the chore herself. She couldn't imagine John-Henry sitting around while she was struggling to do something; hadn't he taken the mixer out of her hands that night and restored it himself?

Remembering the quick embraces, the all-too-brief kisses, and her fevered responses even to such simple gestures, Paula sometimes wondered what would happen if she just threw caution to the winds and let herself fall in love with John-Henry. But she only wondered this when her guard was down, or she was particularly tired and feeling vulnerable; at other times, she refused to consider the idea. She had planned her future; she had locked in her goals.

And if she wavered, she thought, all she had to do was remember what she had learned about Camilla, John-Henry's wife. Like a fool, she had gone to the library archives soon after meeting him to satisfy her curiosity by reading through old newspapers. She had found out more—much more—than she ever wanted to know about the woman John-Henry had married. Camilla had been everything she was not: petite and blond, with a gorgeous figure and a perfect patrician profile. Only when caught full-face by the camera did she seem just the slightest bit petulant and sulky, but even on microfiche, Camilla was the epitome of glamour and sophistication. Staring down at those flawless features, Paula couldn't imagine her doing dishes, or cleaning the house...or making cookies, and with a snap, she'd turned off the viewer light. She had seen all she needed to see.

Feeling more keenly than ever that John-Henry was out of her league, the only communication she allowed herself was a polite note thanking him for having had her car fixed. It seemed the safest approach, although she still found herself thinking about him far too often.

But while she might struggle to put John-Henry out of her mind, she wanted to remember what she had learned from Henrietta Hennessey. She didn't forget that beautiful house, and all those lovely things John-Henry's mother possessed, and in daydreams, Paula saw her grandmother in Henrietta's place. Heddy deserved such splendid surroundings, even if Paula hadn't known what Mrs. Hennessey was talking about half the time. Louis XVI—or was it Louis XIV? Regency. Aubusson. After being exposed to all those fine things, she realized how ignorant she was, and decided it was time to learn more.

Heddy was appalled when she learned that Paula had signed up for night school. She was going to take classes in art history and art appreciation, she said one night, and because she needed more business skills, some accounting and management classes.

"But when are you going to have time, Paula?" Heddy asked anxiously, when Paula told her about the new plan.

"I'll make time, Grandma," she said, although she had wondered that herself. "It's important."

"Your health is important, too," Heddy reminded her. "If you keep on like this, you're going to have a nervous breakdown!"

"I'm strong as a horse!" Paula boasted, and then had a sudden thought. "Speaking of horses, I haven't heard you mention the racetrack in quite a while. I hope these new friends of yours at the Senior Center are keeping you too busy to go."

"Yes, well, they are a bunch, I'll give you that," Heddy said, reddening slightly, although Paula couldn't imagine why.

"Well, I'm glad you're having a good time," she said. "I did so worry about you when you went to the racetrack, Grandma. I never did think it was the place for a cozy little grandmother like you."

"I'm not a cozy little grandmother," Heddy said tartly. "I can take care of myself."

Seeing she'd hurt Heddy's feelings, Paula gave her a hug. "I know you can. But still, I feel better now that you're not spending so much time there. You know what? You haven't told me very much about your new friends. Tell me something about them. I know! We can have a little party. Would you like that?"

"No, no, I don't think so, Paula," Heddy said hastily. "Not yet. I mean, we hardly know one another."

"But that's silly! You've been going down there practically every day for months!"

"Well, yes, but . . . I don't want to rush anyone. Old people get a little set in their ways, you know? They don't like to be told what to do or where to go."

"It's only a party, Grandma! It's not an inquisition!"

"Yes, yes, I know. But . . . well, it isn't that simple."

"Why not?"

Looking more uncomfortable by the minute, Heddy said, "Paula, about the Senior Center . . ."

"Yes?"

Heddy hesitated. Finally she said, "Never mind. It wasn't important." Then she shook her finger at Paula. "The important thing is that I think you're taking on too much, girl. When are you going to admit you can't do everything?"

"When I find I can't, Grandma," Paula said, giving her a goodbye kiss. "I've got to run. Did I tell you I'm thinking about expanding?"

"Expanding! You don't mean another store!"

"I do, indeed," Paula said, looking excited as she paused at the door. "My clip-ons—those little baggies

with clips that I designed to carry one or two cookies?—
took off so fast, along with everything else, that my accountant says I can expand if I'm careful, and I have already found a site for another store.''

"And you're going to? Oh, Paula!"

"Well, I said I'd think about it. I'm not sure I want to
take on so much just yet."

"Thank heaven for that!" Heddy said, looking relieved. "Have you talked to John-Henry about it?"

Paula went still. "Why mention him?"

"Well, he is your banker, isn't he?"

"Yes, but I don't see what that has to do with it."

"I think you'd better talk to John-Henry, Paula,"
Heddy said, nodding vigorously. "I don't know about all
these high finances, but I'm sure he'd want to know you
were thinking of expanding. Won't it have some effect on
the loan he gave you?"

"Only in that I'll be able to pay it off faster," Paula
said firmly. "Now I've got to go."

"You never said where the new place might be,"
Heddy called, as Paula headed down the walk.

Paula turned briefly, a mischievous glint in her eye.
"You won't believe this, Grandma, but it's right across
from the racetrack. Isn't that a coincidence? I've objected to you going there for years, and now I'm going to
be practically in their back pocket. Isn't that a hoot?"

"A real knee-slapper," Heddy said faintly, as Paula
ran down the walk toward her car. She was in such as
state of shock that she forgot to wave as Paula honked
and turned the corner.

PAULA'S SECOND STORE OPENING only six months after
she had opened the doors on the first, was a smash. It
came a little soooner than she originally planned, but she

decided to go ahead because she wanted to take advantage of Oklahoma's long autumn days. Too soon it would be cold and wintry; people were out now enjoying the fine weather, and, she hoped, her cookies.

She needn't have worried about her timing. To her delight, word had spread, and she had customers waiting outside even before ten o'clock, the hour she had planned to throw open the doors on Sweet Temptations Two. Such a mob showed up that before the day was over she almost ran out of cookies. Almost. She was wiser now; she knew more, and she planned things better. No more handwritten notices tacked up in store windows throughout the mall; no more tiny ads in free supermarket throwways. With night classes in marketing, business administration and financing and advertising under her belt, she knew what she was doing this time.

Promotion was the name of the game, and she had learned her lesson well. When Sweet Temptations Two greeted the first customers, Paula was ready for them. Free coffee and free samples of cookies, muffins, and brownies abounded; a free clip-on baggie was given to every customer who brought a friend, and another to those who came back for more. She'd had buttons made up that said I Had a Sweet Experience at Sweet Temptations, and she passed those out by the handful to whomever passed by, along with a free cookie. Carefully selected music played constantly from the stereo she'd brought from home, and the dozens of balloons on strings that she and Rodney had spent half the night blowing up, wafted gently in the heat from the ovens that had been in use since four that morning.

Remington Park, once her nemesis because of Heddy's fondness for the racetrack, stood just across the way; viewing it with new eyes as a potential source of revenue, Paula had secured permission for the two high school girls she had hired to stand outside the gates as soon as the park opened for the day. The girls wore uniforms Paula had sewn herself—demure red-and-white petticoated dresses with laced bodices—and passed out free clip-on baggies, compliments of Sweet Temptations Two, to racegoers who then had to buy the cookies themselves from the gaily decorated trays the girls carried, suspended from ribbons around their necks.

Paula, dressed for success in a slightly more sophisticated uniform than her high school employees wore, dashed back and forth between the racetrack and the new store, making sure the girls were all right, that both they and the store had enough of everything, and that people kept streaming in for more. During all those nights of study, she had learned another valuable lesson: the art of the self-sell. Gone was the reticent young woman who was reluctant to push herself; in her place was the self-assured owner of a successful business, looking confident as she greeted customers and even inquisitive onlookers, with a big smile and sparkling eyes. She introduced herself, asked their opinions. The people loved it, and told their friends, who came to see for themselves what was going on. Those people told others, and so on, and so on, and so on, until a constant crowd was milling around the store. She couldn't have asked for more.

Rodney had been delegated to supervise activities at the other store, and in addition to other promotional gambits, like coloring books for the kids, and two extra cookies per dozen, Paula had printed up free coupons for him to hand out to those who wanted to visit the new store. When *those* people started coming, and Paula saw the coupons, she made another of those instinctive decisions that had given her two successful stores in less than a year. She had originally planned for the grand opening day celebration to end at closing; now she decided to extend it through the week. When she called Rodney during a short break to tell him, he was appalled.

"Keep up these giveaways an entire week?" he cried. "You'll go broke!"

Paula laughed. "I don't think so. Now, do you have enough coupons, or should I order more?"

With a sigh, he surrendered. Gloomily, he said, "You'd better order more. I hate to admit it, but things are going so well here that I've only got about six left."

"Out of all those hundreds I had printed?"

"You said, give 'em out," he reminded her. "And that's what I did."

"And that's what I want you to keep doing," she said with a smile. "I've got some more in my car. I'll stop by in the morning."

As soon as they hung up, she was immediately engulfed by customers. By the time she looked at the clock again, it was closing time, and by the time she checked it again, after tidying up, it was nearly midnight. Tired, but still exhilarated at the thought of her success today, she locked up and went out to her car. It was not until she was inside and on her way home that she allowed herself to think of John-Henry, and how much she missed him.

"Well, it's your own fault, girl," Heddy had said tartly, when Paula reluctantly told her about the quarrel she and John-Henry had had about her opening another store so soon. "You can't treat a man as if he's got no feelings. It isn't right."

"I don't know what you mean," she'd said, stung. "I told him right from the beginning what my goals were."

"He didn't know you were going to open a second store so soon," Heddy reminded her.

Paula lifted her chin. "Well, neither did I. But it so happens that he was the one who told me I had to seize the opportunity when it came by, and that's exactly what I did. He has no right to be angry with me about that."

"Maybe that's not what he's angry about, Paula," Heddy had said.

Remembering that conversation, which had taken place several months ago now, Paula clenched her fist on the steering wheel. Now all her elation at her successful second grand opening went stale. John-Henry hadn't been here to share it with her, and Heddy was right: it was all her fault. She shouldn't have told him to mind his own business when he advised against her opening another store so soon, and if she hadn't been so busy with all these endless details and demands, she would have called and apologized long ago. Where had the time gone?

She had even deserted Heddy, she thought guiltily. She couldn't remember the last time she'd seen her grand-mother before today; with all the night classes, and countless arrangements she'd had to take care of to open the new store, she hadn't had time for anything but work. She'd been rushed even this morning when Heddy stopped by for the opening. She'd given her grand-mother a quick hug and a kiss and promised to come and talk when she had more time. She wanted to show Heddy around, but then some crisis had claimed her attention, then it was something else, and something else again. By the time she looked up, her grandmother had gone.

"Oh, Grandma," she sighed, and looked at her watch. It was after midnight, far too late to call Heddy and apologize. She'd just have to do it tomorrow, she thought, and was suddenly angry with herself. What was the matter with her? Couldn't she have taken two minutes out of her day to visit with her grandmother?

And what about John-Henry?

Feeling the sting of tears behind her eyes, she put the car in gear and drove home. She had treated John-Henry shabbily, and she was ashamed. But at that time, she hadn't been able to see beyond her ambition to move ahead with that second store. Sometimes she felt as though she'd spent her whole life...waiting...for something to happen, and now that it had, she was terrified that the opportunity would slip out of her grasp before she could make it hers.

Well, now she had her two stores. Everything had worked out just the way she'd planned—better than she'd planned. She was a bigger success than she'd even dared anticipate; she should be elated, ready to rush out and celebrate. Instead, she felt miserable, too tired and guilt-ridden now that the excitement and all the hoopla had died down, to do anything more than drive home...alone.

JOHN-HENRY WAITED A WEEK after Paula's second opening before he decided to take matters into his own hands. She had put him off time and time again when he'd called, saying she was far too busy even to talk, much less go out somewhere, and now he knew that if he wanted to see her again, he would have to be the one to make the first move. The thought did not do much for his self-esteem, as Heddy noticed when he came out to the track to see how No Regrets was getting on.

Otis had put the horse in training again, starting him out with long, slow gallops to build up his strength and endurance, and gradually increasing the sessions to "breezes," with an occasional "hard work" timing run for three-eights, then one-half, then five-eights, of a mile, but no more.

"There's plenty of time," he'd say, when Heddy fretted at how long all this was taking. "He'll come along slowly, and be better for all that."

John-Henry agreed with the philosophy—as far as racehorses were concerned. His personal life was a different story, he thought that day, as he leaned against the rail and watched the horses at their morning workouts. He had tried being patient with Paula, but since that obviously wasn't getting him anywhere, new tactics were clearly required.

He still hadn't decided on his best approach when he went back to the shedrow, where Heddy was sitting on a hay bale, enjoying the morning sun. As always, she was direct.

"You and Paula haven't patched up that misunderstanding you had, have you?"

She knew all about the disagreement he'd had with Paula; if Paula hadn't said anything, he'd told Heddy himself. The old woman saw too much with those bright blue eyes of hers, and he had to have some explanation for his black mood of late. It was obvious he needed help with his problem—a dark-haired, dark-eyed dynamo who couldn't seem to spare anyone the time of day because she was too busy building a one-woman cookie empire. Thinking glumly that if anyone had told him last year he'd be in such a predicament, he would have laughed in their face, John-Henry grabbed a nearby rake. Since getting involved with Heddy, Otis and No Regrets, he'd found himself coming out to the racetrack more frequently—especially of late. There was something soothing about being around horses again, he thought, and realized he had avoided anything remotely to do with the animals since Camilla's death.

Realizing that Heddy was still waiting for an answer to her question, he shook his head and began to rake up the aisle. "No, I haven't talked to Paula in some time," he said.

Heddy nodded. "I sort of figured that."

He leaned against the rake. "You got any ideas?"

"Sure do. Call her."

He frowned. Even though he'd been thinking the same thing, he said, "I'm not sure I want to intrude."

"Oh, pucky," Heddy snorted. "Intrude! Why don't you tell me the real reason? And don't say it's none of my business again. I know you think I'm a nosy old woman—"

"You *are* a nosy old woman," he said, smiling despite himself.

She smiled, too. "Well, all right, I am. I admit it. And when you've reached the age I have, you can be a nosy old man. But until then, give me my due and tell me why you haven't called my Paula."

He felt stubborn. "Paula has my number."

"Yes, that's so. But since she hasn't used it, maybe it's time you used hers."

"I don't know. You said yourself she's so busy with the new store."

"Or maybe too proud, just like you," Heddy said, and squinted at him. "Have you ever considered that?"

He had considered it. In fact, he had thought of dozens of reasons why she hadn't called him, dozens more why he should just pick up the phone and call her. "How do I know she wants me to call?" he hedged.

"I'm her grandmother, aren't I?" Heddy said. "Now, go on. Get yourself to a phone. Or do you want to borrow a dime?"

"I've got a dime, Heddy," he said, glowering. "But since you're so full of ideas, maybe you can suggest what I should say."

"Oh, you'll think of something, John-Henry," she said complacently, and then gave him a wink. "But maybe this'll help. Paula's been working hard lately. She might need a little time away to get a new perspective. What do you think?"

He was thinking of it even before she stood up from the hay bale and gave him a little wave before disappearing into the tack room to watch her morning television programs. Long ago, when John-Henry had seen how bleak that little room was, he had brought in some comfortable chairs, a little refrigerator, and a portable TV.

"All the comforts of home," Otis had said admiringly, testing one of the chairs. "Thanks, John-Henry. You really know how to spoil a person, don't you?"

Yes, he did, John-Henry thought, remembering what Otis had said. His car was parked at the end of the shed-row, and as he strode toward it, eager to implement the plan that was forming in his mind, he didn't see Heddy peeking out the tack room door. She was smiling in satisfaction when Otis came around the end of the barn and saw her there.

"Heddy, what are you doing?" he called out.

She checked quickly, but John-Henry had already gone. Emerging from the tack room, she told Otis what she had done.

"Oh, Heddy, do you think you oughta done that?" he asked. "What's Paula gonna say?"

Heddy didn't know, but she hoped that whatever John-Henry had in mind, Paula would accept. She and her granddaughter hadn't been getting along lately—well, they were *getting along,* it wasn't that. It was just that Paula had been too busy for her these past few months. She understood—or tried to, but she was worried all the same. Despite her obvious excitement and pleasure at what she had accomplished, Paula had still looked tired and harassed behind that bright smile when Heddy had dropped by on the day of the second store opening last week. That's what had made her decide to give John-Henry a little push. Paula needed to take some time off, whether she realized it or not. And, thought Heddy in satisfaction, John-Henry was just the man to see she did just that.

"Heddy?" Otis said.

She turned to him. "You tend to your business, Otis," she said. "And I'll tend to mine. There's nothing wrong with giving two young people a nudge in the right direction, if they need it, not to my mind."

"I guess you're right," Otis said, and hesitated. "Heddy, have you told Paula about No Regrets yet?"

"Well, now, that's another thing," Heddy said, knowing her cheeks were pink. "I intended to tell her, but I just haven't had the time lately. She's been so busy and all with the new store, that I . . . I just didn't have the heart."

"You mean we're gonna have to go on sneakin' in and out of the track?" Otis said reproachfully. "Oh, Heddy!"

"Don't you 'Oh, Heddy!' me!" Heddy said, but she knew he had a point. Since she hadn't told Paula about the horse, she had made Otis and John-Henry promise to use only the back gate, just in case Paula happened to be going in or out of the new store. Things would be even worse if Paula found out by accident, and she really had intended to tell her; she just hadn't found the right time.

"Well, you'd better tell her soon," Otis said, his face breaking into a wide grin despite himself. "'Cause our horse breezed a mile today in a minute, thirty and change, and pranced off the track fit as a fiddle."

Heddy looked at him a moment, wondering if she dared believe the good news. "If you're pullin' my leg, Otis—" she warned.

Dramatically, he crossed his heart. "No foolin', Heddy. God willin' and the creek don't rise, soon that horse is gonna be ready to run."

"Oh, Otis!" she cried, and gave him a kiss that made him go red.

"Aw," he said, embarrassed.

But Heddy just laughed. Color rose to her cheeks again, but this time with delight and happiness at the thought that her long-awaited dream was about to come true at last. She looked, for a moment, just like the girl she used to be.

PAULA FELT AS THOUGH she were a hundred and fifty years old. If owning and operating one store had been difficult, doing the same for two seemed impossible at times. Excitement, as well as the thought of fulfilling another ambition, had carried her through the demands of that second opening, but now exhaustion was setting in, the strain of the past months starting to tell barely a week after Sweet Temptations Two opened its doors. When she asked herself why she was so tired, she realized that she hadn't had a day off in months—not since she'd first obtained her loan to start the business.

Wishing she hadn't thought of that, since it only reminded her achingly of John-Henry, she rubbed the back of her neck as she bent again to the task of writing down her recipes. She had never thought of documenting; until now she had just kept everything in her head. But with the second store, that approach was no longer feasible. She couldn't continue running back and forth between both places preparing batches of ingredients because she didn't trust anyone else—not even Rodney—to do it; and it was too hard to premix everything and deliver it. With both stores so busy, she was already driving herself crazy keeping up with the demand. Clearly, it was time for another approach, and so she had reluctantly decided she would have to start using suppliers.

Just thinking about it made her nervous. It wasn't the cost; with the stores doing so well, she could afford it. The trick was to find suppliers she could trust. She had worked hard on her recipes; they were originals, not meant to be duplicated. And since a recipe is a trade secret, she had learned through one of her classes that one way to protect it was to develop her own formula for every ingredient—and to find suppliers who would scrupulously maintain secrecy about those formulas. The idea was to create something unique so that, even if someone obtained the recipe, the cookies could never be reproduced exactly. In her own endless trial-and-error sessions, she had finally come up with certain combinations of flours, assorted sugars, even a certain type and consistency of chocolates that made her cookies one of a kind. Now she had to find suppliers who would prepackage all those ingredients.

But first she had to write out the codes for all the recipes, and she was just reaching for a fresh sheet of paper when she was sure she heard John-Henry's voice outside by the counter. Her hand froze.

No, it couldn't be, she thought. She hadn't heard from John-Henry in weeks, ever since that stupid quarrel. Since that time, she had picked up the phone a dozen times only to put it down again. If he wants to talk to me, *he* can call, she had told herself. But he hadn't, not even when she had begun making double and then triple and finally, quadruple payments on her loan. She sent the checks directly to the bank, but soon, when the loan was paid off completely, she wouldn't even have that tenuous contact with him.

She had tried to tell herself that it was better this way; after that last argument, and her own growing preoccupation with the stores, it was even more obvious to her that she just didn't have time for a relationship. But that didn't stop her heart from hammering when she heard his voice just now, and she hoped she had made a mistake as she strained to hear.

It was John-Henry all right, and he was talking to another of her high school helpers, Margie, who happened to be out at the counter today. From the high-pitched giggle that ensued after he said something, Paula knew that the normally unflappable Margie was flustered.

Feeling flustered and slightly giddy herself at the thought that he had actually broken this strained silence between them, Paula knew she couldn't cower at the back of the store, trying to pretend she wasn't here. Before she lost courage, she got up and went through the swinging doors to the front of the store. He was standing by the counter, and looked so handsome that her breath caught.

"Hello, John-Henry," she said—casually, she hoped.

She noticed then that Margie's plump cheeks were bright red. The girl was an honors student at the high school, and studied physics in the rare moments when she was on duty and the store wasn't busy. But she stuttered and stammered right now, as she turned to Paula and said, "Uh...this man...er...Mr. Hennessey? He wants to see you, Paula. Oh...you're here. Excuse me, I'll...be in the back."

Then she giggled that high-pitched giggle again and disappeared through the doors, letting them fly back with a bang. Paula hardly noticed; she couldn't stop looking at John-Henry. Why does he look so different? she wondered, and then realized that his hair was longer, and he wasn't wearing the suit he normally wore during the day. In fact, she thought, puzzled, he wasn't wearing a suit at all. Today he had on jeans and a sportshirt under a jacket, and he smelled faintly of...horses?

She made herself approach the counter. She hadn't allowed herself to think how much she had missed him, how much she had longed to see him again until now, when he was standing such a short distance away. Then she knew how futile it had been to think she could simply put him out of her mind. The truth was that no matter how hard she worked, or how many strenuous hours she put in, she was never too tired to think of him. There had been so many nights these past weeks when she tossed and turned in bed, thinking of him and yearning for his touch. She had heard his voice in her dreams; she had felt the strength of his arms; she had tasted the warmth of his lips.

But that had all been in dreams. Nothing she had fantasized had prepared her for seeing him unexpectedly today. His sudden appearance unnerved her, and it was all she could do not to throw herself across the counter and beg his forgiveness. How could she ever have contemplated not seeing him again?

"Hello, Paula," he said. "Do you have a minute?"

Now that he was here, she had all the time in the world. "Of course," she said. "Would you...would you like to go get a cup of coffee, or something?"

"You have that much time?"

Because she felt so happy at seeing him, and so guilty and off balance and defensive all at the same time, she was more abrupt than she intended. "Not if you came here to be sarcastic."

"I'm sorry," he said at once. "I didn't mean to say it like that. It's...just that it's been a long time, I guess."

Immediately she felt contrite. Lowering her eyes, she murmured, "Yes, I know. I'm sorry, too. I've been so busy...." Her voice trailed away. It was a lame excuse.

"I figured that. That's why I came."

Slowly, she raised her eyes again. "I'm glad you did."

"Are you?"

"Yes, I am."

"In that case, do you think we can start over?"

Now that he was here, she was willing to do anything. "Do you?"

He held her eyes. "I'd like to."

She couldn't look away from him. Shakily, she said, "So would I."

He looked so relieved that she wanted to laugh from sheer joy. "I know it's sudden notice," he said, "but I thought you might be able to get away for a few hours."

"Now?"

"I know you're busy..."

She was. When she thought of all she had to do... Then she looked into his eyes again and knew that no matter what needed to be done, it could wait. Nothing was more important to her at this moment than John-Henry. "Where do you want to go?" she asked.

She saw her feelings reflected in his eyes, but he seemed determined to keep the invitation casual.

"How about a picnic?" he suggested.

"A picnic!" she said in dismay. She thought they'd just go out for coffee.

"Well, if not that, then how about the...Cowboy Hall of Fame?"

He couldn't be serious. "Why would I want to go there?"

"Not a loyal Oklahoman, I see," he said teasingly. "All right, how about the Will Rogers Memorial? Or the Stockyards?"

"The Stockyards! That's even worse! What about that little coffee shop down—"

"Or," he said, with a twinkle in his eye, "we could just play it by ear."

It was that twinkle that decided her. With him looking at her like that, she would have gone anywhere with him. But because she couldn't let him know how easily she had surrendered, she pretended to consider his suggestion. "I can't be gone long. I have to close up tonight."

"Margie already said she'd handle that."

"So now you're arranging my employees' schedules?" she asked indignantly.

"Just trying to anticipate. Any other objections?"

"Well, I don't know—" she started to say.

Something changed in his eyes. He obviously thought she was serious, for he suddenly straightened. "We're going," he said quietly, but with purpose, "if I have to throw you over my shoulder and carry you, kicking, screaming and yelling your head off through this entire mall. Now, what do you say to that?"

What could she say to that? Her hands on her hips, she lifted her chin and said, "I've never yelled my head off in my entire life. If you'll wait, I'll get my coat."

CHAPTER ELEVEN

PAULA AND JOHN-HENRY hadn't reckoned on Oklahoma's changeable weather. When they left the mall and headed for his car, the day was sunny and breezy, but long before they reached their destination, black clouds had covered the sky, and the rain was beginning to fall.

"John-Henry," she said at one point, watching the wipers struggling to keep the windshield clear, "I don't think it's a very good day for a picnic."

Leaning forward, he peered up at the sky. With the rain had come a chill, and he turned the heater up just as a gust of wind buffeted the car. "I don't know why you say that," he said. "Looks like it's going to clear any minute to me."

Amused, she said, "You think so?"

He glanced across at her. "You want to go back?"

"I've got no regrets. How about you?"

A strange look crossed his face before he turned back to his driving, but he said, "Not me."

Paula was feeling too surprised at herself to wonder about John-Henry's expression. It was the strangest thing, but once she had agreed to go with him, it was as though she had thrown all responsibility aside. She didn't even feel guilty at the thought of all the work she had left behind. Instead, as the Jaguar purred along the Turner Turnpike, the only thing she felt was...relief. A whole afternoon! she thought blissfully. It had been so long since she had taken time off that she could hardly believe she was on her way. She loved her stores, but as she looked out at the storm-blurred outlines of the oil derricks they were passing—a permanent part of the city's landscape—all she could think about was how good it felt to be getting away, even in the rain.

Sighing with pleasure, she put her head against the soft leather car seat. She hadn't realized until now how tired she was even of the pleasant smells of cooking. She had always enjoyed walking into a place and catching a tantalizing whiff of something in the oven, but as she had discovered these past few months, home cooking was completely different than commercial baking. Now there were times when she thought she'd choke if she ever saw another cookie, much less had to taste one; or she would scream if she had to fill yet another of those endless cookie trays. At night, instead of counting sheep, she was seeing chocolate chips in her sleep.

Settling luxuriously into an even more comfortable position, she felt like a child suddenly given a holiday from school—until she glanced across at John-Henry again. Then, slowly, she sat up again. She couldn't just ignore the silence that had existed between them the past few weeks; if she didn't say something about it now, the memory would be hanging more threateningly over their heads than the dark clouds that were scudding across the sky.

"John-Henry," she said, her voice subdued. "I'm sorry we disagreed."

He looked at her. "So am I."

"And I'm sorry I didn't call."

"I knew you were busy."

"That's no excuse," she said. "I got so preoccupied with the stores that I couldn't—didn't—think of anything else. I know I treated you badly, and I regret it."

Without speaking, he reached for her hand. "It's all right," he said. "You're an intense person, Paula. You . . . get involved."

She felt chagrined. She had always become totally absorbed in anything that caught her interest; once she was committed to a project, she became—obsessed was too strong a word, she thought—but maybe not. She had certainly been obsessed with the stores. Heddy had always told her that her intensity was both her strength and weakness, and Paula knew it was true. Unfortunately she didn't know how to change that aspect of herself, or even if she wanted to try. That quality had stood her in good stead these past few months; without her single-minded commitment, the stores wouldn't be the success they were. But at times like this, she wished she could tone it down a bit.

"I know I get involved," she said. "But that's no excuse for treating a friend shabbily."

His fingers seemed to tighten over hers. "Is that what we are—just friends?"

She looked down at their hands, clasped on the seat. How many times had she held hands like this with Randy? she wondered, and yet had never felt the strength and comfort from him that she felt from John-Henry right now. It wasn't even a sexual thing, she thought—although heaven knew, in the past a simple touch from John-Henry could send her into a tailspin. At the moment, though, she just felt connected to him, as though he would protect her with his own strength, and she could draw from him to fortify herself.

Not sure how comfortable she was about that, she said slowly, "No, I think we're more than friends, don't you?"

When he looked at her again, his eyes seemed very blue. "I know what I'd like to be."

She couldn't hold that powerful gaze. It was too much like a caress, and she was starting to feel shaky enough as it was. *Now who's being intense?* she thought. But she couldn't quite make herself ask him what he meant, not yet. She wasn't sure she was ready to hear the answer she had already seen in his eyes. *And felt in her heart?* Quickly she turned to look out the window. Instead of pursuing the subject, she said, "Where are we going?"

He seemed to realize that she wasn't ready to continue the discussion. "You'll see."

"You're being very mysterious."

"I'm a very mysterious kind of guy."

She knew he was doing his best to lighten the mood and she was grateful. Thinking that "mysterious" was the last adjective she would have used to describe him, she leaned forward to look out the windshield again. The weather was so bad now that all she could see of the car in front were the taillights. Playing the game, too, she asked, "Do you think you can find your way in the dark?"

"Do you want to go back?"

Vehemently, she shook her head. "Absolutely not."

"Then leave it to me," he said, and a few minutes later took an exit off the turnpike. It was still pouring, the rain coming down so hard she had no idea where they were going, much less where they were.

"We're almost there," John-Henry said. "I hope you're hungry."

To her surprise, she was. "I am," she said. "Are you still determined to have a picnic?"

"No, that was just a ruse to get you out of the store. I've got something much better in mind—especially in this storm."

It seemed he did. They had turned off the main highway by this time and were heading down a two-lane road, bordered on either side by dripping trees. It was like being in the middle of a forest, and Paula turned to him. "Do you know I've lived in this area all my life and I've never been here? It's beautiful!"

"Yes, it is," he agreed. "My parents used to come here when they wanted to get away for a few days and didn't have time to make a longer trip. At the end of this road is a lovely old place called Heritage House."

"A house?"

"A guest inn, actually," he said, and added quickly, "With a public dining room."

Before she had time to reply to that, they were driving between two tall brick pillars that supported elaborate wrought iron gates. At the end of a gently curving driveway, she saw a structure that had to be the inn. At her first glimpse, she held her breath. She didn't know much about architecture, but the place was beautiful. Built of white-painted wood with green trim, it had two stories, pointed roofs, tall gables, and a wide porch under an overhang supported by columns. The front of the house appeared to have been built around a large semicircular stained glass window over double doors of paned glass. Because of the gray day, glass carriage lamps glowed all around, giving the place a fairy-tale quality.

"Goodness," Paula murmured, wide-eyed. She could see why John-Henry's mother enjoyed coming here. It looked like something out of another era... another century.

John-Henry stopped the car under the portico. "You go ahead so you won't get wet," he said. "I'll park the car and meet you inside."

Suddenly conscious of her casual attire—slacks and blouse under her coat, the old loafers she'd thrown on in the dark that morning, Paula didn't want to go in. "Oh, John-Henry, I don't think I'm properly dressed."

"It's very casual here, you'll see."

"But still—" She glanced nervously up at the elegant stained glass doors.

"I'm wearing jeans," he pointed out.

Well, that was true, she thought, and tried to tell herself that if John-Henry, who normally looked so proper and formal in his suits, could go in dressed as he was, she could enter wearing slacks. But she still felt out of place as she got out of the car, and the only reason she went inside without him was because she felt sillier standing in the rain than she did going in.

The interior was more intimidating than the outside. As she hesitated in the foyer, she could see the dining room to her left, and what looked like a hotel lobby to her right. A reception desk stood at one end of that, the long oak counter gleaming as wood does when it has been carefully and faithfully tended for years. Indian rugs covered the parquet floor, and here and there were clusters of overstuffed sofas and chairs under tall antique brass lamps. Plants were scattered around: ficus and rubber trees in ornate pots against walls papered with tiny Victorian prints. Hunting and still-life scenes framed in gilt and scrollwork hung on the walls, and as she was taking in all this splendor, John-Henry joined her.

"This way," he said, taking her arm. "I requested a table in the solarium."

The solarium seemed even more elegant and ornate than the dining room through which they passed. As Paula entered, she looked up in awe. The entire room was made of glass panels that curved and stretched into a dome high above. With the rain beating steadily down, it was like being outdoors inside, or indoors outside, she couldn't decide which. The air was warm and slightly moist because of the profusion of plants in flower boxes around the periphery of the room; even in here the atmosphere was garden-like. She had never seen anything like it, and when she was seated, she looked in wonder across the table at John-Henry.

"This is like something out of a book," she whispered, after the waiter had left their menus and disappeared.

"I'm glad you like it," he said with a smile.

"Like it! I feel like I've suddenly awakened in another dimension. I never realized something like this existed, especially so close to home."

"My mother felt the same way when she discovered it. She made Claude come as often as possible."

"I can see why," Paula said, glancing around again. Every table was covered with pristine white damask, with gleaming silver and delicately tinted rose-colored china settings. Beyond the glass walls, a lake glinted through the trees, and Paula couldn't help thinking that if it was this beautiful at this time of year, it would be spectacular in the spring. Wide-eyed, she turned to John-Henry again. "What about you?" she asked without thinking. "Do you come here often?"

A strange expression flashed across his face, making her sorry she had asked. But his thought, whatever it had been, seemed to pass, for he said easily, "I used to come here with my parents. But I haven't been back since...for several years."

Since his wife died, Paula thought, and glanced down, embarrassed. She took a quick sip from her water glass.

"It's not what you think," he said, reading her expression. "The reason I stopped coming was that... that Camilla hated the place." His expression turned ironic. "She said it was too tame for her. And, I have to admit, at that time, I felt the same way."

Paula looked up. "And now?"

Reaching for her hand, he said quietly, "Now I find it peaceful and beautiful again."

She could hardly say it. "Why?"

He held her eyes. "Because I knew you would."

They were still looking at each other when the waiter appeared at their table. "Have you decided," he asked cheerfully, "or would you like a little more time?"

Paula hadn't even looked at the menu; with John-Henry gazing at her so intensely, she couldn't have ordered anyway. "I can't decide," she murmured. "You order for me."

"Taittenger's," John-Henry said, without looking away from her face.

"Champagne?" the waiter said, glancing smiling from one to the other. He seemed to realize then that he had stumbled into something very private. "Immediately, sir," he said, and went away.

"Champagne?" Paula echoed. "But it's the middle of the day."

"I owe you a celebration, remember?"

"Oh, that," she said, remembering her nonsense about the rain check. "You don't owe me anything, John-Henry."

"Indeed, I do," he said, reaching for her hand again. "More than you know."

Overwhelmed again with the same confusion she had felt in the car, she glanced away. Things had seemed so clear to her before she met John-Henry, she thought. Now she had trouble keeping her priorities straight. When she was with him, it was too tempting to forget her ambitions and her plans and just surrender to the pleasure of being with him. It was only when they weren't with each other that she seemed able to put things in perspective again; in his powerful presence, she wasn't sure what she wanted.

But she couldn't give in to that feeling, she told herself; she couldn't forget what her responsibilities were. There was only one reason she was working so hard: Heddy. Her grandmother had given her so much; it was time to give some of it back.

But John-Henry could take care of both you and Heddy.

The insidious thought came out of nowhere, startling her and making her feel ashamed. She didn't *want* John-Henry to take care of her—or Heddy either, she thought, and knew her cheeks were red when he looked at her curiously. She couldn't tell him what she'd been thinking, so she said the first thing that popped into her head. "I'm sorry. I was just thinking how much I'd like to bring my grandmother here."

John-Henry looked around. "Yes, she'd like it, wouldn't she?"

"How do you know that?" she asked, surprised.

"Oh, well, I don't," he said quickly. "Not really. It just seemed, from the things you've told me about her, that she would."

"Oh," Paula said, but she still looked puzzled.

John-Henry leaned forward. "Paula, there's something I—" he began.

But just then the waiter appeared with the champagne. As it was being presented with the proper flourishes, they were both distracted from what he'd been about to say. When they were alone again Paula forgot about it completely as John-Henry raised his glass in a toast.

"To your success," he said quietly.

Touched, Paula raised her own glass. "To the man who made it possible," she murmured, and clinked her glass with his.

The champagne was a perfect complement to the consommé that came later, followed by Chicken Kiev. But as the meal started to come to a close, Paual could feel herself getting nervous and didn't know why. She glanced at her watch and realized how late it was.

"Good heavens!" she exclaimed. "Look at the time!"

John-Henry looked up from the dessert menu he had just been given. "What?"

She gave him a stricken look. "I hadn't realized it was so late! We have to go back!"

He put the menu aside "Why?"

But she was already glancing around for the waiter. "Why? Because I've got to start the afternoon baking, that's why! Didn't you hear what I said?"

"I heard you," he said calmly. "I just don't understand what the panic is."

She looked at him without really seeing him. In her mind's eye, she could see all her customers lined up, waiting for something to come out of her cold and empty ovens. Since opening the first store, she had prided herself on serving an endless stream of hot and fresh cookies.

"I told you, I have to get back," she said. "I'm sorry. I should have thought of it before, but you surprised me by showing up unexpectedly, and I just didn't think about it."

He was still being calm. "I don't understand why you're in such a rush. Can't someone else take care of it?"

"Someone else! But it's *my* responsibility!"

His patience was wearing a little thin. Leaning forward, he said reasonably, "Don't you think you're being just a little overprotective, Paula? You can't be there every minute to supervise your people, and you can't do everything. Isn't that why you have employees?"

Completely forgetting that she had recently decided to contact suppliers who would pre-mix everything so she would have less to do, she looked at him fiercely. "I have employees to help out at the counters and keep the trays supplied. But *I* do all the baking. I always have!"

Since she looked like she was about to leap up and dash from the dining room, he reached over and took her hand. "Listen to me," he said quietly. "You're running yourself ragged with those stores. Don't you think it's time to give your employees some responsibility?"

She *had* thought of that. Especially during all those midnight hours when she was finally able to close up shop and drag herself wearily home, almost too tired to shower before she fell into bed.

"Yes, I do," she said. "But not today!"

"Why not?"

"Well, because..." She stopped trying to think of a reason—any reason, other than the one that was really pushing at the back of her mind: her fear of being alone with him. She wasn't worried about the stores running out of cookies; every day she checked the emergency containers she made up and kept in the back. After all, she never knew when she might be called away. If Heddy got sick, or, heaven forbid, something worse happened, she was prepared.

What she wasn't prepared for were these conflicting feelings about John-Henry. Even though she was sure she had managed to hide it, all through lunch she had been fighting an increasing desire for him. In fact, she had been so keenly aware that this was an inn that she had had to force herself not to look through the open doorway into the hotel lobby. How easy it would be to suggest . . .

But she couldn't, she told herself again and again. Once she did, there would be no going back. If she allowed her feelings for John-Henry to override her common sense, she could no longer pretend that they were just . . . friends. And wasn't that what she wanted them to be?

She didn't know. She didn't know anything at this point except that one look from him could send her into a tizzy; one touch from his hand could make her feel so weak she couldn't hold onto any resolve, much less remember her responsibilities to the store, to herself, to her grandmother. Somehow John-Henry made all that seem less important. And, she couldn't allow that. She had to remember who she was and where she was going; even more importantly, she couldn't forget who *he* was, and where he had been. She'd told herself over and over that he was out of her league.

"Paula," he said just then. "Surely you can let your people handle it just once—just for today."

And because she was too aware of his hand over hers, and much too much aware of his nearness, and how badly she wanted him, she blurted out without thinking, "No, I can't, John-Henry. I'm not ready. It's too soon!"

He didn't say anything for a moment. Then he let go of her hand and said, "Are we talking about the same thing?"

She could feel his eyes on her, but she couldn't raise hers to him. Staring hard at her plate, she muttered, "I don't know what you mean."

Again he hesitated. "I was talking about the cookie stores, but I have the feeling that you meant something else when you said you weren't ready." He stopped, and then asked, very quietly. "Do you really mean that you're not ready for me?"

"I don't know," she said desperately. "I don't know what I'm feeling. I get so confused every time I'm with you that I don't know what to think!" She looked up at him then, her amber eyes dark with emotion, with fear. "I'm sorry," she said. "But I...I think we should leave."

And before he could respond, she threw her napkin on the table and quickly left the dining room.

Caught off guard by her sudden departure, John-Henry stood and reached for his wallet. Throwing some bills down on the table without looking at them, he followed Paula. He caught up to her as she waited on the porch, her arms hugging her waist, staring out at the rain.

He was angry at the way she had left him, but when he saw how miserable she looked, his anger changed to tenderness, and he gently put his hand on her arm and turned her to face him. "Let's talk about it."

She wouldn't look at him. "I don't want to talk about it."

"I do," he persisted. Realizing they were blocking the way, he took her aside, and made her look up at him. "You're not the only one who's feeling confused," he said. "I don't know what I'm feeling, either. I just know that I want to give whatever it is a chance—"

She pulled her chin away. "I told you I don't want a relationship, John-Henry. Especially not with you!"

He stiffened. "What do you mean—especially not with me?"

Embarrassed, she muttered, "Never mind. I shouldn't have said that."

He couldn't let it go. "Well, you said it. Maybe you should explain."

"John-Henry, I don't think I want to get into this!"

"We already are into it. Now, what did you mean?"

She felt at the end of her rope. "All right, then!" she exclaimed. "Don't you see? The problems is—and always will be—that we don't have the same background! We're not alike at all!"

"So what? That doesn't have anything to—"

"It has everything to do with it! You've lived in that big, fancy house. You drive that beautiful, expensive car—" She could see he was going to interrupt her again, and she clenched her fists. "You own a damn *bank!*" she said fiercely. "The only thing I own is a rundown little house that I gave to you as collateral, and two cookie stores I'm still paying loans on! Don't you see? It's all wrong! We're not the same at all!"

"We don't have to be the same. I thought that was the point."

"I don't know what the point is!" she cried.

"Then why are you acting this way? You've said we're not alike, so what? You've said that we come from different backgrounds, why does that matter?"

"Because it does!"

"Then maybe this will equalize everything," he said, and before she could react, pulled her powerfully toward him.

She struggled, but only for a moment. When his lips came down hard on hers, his tongue thrusting between her teeth into her mouth, she couldn't resist. All the emotion she had been holding back erupted, and she wrapped her arms fiercely around his neck and pulled him to her. Passion met desire and exploded, and they were both gasping when they finally drew apart.

Before he could collect his wits, Paula took a deep breath. "Don't say anything," she said. "That was stupid. I shouldn't have done that."

Still dazed, he shook his head. "Well, you did. You can't change that."

"I can!" she said, her lip trembling. "I must!"

"No," he said, staring down into her eyes. "You can't change the way you feel any more than I can—any more than I want to change it. For a long time now, I've resisted these feelings, too. But I can't any longer. You've made me feel alive for the first time in years, Paula, and I don't want to—"

"No, don't say it! Please, take me back now."

"Do you really want that?"

The look in his eyes made her falter for a moment. She had made him feel alive? she thought. And he had given her a reason to live. "Yes," she muttered. And then, "No..." And finally, "Oh, I don't know!"

"Paula," he said again, and very gently put his hand on her arm again. She trembled under his touch, but she was still too stubborn to give in. "Paula," he said again. "Let's go inside."

"No! I can't!"

"Why not?"

He waited. Finally, she looked defiantly up at him. "It'll change everything!"

He held her eyes. "Everything has already changed," he said quietly, and waited again.

She stood there, agitatedly tapping her foot, trying to make her decision. It was one he couldn't help her with. She either wanted to go inside with him, or she didn't. He wouldn't force her.

At last she said, almost angrily, "I'm not going to continue discussing this out on the porch. We're making a spectacle of ourselves!"

"What do you suggest?"

She wouldn't look at him. "If we go back in, that means we'll take a room, I suppose. Is that what you have in mind?"

"No, we could sit in the lobby and talk, if that's what you want."

"Is that what you want?"

"You know what I want."

She looked away. "If we take a room, what will people think?"

"They'll think we're in love," he said, and barely controlled himself from sweeping her up into his arms and carrying her inside.

IN ADDITION TO THE MAIN HOUSE, the inn comprised a series of private cottages dotted about in secluded glens around the lake. While Paula waited in the lobby, feigning an intense interest in a still-life painting in a corner, John-Henry made the arrangements. To her relief, he had the key in minutes, but then she had second thoughts when she realized they had no luggage. He took care of that, as well, waving off the approaching bellman by telling the man they could find the cottage themselves.

The rain still hadn't let up as they hurried down the path the clerk had indicated. Without umbrellas, and with coats thrown over their heads, they dashed inside as soon as John-Henry opened the door.

"Oh, my!" Paula exclaimed, skidding to a stop.

"What's the matter?" he asked quickly, thinking that if anything went wrong now, he was going to smash something.

She threw off her coat. "Everything is so beautiful, all antiques—and we have a fireplce!"

"So we do," he said, tossing down his own coat, and giving the bungalow only a cursory glance. He was more intrigued with Paula whom he thought looked enchanting with drops of rain on her eyelashes and her hair starting to curl from the damp. He made himself look away. "Would you like me to start a fire?"

"Would you mind?" she said, sounding surprised.

"Of course not. Why?"

She looked at him a moment longer, then she shook her head. "It's nothing. It's just that Randy would never have asked or offered, that's all."

"More fool he," John-Henry muttered, squatting by the fireplace to start arranging kindling. He had the fire going before he realized he hadn't heard anything from Paula the last few minutes. With a feeling of dread, he turned around. She was standing by the big, old-fashioned four-poster bed, whose mattress was so high it nearly reached her waist. She had such a strange expression on her face that he hardly dared ask what she was thinking.

"What is it?"

Swallowing visibly, she shook her head. She seemed so upset that he went quickly to her and took her in his arms. "Paula?"

She buried her face in his chest. "I'm sorry," she said. "It's been so long since I...since I've been with a man that I...that I'm not prepared."

"Is that all?" he said, sighing with relief. "Well, don't worry. I am."

"You are?" She looked up indignantly. "Were you so sure of me?"

"No, no," he said quickly. "I didn't plan for this to happen, please believe me. But...but I wouldn't have been human if I hadn't hoped, would I? I just wanted to be ready, in case. Are you going to hold that against me?"

She stared at him for a tense moment, during which he held his breath in anticipation. But then she began to smile. "Hold it against you? I'm glad one of us had sense," she said.

Laughing, he scooped her up and deposited her on the tall bed, and then he joined her there. The feel of her soft, pliant body in his arms at last was so heady he felt as though he were drowning with desire. Now it was her lips that sought his, her arms that pulled him over on top of her. Even through their clothes, the flame leaped, and when she took his hand and guided it to her breast a moment later, he put his head in the hollow of her neck and closed his eyes in sheer bliss.

"I've dreamed about this so long," he murmured. "I can't believe it's coming true at last."

Her breath was warm against his cheek. "I've thought about it, too," she whispered. "I just hope I don't disappoint you."

Raising his head, he looked into her dark eyes. "Never," he said, and gathered her close. "Never!" he said again, fiercely, and kissed her.

Paula responded instantly, wrapping her arms around his neck, so lost in the sensations he was arousing that she forgot all her fears. John-Henry held her close, and nothing else seemed to matter.

Just for an afternoon, she thought, and gave herself up to the sensation of living the dream she had dreamed and denied herself for so long. Drawing him closer, she inhaled deeply, taking in a heady mixture of soap and faint cologne, and the essence of male that would never be duplicated in any bottle. Loath to leave the bed even to undress, they helped each other, removing garments one by one, delighting in the sight and scent and touch of each other. The flames leaped in the fireplace, filling the room with warmth, touching everything with a soft glow. Flickering images on the walls made a dramatic background, and as John-Henry raised himself on an elbow to look down at her, his face was filled with wonder.

"You're so beautiful," he murmured, his eyes taking in every detail of her slender form. "So beautiful..."

Bending down, he kissed her eyelids, her lips, and then the pulse beating wildly in the hollow of her throat. Gently, his hand cupped one breast, and when he moved even lower to tease the nipple of the other with his tongue, she moaned and arched up against him.

Raising his head again, he glanced toward the fire. "Just a minute," he said. "I'll be right back."

She clutched at him. "Where are you going?"

"To build up the fire. I don't want you to get cold."

Laughing, she looked up into his eyes. "I won't get cold," she said huskily. "Don't leave..."

But he did, for just a moment, rising from the bed with one lithe movement. She couldn't keep her eyes off him as he walked across the room to the fireplace. Thinking what a wonderful body he had—those long legs, and broad chest and tight buttocks, she smiled. She could have stared at him forever. Rising on one elbow, she watched, noting the play of muscles in his arms as he added wood to the fire. Then he stood and turned toward her and she was fascinated by his obvious arousal. Sighing as he joined her again, she thought that he was truly a beautiful man.

She soon discovered that he was a wonderful lover, as well. She had expected him to be experienced, expert in the art of making love; a man as sophisticated as John-Henry would be, she'd thought. But she wasn't prepared for the passion he aroused in her with his kisses and caresses, and the careful attention he paid to her every desire. He seemed to know what she wanted, needed and had always yearned for, and, long before he entered her, she was achingly ready for him. One magic moment led to another, and then another, until finally, even his expert caresses weren't enough. She wanted all of him, wanted to feel him inside her, to draw him deeper and deeper within, until the moan she heard came from him, not her, until a cry for release was torn from his throat just as one erupted from hers.

Once, just before desire caught them on the wave and hurled them toward a distant shore, he raised up again and looked down into her face. She could see the sheen of perspiration on his forehead, and how dark his eyes had become with the passion she had aroused in him. "I never thought I'd feel this way again," he murmured.

"I never thought I'd feel this way at all," she whispered, and drew his lips down to hers again. Shadows danced on the wall, the flames from the fire flared higher. She could feel herself being swept away with every glorious thrust from his body, and when he drove into her, deeper and deeper with every answering rise of her hips, she ran her hands up and down his perspiring back, her own fingers slippery with sweat, pulling him down, down, into her, arching her back to present her aching breasts for him to kiss. He bent his head, sucking one swollen nipple, then the other, kneading the soft flesh with his hands. The rising sensations drove her to a frenzy; with a cry, she couldn't hold back any longer, and she took him with her. His moan matched hers, and just as the pleasure surged through her body until she thought she would pass out, he drove into her for the last time. Her body wasn't her own; it had become ethereal, a being that could fly.

Then he laughed softly, and she came reluctantly back to earth.

"Lord," John-Henry said, and collapsed.

PAULA WOKE WITH A START, not knowing where she was. But then she realized John-Henry was staring at her, and she smiled. "Why did you let me sleep?"

"Because you looked so beautiful," he said.

"What time is it?" she asked, sitting up and pushing her tousled hair back with both hands. In the process, the blanket that had been covering her slipped down to her hips.

Seeing the lovely sight of Paula naked to the waist, John-Henry reached for her and pulled her down again. "Who cares?" he murmured, beginning to caress her.

Paula had cared until she'd felt John-Henry's touch. "Well, I . . . I have to get back," she said, trying to talk around the kisses he was showering on her lips. She pulled away. There was just enough light for her to see the gleam in his eyes. "It must be late."

He began kissing her again. "In that case," he whispered, "maybe we'd better make up for lost time. . . ."

They made love again, slowly now, taking time to savor the anticipation. She hadn't thought anything could top that first cataclysmic coming together, but it seemed she had underestimated John-Henry. This time when they finally fell into each other's arms, John-Henry sighed luxuriously.

"That was wonderful."

"I agree," she said blissfully.

"Can I tell you something?" he asked.

She wound her fingers through his thick hair, marveling at the texture of it. "Anything."

"I'm starved."

She laughed. "So am I," she admitted, snuggling against him. "But I don't want to get up and get dressed."

"Neither do I," he said, and reached for the phone.

"I didn't know they had room service," she said, surprised.

"They do now," he said, and ordered enough food to feed an army. He built the fire again and then, with the peaceful sound of the rain drumming steadily on the roof, and the warming crackle of the flames leaping high in the fireplace, they feasted in front of the fire. At last, feeling as though she couldn't eat another bite, Paula sighed and leaned back against the sofa from her position on the floor.

"I can't remember ever having such a wonderful day," she said contentedly.

She had donned his shirt in order to eat supper; he was wearing a towel. Smiling wickedly at her, he jerked the knot free and casually tossed the terry cloth aside. "It's not over yet," he said, and pulled her down with him on the rug in front of the fire.

When Paula woke briefly during the night, she wondered sleepily how she'd gotten into bed. The last thing
she remembered was making love to John-Henry in front
of the fire, a fitting end to a wonderful day. The flames
had died down to a warm glow, matching the afterglow
of their spent passion, and they had lain on the rug, his
arm around her, her head on his chest, both gazing into
the glowing embers. She must have fallen asleep, but she
didn't remember getting up again. Then John-Henry put
an arm around her in his sleep and drew her closer, and
with a sigh, she snuggled against him and drifted off
again. It was too late to go home now, anyway, she
thought. For once, the cookies could just take care of
themselves.

CHAPTER TWELVE

WHEN PAULA WOKE AGAIN it was morning. Smiling to herself, she glanced out the window. They had forgotten to draw the blinds, and through the trees she could see a clear sky. Sometime during the night it had stopped raining, and far off the lake was glinting in the sunshine. It was going to be a beautiful day.

Then she glanced at the clock and saw to her horror that it was nearly eight.

"John-Henry!" she cried, shaking him awake before she jumped out of bed. "We've got to leave, right now!"

Awakened from a sound sleep, John-Henry blinked and sat up. "What time is it?"

"It's late!" Pausing in her dash around the room picking up all her clothes, she saw him still sitting there. "Didn't you hear me? We've got to get going!"

He snagged her as she ran by, pulling her head down onto the bed. By this time she had on her lace panties and bra, and he ran his finger over the swell of her breast. "Why the hurry?"

As tempting as it was, she couldn't give in. Pushing his hand away, she stood up and ripped the covers off the bed. "Out!" she commanded. "If you're not ready in five minutes, I'm leaving you behind!"

"Without the car keys?"

Just out of reach, she held them up. "Five minutes," she said, and locked herself in the bathroom to finish dressing without interruption.

They were on their way soon after that, John-Henry protesting that they could at least have stopped for coffee. But Paula had been away long enough; the guilt she'd set aside last night had returned full force today. All she could think about was how she was going to make up the time and get the stores ready for the day.

It turned out she had more to worry about than that. Because she insisted, John-Henry took her directly to work, and when she found Margie waiting at the store, wringing her hands in tears, Paula had the first premonition of disaster.

"Oh, I'm sorry, Mrs. Trent!" the girl wept as soon as Paula and John-Henry came in. "It's all my fault!"

Paula glanced quickly around. Nothing seemed to be amiss, and she couldn't imagine why the girl was so upset. Thinking that Margie had broken something, she said briskly, "Whatever it is, it can't be as bad as that."

"It's worse!" Margie wailed, holding up the empty cashbox. "All the money's been stolen, and I'm the one to blame!"

Trying to be calm—and to give herself a precious few seconds to think—Paula took the cash box. Carefully she said, "What do you mean, it's all your fault?"

Margie burst into fresh tears. Silently, John-Henry handed her his handkerchief, which she took with another sob after looking up at his sympathetic expression. "I'm sorry!" she told him mournfully. "I just forgot!"

Very quietly, Paula said, "Why don't you just tell me what happened?"

She finally got the story between gulps, sobs and fresh tears. It turned out that Margie had completely forgotten she was supposed to baby-sit her younger brothers and sister the night before when she had promised John-Henry that she would stay until closing—something Paula normally did herself if Rodney was at the other store. By the time Margie had realized her mistake, her parents had already gone off to their meeting, so she had phoned the new girl Paula had hired, another teenager named Kim, and asked her to come in for a couple of hours and lock up at closing time.

"She told me she could do it, Mrs. Trent," Margie wept into the sodden handkerchief. "I never would have let her if she hadn't told me that!"

Thinking that there would be time enough later to affix any blame, Paula just wanted to hear the entire story. Handing Margie a roll of paper towels to blot up her flowing tears, she said, "Go on."

"There's nothing to go on with!" Margie wailed. "I called Kim at closing, and reminded her to put the cash box away so it would be safe. She said she would, and I believed her. Why wouldn't I? But then...but then, I thought I'd better check this morning myself. I'd said I would, after all. But when I came in, all I found was...this!"

And with that, she handed Paula a wrinkled piece of paper. With rising anger, Paula read the misspelled note that had been written in pencil. It said:

Thanx for the money. I been waiting for this chance. I'll send it back with interest when I hit it big in Calfornya. Love ya.

                                        Kim.

Closing her eyes against her fury, Paula crumpled the note. *Why,* she wondered, did everyone who left this town think they were going to make their fortune in California on *her* money?

"It's not your fault," she said to the desolate Margie. "You didn't know that Kim would steal the money."

Margie burst into another fit of weeping. "I know, but it was my responsibility!"

Her face tight, Paula shook her head. "No, it was mine."

John-Henry waited until she had shown Margie out the door, assuring her that she still had a job, before he said anything. I'm sorry, Paula. I feel that I'm to blame."

Paula's mouth tightened. "The store is my responsibility," she said. "No one else is to blame but me."

"You couldn't have known this would happen!"

"It doesn't matter," Paula said. "I should have been here."

"You can't be here all the time."

"Oh, yes, I can," Paula said grimly, "And from now on, I intend to be. This isn't going to happen again!"

"I understand that you're upset, Paula," he said. "But don't you think you're taking this to extremes? Surely you don't intend to be here every minute. What about us?"

Paula had been holding herself under tight rein during Margie's story, but her emotions boiled over now. A part of her knew she was overreacting, but she was filled with guilt because she'd been off enjoying herself while a new employee robbed her of an entire day's earnings. Well, no more, she thought, and turned accusingly, and unfairly, to John-Henry. "I knew something like this would happen if I listened to you!"

"Now, wait a minute," he said reasonably. "What do you mean, you 'knew?' You couldn't have predicted this would happen."

She wasn't going to listen to anything he had to say. She'd already listened to him once, and this was the result. She didn't know exactly how much had been lost, but a day's receipts were not to be taken lightly.

"I think you'd better go, John-Henry," she said tightly.

"Paula, I think we should at least talk about it."

She didn't want to talk about it; she couldn't afford to let him persuade her with that logic of his that she was overreacting, and that this was just one of those things. It wasn't one of those things, she thought fiercely, and she couldn't allow herself to weaken.

"I don't," she said. "I knew it was wrong to go off and leave the store like I did, but I went anyway, and see what happened? Well, it's not going to happen a second time!"

Despite his own effort at self-control, his face was turning red. Well, she didn't care. Let him get angry. She was angry, too!

"I think you're overreacting, Paula," he said. "How much money can it be? It's not as if—"

That did it. Furious because he seemed to be dismissing something that was so important to her, she cried, "What do people like you know about it? What can you possibly know about having to worry about money?—you who live in big, fancy houses, and who drive imported cars! You, who go off to resorts when the mood strikes you! Do you worry about bills, or how you're going to buy the week's groceries, or what you're going to do if your grandmother gets sick?"

John-Henry controlled himself. He knew Paula was upset, but he felt she was going off the deep end and he could project what that would mean to him. He would never see her again outside the store, he thought, and tried to reason with her. "I know that your grandmother wouldn't want you to deny yourself everything just to bury yourself in work!"

"What do you know about my grandmother?" Paula cried, whirling on him. "For that matter, what do you know about me? Not much, if you could dismiss this so lightly! You see, I know what not having money is like, John-Henry. I know what it is to have to worry about how I'm going to keep my house, or what I'm going to do if my car breaks down or how I'm going to pay the light bill because my husband walked out on me and stole all the money. I *know* these things. What do *you* know?"

His jaw tightened. "Is this about Randy?"

Defiantly, she lifted her head. "No, it's about me not depending on Randy, or you, or anyone else but myself, *that*'s what it's about! So go, and leave me alone. I've got work to do!"

By this time he was so angry he didn't trust himself to say more, so he left, banging the door behind him. Seconds later, Paula heard the Jaguar's engine roar, and she clenched her fists.

"Oh, damn and blast all men straight to hell!" she cried, and then looked down at the table. The empty cash box sitting there seemed to mock her, and with another cry, she swept it onto the floor. Then she threw herself in the chair and burst into tears.

JOHN-HENRY WAS SO ANGRY after leaving Paula at the store that he headed the Jaguar toward the turnpike and drove halfway to Tulsa and back just to give himself time to calm down. He didn't remember the board meeting at the bank until he got back to town; by then it was too late to drive back to his apartment to change.

"To hell with it," he muttered. At the moment he didn't care what he looked like. After pulling into the private parking lot behind the bank building, he took the elevator up to his office with a scowl that sent everyone scattering. Only Mrs. Adams stood her ground, too well-trained to betray, even by a flicker of an eyelash, her surprise at his disheveled appearance.

"There you are, Mr. Hennessey," she said, stopping him in midstride. He recognized a warning when he heard one and he turnd to her.

"What is it?"

She gestured with her head. "Mr. Evers is waiting in your office."

"With a board meeting in five minutes?"

"He insisted on seeing you privately."

John-Henry felt more grim than ever. "I see," he said. Well, he would take care of Mr. Jefferson Evers, he thought, and opened the door to his office with a bang.

The man waiting jumped, his prim expression turning to one of astonishment when he saw John-Henry's somewhat rumpled appearance. "I...er..." he stuttered, and looked curiously at John-Henry. "Is everything all right, Mr. Hennessey?"

"Everything is fine," John-Henry growled as he went to the desk to get the papers he would need for the meeting. "Why?"

"Well, you look...that is... I'm afraid this is a bad time."

Jefferson Evers was a small man, dressed in meticulous detail from his pencil-thin mustache to the tips of his polished wingtips. John-Henry had always disliked him, but never more than at this moment. Impatiently, he looked up from the papers he was shuffling. "What is it, Jefferson? Can't it wait until the meeting?"

Evers swallowed, his prominent Adam's apple moving up and down like a yo-yo. "Well, that is, I . . . er . . ."

John-Henry slammed down the folder he was looking through. Thoroughly aggravated and out of patience, he commanded, "Damn it, Jefferson, spit it out!"

With an effort, Evers took control of himself. After all, he had the support of the entire board or he wouldn't be here. They had elected him their representative, and on that proud thought he straightened to his insubstantial height. "The board—" he began pompously, but John-Henry cut him off.

"I'll hear what the board has to say in three minutes when I walk down the hall to the conference room," he said tightly. "You have until then to tell me what exactly is on your mind. Do you want the opportunity or not?"

Pushed to the wall, Evers abandoned all decorum. It was no secret that he and John-Henry had never liked each other, and he would not be treated like a common teller, which he had been at one time. He was an officer of the bank, and as such, he leaned forward aggressively. "I certainly do want the opportunity," he said nastily. "I came to talk to you about your outrageous plan to sponsor..." He could hardly believe it now, so he repeated it, "To sponsor one of the races at Remington Park!"

So that was what this was all about, John-Henry thought, and wondered where Evers had gotten hold of that insignificant piece of information. As his mother had often amusedly said, the man's network was even more extensive than her own. He believed it now.

"Yes?" he said.

Evers looked nonplussed. "Yes? That's all you can say?" he said incredulously. "Aren't you going to explain yourself?"

"I don't have to explain myself to you, Jefferson," John-Henry said. "If I want to sponsor a race, I'll do it. I can't imagine why you think it should concern you."

The little man's eyes bulged. "But it does concern me!" he sputtered. "It concerns everyone here, the reputation of the entire bank! My heavens, what will people say when they see the Hennessey name slashed across that cheap little paper all those people follow—"

"The *Daily Racing Form?*" John-Henry supplied, enjoying himself for the first time since entering the room.

"Does it matter what it's called?" Jefferson said, outraged. "The point is—"

"The point, Jefferson," John-Henry cut in, "is that the Hennessey name belongs to me, not to you. And with it, I have decided to sponsor a race. Now, since I have already said that it doesn't concern you, this conversation is a waste of time. I have a board meeting to attend."

Evers was red-faced now. "But won't you even tell me why?"

John-Henry gathered together the papers he was going to need. He glanced at the little man. "Yes, I can do that," he agreed. "I arranged to do it because of the publicity."

Jefferson looked apoplectic. "The publicity! But we don't advertise!"

"No, but it doesn't hurt to let people know that The Hennessey is involved in the community."

"The racetrack is not the community! It's a place for shysters and gamblers and heaven knows who! I can't imagine why—"

"That's your problem, Jefferson," John-Henry said calmly. "You can't imagine." He gestured toward the door. "Now, do you mind?"

"Wait! There's one more thing—"

John-Henry sighed. "What?"

That Adam's apple bobbed again. "Is it true that the race is going to be called the Hennessey Stakes?"

"It is." John-Henry had spoken to the racetrack's board of directors when he had first conceived the idea of the bank sponsoring a race for the meet. Since he had offered a substantial amount of money, they had agreed to call it anything he liked. Thinking that Claude would have approved, John-Henry had chosen the most obvious.

"And the . . . the—"

"The purse?" John-Henry said calmly. "Well, I didn't want to have anyone think the bank was cheap. After all, as you pointed out, we have a reputation to maintain. So I thought a hundred thousand dollars was a nice round sum. What do you think?"

"I think," Jefferson said faintly, "that I need a drink of water."

"Fine," John-Henry said. "Tell the board members I'll be with them shortly."

As soon as Evers had scuttled out again, John-Henry went to the bathroom/dressing room that had been installed just off his office. He kept a change of clothes on hand for emergencies, but as he reached for a fresh shirt, memories of the night with Paula flashed without warning into his mind. He could see her so clearly, her features outlined by the firelight, those beautiful eyes with the long, thick lashes shining for him. Without even trying, he could feel the texture of her hair, remember how silky-soft her skin was. She'd been like a reed under his hands, so delicate and fragile that he had almost been afraid of hurting her—until she'd responded like a young tigress, full of life and passion, demanding as much as he could give. Just thinking about it now made his loins burn with desire and his arms ache to hold her again. His mother had said it before, and he knew she was right: Paula had changed something in him. For better or worse, she had changed his entire outlook, his whole life, and he couldn't imagine living without her beside him.

She can't forget what happened last night anymore than I can, he told himself, and hoped that all she needed was a little time to herself to realize it before she came to him again.

Came to him? He nearly laughed at the thought of his independent Paula swallowing her pride and admitting she needed him. No, she wouldn't come to him, he thought. But that didn't mean he couldn't figure out a way to get close to her again.

Hoping that some foolproof plan would occur to him—soon—he changed quickly, ran the electric razor over his face, and left his office again. When he entered the conference room, as polished and immaculate as he always was at these meetings, he glanced around the big table. On the way in, he had decided that as soon as the meeting was over, he was going to call Paula and have it out with her. That resolved, he nodded to those assembled and said calmly, "Good afternoon, gentlemen, ladies. Shall we begin?"

DESPITE HIS RESOLVE, John-Henry didn't have a chance to get together with Paula for nearly a month after their disastrous return from Heritage House. For the first two weeks, she refused his calls; when, by chance, he did manage to get hold of her, she fobbed him off saying she was too busy to talk. The third week he had meetings stacked back-to-back, and then he had to go out of town for a few days. By the fourth week, he was desperate enough to stop by the shop, only to become immediately embroiled in a furious argument with her. The first thing she said infuriated him, and from that point on, things only got worse.

He had timed his arrival so that she was just closing the shop. He knew the store would be empty, or nearly so, at that late hour, and he'd hoped they would have a chance to talk. One look at Paula's face when she saw him made him realize the folly of that.

"What are you doing here?" she demanded belligerently.

It was obvious that she still hadn't forgiven him for their last quarrel. Glad he hadn't brought flowers as he had planned, he told himself to be calm. "I came to talk to you."

Those beautiful amber eyes narrowed. "I told you, John-Henry, we don't have anything to talk about."

He was determined to hold onto his temper. "You can say that, after what happened out at Heritage House?"

Reddening, she glanced away. "That was a... mistake."

Despite himself, a muscle jumped in his cheek. "I don't believe you mean that."

She turned back fiercely, "I do! I told you, John-Henry, I don't have time for a relationship, especially now that I'm thinking of—"

When she broke off guiltily, he couldn't let it go. "Of what?"

"Of expanding," she said sullenly.

He stared at her, hoping he hadn't heard right. "You're joking, of course."

She narrowed those eyes again. "Do I look like I'm joking?"

Beginning to feel that he was definitely losing control of the situation, he tried again. "I don't understand. You've just opened another store. Aren't two enough?"

He realized he had made a bad mistake when her cheeks turned red again. But, despite the fact that she was angry, she looked so beautiful standing there, with her dark eyes flashing amber sparks and her slender body practically quivering with indignation, that he wanted to gather her up in his arms and tell her that they had to make things right. He never got the chance.

"Ten stores wouldn't be enough!" she declared, lifting her chin defiantly. "A dozen. *Two* dozen! I told you, John-Henry, I'm going to be a success!"

He knew he was losing her, but he didn't know how to make her listen to him. "But you are a success. Look what you've done so far!"

"I told you, it's not enough!"

Reigning in his temper, he tried once more. "And what about us?"

"There is no us!" she cried. "Oh, why are you doing this to me, John-Henry? Why can't you just accept that and let it go?"

"Because I don't want to let it go. I told you—"

"Don't say it. Don't say anymore, please! It won't do any good, and it will only prolong..." She stopped, her voice catching. When she resumed, her voice was harsh. "Look, I'm sorry, really I am, but there's no point in going on. I told you, right from the beginning, what my goals were, what I intended to do."

"And nothing that happened between us is going to make any difference, is that right?"

She wouldn't look at him. "No, I'm sorry—"

He wasn't going to beg, not even for her. "So am I," he said harshly. "So am I. I thought we could work it out if we tried, but I see I was wrong. Well, good luck, Paula. I hope you enjoy great success with your stores."

She looked at him quickly. "I didn't mean for it to be this way, John-Henry," she said.

He had already started out, but he turned back at the door. "Neither did I, Paula," he said, his eyes burning. "I guess I was wrong about that, too."

"John-Henry!" she cried after him.

But he was already gone.

CHAPTER THIRTEEN

AS SOON AS SHE HEARD Paula's car in the driveway, Heddy came out onto her front porch. Waving gaily, she locked the door behind her and bustled down the walk. It had been so long since she and Paula had had a talk. When Paula called last night and said she had a surprise, Heddy had been so happy to hear from her that she didn't even ask what it was. They had arranged to meet at ten this morning, but she'd been so excited that she'd been ready for over the past thirty minutes; she'd spent the time looking out the window and trying to finish crocheting a doily at the same time.

"Oh, Paula, it's so good to see you!" Heddy said, squeezing her granddaughter's arm when she got into the car. "It's been so long!"

"Yes, it has," Paula said, sounding guilty. "But I've been so busy since that theft from the store."

That had happened nearly two months ago, but Paula still sounded grim whenever she spoke of it, and Heddy didn't like to pry. She didn't know the whole story, just that one of the new employees had helped herself to the day's receipts and gone off to California to make her fortune. *Just like Randy,* Heddy had thought, and had tried to be as comforting as she could. But it had been a bleak few weeks until Paula started to get over it, and just when she thought things were better again, that darn fool racehorse had scared her half to death by getting his foot

wedged under one of the rails in the stall one night. Fortunately, Fernando, sleeping in the tack room, heard the
ruckus. He managed to free No Regrets before the horse
did any serious damage, but the animal had been lame
again for a while, and Heddy had begun to doubt that he
would ever run. Naturally that meant that she couldn't
tell Paula as she'd planned, but it didn't seem to matter.
Paula, too, had a lot on her mind.

But that was all behind them now, and Heddy turned
eagerly to Paula as they drove away from the house. "So,
what's the big surprise?" she asked. "Are we going
shopping?"

Laughing, Paula glanced fondly across at her grandmother. "You could say that, Grandma. You could say
that."

Paula was in better spirits than Heddy had seen her in
a long time, even if, to Heddy's sensitive eye, her granddaughter looked a little thin and tired. She had lost
weight again, and there were faint circles around her eyes.
From working at both those stores all the time, Heddy
thought, and then reminded herself to stay out of it. She
and Paula had argued about it before, to no avail, and,
as worried as she was, she knew Paula wasn't going to
take her advice—not now. Her granddaughter had always been a hard worker, but, ever since the theft, she'd
been like someone possessed. Heddy knew she was putting in twelve- and fourteen-hour days, and while she
couldn't deny that it wasn't paying off—the stores were
jammed whenever Heddy dropped by—all that hard
work was taking its toll.

And then there was John-Henry, Heddy thought, and
shook her head sorrowfully. He'd been out to the track a
couple of times lately, but he looked so grim that she'd
finally asked him what was wrong.

"I'd just like to know one thing," he said.

"What's that, dear?" she'd asked.

"Why does Paula have to be so damn stubborn?"

She hadn't said much about Paula after that, but as the days went by, she could see by his expression that the situation hadn't improved. What was wrong with Paula? she wondered. Didn't she see that John-Henry was so in love with her he didn't know what to do with himself? Why couldn't she take time to notice that?

"You seem happy today, Paula," she said. "Have you and John-Henry made up your quarrel?"

Paula gave her a sharp glance. "Who said John-Henry and I quarreled?"

Oh, my, now she'd almost done it! "Why, you did, dear," she said, crossing her fingers. "Don't you remember? You told me about it yourself."

Paula returned her attention to her driving. "Yes, that's right," she muttered. "And no, we haven't made up. I doubt we will. He just doesn't understand."

"Oh, I'm sure that's not true," Heddy said, and subsided when Paula shot her another fierce glance. "But dear, it was a long time ago, and he's tried to make it up since. You know he has. Why won't you see him?"

"Because I don't have time for a relationship, Grandma," Paula said. "I've told you that before. Do we still have to talk about it?"

"No, no, not if you don't want to," Heddy said and glanced out the window. Even so, she couldn't prevent a muttered, "But I still think it's a shame."

"Yes, well..." Paula said impatiently, and then shrugged. "Besides, even if I wanted to, I wouldn't have time now, Grandma," she said. "Not when I open my third store."

Dismayed, Heddy turned to look at Paula. "A third store?"

"Yes, I've been scouting locations for two weeks," Paula said, beginning to sound pleased again. "Didn't I tell you?"

"No, you didn't," Heddy said. She was so concerned that she asked tentatively, "Don't you think a third store is a . . . little too much?"

"You sound just like someone else I know."

Heddy knew she meant John-Henry, but of course she couldn't say so. "It's just that I worry about you, dear."

"Why? I thought you liked people with 'gumption.'"

"I do. I do. It's just that you work so hard now. With a third store, it will be that much worse. Why can't you be satisfied with the two you've got? You've said yourself that both of them are doing well—"

"And that's just the point, isn't it? Now that I know I've got a market, there's no limit, don't you see? I can have a chain if I want. I can have stores all across the country!"

Heddy was horrified. "Do you really want that?"

"I don't know. That's in the future, isn't it?" Paula said, and didn't fool Heddy with her bright smile. "I still have to find a location for the third store, after all—and I have to show you my surprise. Close your eyes, Grandma. We're almost here."

Heddy had been so involved in this distressing conversation that she hadn't paid any attention to where they were going. Now she looked around and saw that they had come to a modern section of town, with new houses, many of which were still empty. Bare lots dotted the block, and other structures were in various stages of construction. Wondering why Paula had brought her here, she obediently put her hand over her eyes. "What's this, Paula? Why—"

"We're here," Paula said, braking to a stop. "You can look now!"

Dropping her hand, Heddy looked around. Paula had parked in front of a house so new the paint still looked wet. The builders hadn't yet done any landscaping work, but the two-story modern house, with mullioned windows sparkling in front, and a huge brick chimney rising from the steeply pitched roof, was complete.

Heddy didn't understand. "What is it you want me to see?"

Paula's eyes sparkled with excitement. "Your new house, before I put a down payment on it!"

"My...new...house?" Heddy said.

"Yes, Grandma, all yours," Paula said, squeezing Heddy's arm in delight. She gestured at various other empty houses around the block. "Or that one. Or that one. You can have any one you choose, Grandma. I'll buy you the one you want."

Heddy still didn't understand. "But Paula, I have a house."

"You have a little cottage that's about ready to fall down around your ears, Grandma," Paula corrected her. "It's nothing like any of these!"

"But...but it's my home," Heddy said, and looked around at the empty lots. "And it's mine," she added. "All mine."

Some of Paula's excitement was fading. "But this one will be yours, Grandma," she said. "I'll put the papers in your name."

Heddy hated to hurt Paula's feelings, but she just couldn't go through with such a crazy plan. "But it won't be the same, don't you see, Paula? Seth left me that little house. I love it. I'm comfortable there. It's mine."

Seth had been Heddy's husband, Paula's grandfather. Swallowing, Paula said, "Grandpa didn't intend for you to stay there forever, Grandma. Especially now that I can afford to buy you something so much better."

Gently, Heddy put her hand over Paula's. "Listen to me, my dear," she said softly. "I know you wanted to give me something to share your success. And a house is surely a wonderful present. But Seth built that cottage with his own two hands, and I intend to stay there until I die."

Tears were filling Paula's eyes. "But, Grandma—"

Tenderly, Heddy reached up and wiped away Paula's tears. "You're the one who should have the new house, love," she said. "You're young, you deserve it. You should have something to show for all your hard work. But you don't have to prove anything to me."

"I wasn't trying to prove anything to you, Grandma! I thought you'd like the house! I thought this is what you'd want!"

Heddy was gentle, but firm. "No, darling, this is what *you* want, or think you want. You've been running so blindly after success—"

"No, I haven't! But even if I have, what's wrong with that?"

"Well, sometimes when you run so hard, you forget what the race was about in the first place, darling. You lose sight of your priorities—"

"Are you saying I've done that?"

"I can't say, Paula. Only you can judge that." She hesitated. Then she decided now was as good a time as any to confess. "As for me, I've got No Regrets—"

"Well, I do!" Paula said bitterly, and before Heddy could explain what she meant, she turned away and started the car again. A tear trailed down her face and she brushed it away angrily. "I wanted to give you a present, Grandma," she said. "I wanted to show you how much I appreciate everything you've done for me all these years. But I never thought . . . I never thought . . ."

She couldn't finish; her tears were spilling over, making it impossible to talk. Putting the little car in gear, she pressed down hard on the accelerator.

Heddy tried again. "Paula—"

"I don't want to talk about it, Grandma!" Paula said, her voice muffled. "Please, let's just not talk about it!"

Against her better judgment, Heddy sat back. She hoped that before they got home, they would have a chance to talk about this, but Paula didn't even look at her when she pulled up in front of the cottage.

"I'm sorry, Paula," Heddy said, as she got out of the car.

"So am I," Paula said, and drove away.

Heddy stared after her for a long time, remembering the hurt in her granddaughter's eyes, the pain, the shock. Then, with the weary wisdom of someone who had lived through those things many times before, she sighed and slowly went into the little house Seth had built so many years ago.

"Oh, Seth," she whispered, glancing around. "What am I going to do now?"

PAULA FELT SO AWFUL about that scene with her grandmother that she didn't sleep all night. By morning she knew if she didn't run over to Heddy's and apologize she would feel terrible all day. But first she had to find two aspirin for the raging headache she had developed, and as she was taking them she wondered what was wrong with her lately. She loved her grandmother; she couldn't understand how she could have treated her so badly. If she hadn't been so disappointed by Heddy's reaction to the house...

No, that was no excuse. She had deserved that reaction. Guiltily, she realized that she hadn't considered her grandmother's feelings at all; she'd been so eager to prove her success by buying that grand house that she hadn't thought how Heddy might feel about leaving her cottage.

Feeling worse than ever, she went downstairs to the kitchen. It was barely six o'clock, but out of habit she sat down at the table and began to plan which batches of cookies she'd start on when she got to the store. Then she remembered that she didn't have to rush any longer. Her idea to find a supplier to prepackage all her ingredients had really paid off. Now, instead of having to mix everything herself, she ordered it all in bulk and divided it between the two stores. Rodney, the still-penitent Margie, and a new woman, Audra, a retired schoolteacher, could handle the mixing chores without her help, freeing her to do other things.

Another innovation was the computer she had finally ordered. She had debated about it for ages, but had finally taken the plunge, and it would be here next week. She still felt a little intimidated by the thought of operating it by herself, but she had taken a class, and she knew that once she got the hang of it, it was going to make all her bookkeeping chores so much simpler. Like the prepackaged ingredients, the computer would save her time on inventory control, accounting, taxes—all the numbers she'd had to learn to deal with since starting her business. Sometimes she wondered whether she would have had the courage to open that first store, if she had known how much was involved.

But now she had two stores, and some new decisions to make. The stores had exceeded even her expectations. In fact, they were doing so well that they had attracted the interest of the giant food company, Freedom Foods International, based in New York.

At first Paula had thought it was a joke when someone, identifying himself as a vice-president in charge of marketing for FFI—the company's initials, he explained later—called and said he would like to talk to her. But once he had convinced her that it wasn't a prank, she could hardly believe her ears. FFI was interested in expanding their retail outlets, and he wanted to know if she'd ever thought about franchising her business.

The thought had never occurred to her. Ashamed to admit that she wasn't even sure what franchising meant, let alone what it might entail, she had agreed to think about it and promised to call him back at the end of the week. Then she had rushed to the library.

But reference books and articles could tell her only so much, and as she returned the material to the librarian, she thought wistfully of John-Henry. If anyone would know about the subject, he would, and she wondered if she could swallow her pride long enough to call and ask his opinion.

Then she decided against it. She didn't want to start up with John-Henry again, not when she had spent these past weeks filling every minute with activity in an effort to forget him—or at least put out of her mind that wonderful afternoon and night at the Heritage House. But every time she thought she had succeeded, she would find herself remembering some little detail or other—something he had said, or how he had looked in a certain light . . . or how good his body had felt, and she would have to start all over again.

It just wasn't meant to be, she told herself; she knew it, even if John-Henry didn't agree. As much as she might want to deny it, the fact was that because they had been raised in such different circumstances, they would never view things in the same way. He was the son of a wealthy banking family who had everything. On the other hand, until she'd gone to him for a loan, she had been having trouble making ends meet. Even if she ever reached the point where she didn't have to worry about money, there would still be a wall between them, unassailable, too high to climb, too far to go around. As successful as she might become, she would never believe John-Henry's assurance that things would turn out right because he had the power to make them do so. And he would never understand her drive to succeed, her ambition to provide for herself and her grandmother without having to depend on anyone. He thought it was money she was after, but that wasn't it at all. Money was only a symbol to her; it was the security that she craved. But she couldn't explain that to someone who had grown up in the privileged atmosphere John-Henry had enjoyed.

And so if that meant she had to deny her feelings for John-Henry, then she would—somehow. She had her stores, and a future to plan, and she hadn't spent so much time and energy trying to get over him just to break down and call him now because she didn't know what to do about the franchise. That was something she was going to have to decide herself.

But first she had to make up with her grandmother, and she thought that an appropriate peace offering would be some of Heddy's favorite spice cookies. As she gathered together the ingredients, she started to smile. It had been a long time since she'd had time to make cookies at home, and she wondered if she could still remember the old recipe.

To her relief, the cookies looked just fine. Tasting one to make sure, Paula tried to call Heddy, but there was no answer. Since it was now after eight, she figured her grandmother was probably at the Senior Center, so she decided to stop there before she went to work. She would apologize for that business with the house, admit she had made a mistake, and ask if they could just forget the whole thing. Heddy could stay in her beloved cottage, and she and Paula would be friends again. Oh, she wanted that. She hated this feeling of estrangement from the person she loved most in the world, especially when it had all been her fault.

The Senior Center was just off Meridian, not far, in fact, from Remington Park. Paula could see the sandstone-colored four-story grandstand at the track when she turned off, and couldn't help feeling glad that Heddy didn't frequent that place anymore. She was probably being overprotective, but she preferred to think of Heddy safe at the Senior Center.

But Heddy wasn't at the Center. A group of oldtimers, whom Paula recognized from a previous visit, were sitting around the sun room playing cards, but her grandmother was nowhere in sight. One of the men looked up and waved.

"Well, bless my soul," he said. "It's Paula Trent, isn't it? Heddy Bascomb's granddaughter."

Marveling that he not only remembered her, but her name as well, Paula smiled. She remembered his, too. "Hi, Mr. Killigan," she said. "How are you?"

"Oh, can't complain, can't complain. What can we do for you, Paula?"

"I'm looking for my grandmother," Paula said, holding up the bag of cookies she'd brought. "I thought I'd bring her some cookies to pass around. Do you think she'll be in soon?"

Killigan screwed up his wrinkled little face. He was ninety-five, if he was a day, but as the mound of poker chips in front of him attested, he still had all his faculties. "Well, now, I can't rightly say, dear," he said, glancing around the table again. "We haven't seen Heddy for some time now. Don't know where she's been. In fact, we was startin' to think she might be sick." He looked anxiously at her. "She's not been sick, has she?"

Not as of yesterday, Paula thought, a suspicion forming in her mind. "No, she's just fine, Mr. Killigan," she said. "But you say she hasn't been around for a while? I thought she was coming in nearly every day."

"Every day! Oh, my, no! If that were the case, why she'd be the one who'd have this stack of chips in front of her, don't you know? That grandma of yours—she might look all sweet and innocent, but there's no one that can play poker like she can!"

And no one that can keep secrets like her, either, Paula thought grimly, remembering her glimpse of Remington Park just now. Sweet Temptations Two was across the street from the main gate, but there were other gates. Even if they were manned by guards, it wouldn't be a problem for someone like Heddy to slip by. After all, who could refuse a sweet little old grandmotherly type, who perhaps handed out cookies on the way in? Was that where all those bags of cookies had gone?

"If you see her, would you please tell her I stopped by?" she said, and remembered the bag in her hand. She held it out. "Oh, and please take these. I brought them for all of you."

Killigan looked inside the bag. "Cookies! Well, I'll be. They won't go to waste, I promise you. It's been a long time since we had a treat like this, hasn't it, gents?"

There was another murmur of agreement, making Paula narrow her eyes. A long time, she thought. How long? Maybe it was time to find out.

Two minutes later, on a chorus of appreciative thanks, Paula left the seniors happily digging into the cookies and was on her way to the side gate at Remington Park. A guard came out to greet her, and she put on her best smile.

"Hello," she said sweetly. "I'm supposed to meet my grandmother here. Do you know her? Her name's Heddy Bascomb."

Her last hope that she was mistaken vanished when the guard smiled broadly in return. "Heddy?" he said. "Sure. She just came in a little while ago."

The guard directed her to the right barn, and, her expression increasingly grim, she followed his instructions to a shedrow not too far from the gate. She knew no parking was allowed between the aisles, so she found a spot some distance off.

"This had better be good," she muttered to herself as she parked the car and got out. She had to pick her way across the muddy ground, jumping out of the way as a horse and rider went by. Watching the pair jog easily down the road, she wondered what in the world she was doing at the backside of the track.

Even more to the point, she thought, was what Heddy was doing here. The gate guard obviously knew her well and had even known where she might be found. It was obvious that her grandmother had been coming to the track all along, and Paula's mouth tightened as she saw the barn number she needed. Keeping her eyes down to make sure she didn't step in something she'd rather not, she rounded the building thinking that Heddy was going to have some explaining to do. She was so deep in thought that she didn't see someone step out into the aisle until they had nearly collided.

"Oh, I'm sor—" she started to say, and then froze when she saw who she had run into. What was John-Henry doing here, in muddy boots, with a rake in his hand?

She was so stunned that she was still staring when someone else emerged from a doorway farther on down the row. The little round man wearing suspenders and boots who came out took one look at her and muttered, "Uh-oh," before disappearing back inside again. Seconds later, Heddy—her own grandmother!—appeared.

"Well," Heddy said calmly, seeing Paula. "It looks like the fox has found the henhouse, all right. Hello, dear. How are you? I know you know John-Henry, Paula, but I don't believe you've met my friend, Otis Wingfield. Otis, say hello to my granddaughter, Paula Trent."

Looking as though he would rather have held out a hand to a striking cobra, Otis hesitantly touched two fingers to a nonexistent hat brim. "How'do, Miz Trent," he said.

Paula was too astounded to speak. Nodding jerkily in Otis's direction, she looked at her grandmother again, but before she could say anything, a young man appeared at the end of the shedrow, leading what had to be the ugliest horse she had ever seen.

"Oh, boy," John-Henry muttered, and set aside the rake.

Paula glanced at him, and then back at the horse. She didn't know much about these animals, but she had always thought they were pretty creatures, with liquid eyes, soft muzzles and expressive little ears. This horse was so far from that image that she almost felt sorry for him. Most gray Thoroughbreds she had seen were a steel-gray, with dappled coats and black manes and tails; this one was a horrible flea-bitten sort of roan, as though the color had run before it had time to set. It had no mane to speak of, and the tail was just an afterthought. Although the coat shone with care it couldn't disguise the ribs and hipbones that stuck out, the huge platter feet, and worst of all, the big ears that flopped with every step. To Paula's untrained eye, the horse didn't look capable of walking into a stall, much less running a race, and she was wondering who would be foolish enough to buy such a horse, when the groom stopped and looked uncertainly at the tight little group.

"You no want me to put the horse away?" he asked Heddy in a heavily accented voice.

Suddenly, all eyes were on Paula. Horrified comprehension beginning to dawn, she looked from the obviously anxious Otis, to a guilty-looking John-Henry, and then to her flushed grandmother. Then she looked back at the horse again. *No,* she thought. *It couldn't be!*

"Now, Paula," Heddy said. "Don't get excited. I can explain."

Paula found her voice at last. *"Explain?"* she exploded. "Yes, that might be nice! What are you doing here, Grandma? Why is that man asking you what to do with that . . . that . . . that—"

She was so upset she was stuttering. To her fury, John-Henry supplied the word she was looking for. "That horse," he said. "It's called No Regrets."

She whirled around on him. "I don't care if it's called the King of Siam!" she cried. "What's going on here?"

"Uh, Fernando," Otis said quickly. "I think we'd better put him up now. Here, let me help."

Otis and the groom started to lead the horse into the stall, but for some reason the animal balked. As it pulled against the lead rope and backed up with those huge hindquarters, Paula shrieked and jumped out of the way. John-Henry immediately reached for her, but she gave him a fierce glance and jerked away.

"I was just trying to help," he said.

"I don't need your help!" she snapped. "But while we're at it, you might try explaining what you're doing here!"

John-Henry glanced at Heddy. "I think I'll let your grandmother explain."

Instantly Paula turned toward Heddy. "Grandma?"

But Heddy was preoccupied with No Regrets, who still refused to budge. "What's the matter with him?" she asked.

"He wants his cookie," Otis whispered.

"What?"

Otis repeated what he'd said, but still too softly for Heddy to hear. "Speak up, Otis! I can't hear a thing you're saying!"

"He wants his cookie!" Otis shouted, unnerved, and then, with a quick, quilty look at Paula, grabbed a very familiar-looking bag. His cheeks crimson, he reached inside.

Feeling as though she'd dropped down a rabbit hole, Paula choked, "What are you doing?"

Otis turned even redder. "He likes a cookie after his workouts," he said, and handed one to the horse. As Paula watched in utter disbelief, the animal delicately took the tidbit between his lips and began to chew contentedly. This time, when the groom tugged on the rope, the horse went willingly into his stall.

Paula looked at her grandmother. Heddy, seeing that expression, sighed. "I guess I should explain now, shouldn't I?"

"Oh, no, Grandma. I think the explanation's obvious," Paula said.

"Now, dear, there's no need for you to be so upset."

Paula didn't care that John-Henry was listening; she didn't care that Otis and the groom were still in the stall. She was upset, and she didn't mind who knew it. "No need?" she cried. "No need? You know how I feel about you coming to the racetrack! How could you have lied to me all this time?"

"I didn't exactly lie, Paula—"

"What do you call it, then? You deliberately let me think you were spending your days at the Senior Center, when you were coming here all the time! Oh, Grandma, how could you?"

Heddy's cheeks were pink; she was distressed, too. She hated to quarrel with Paula, who looked so hurt, and she felt even guiltier than she had before. She knew she should have said something sooner. "I didn't feel I had a choice, dear," she explained, trying to make Paula understand. "I knew how you felt about the racetrack, yes. But I had some decisions to make, too. One of those was No Regrets. And . . . and I did try to tell you about him."

"When?" Paula asked bitterly, and then realized just what Heddy had said. Her voice rose. "What do you mean, you tried to tell me about him? What is there to say?"

Otis chose that moment to come out of the stall. Putting an arm around Heddy's shoulders in silent support, he said, "What Heddy is trying to say is that No Regrets is half ours, Paula."

"Wh-what?" Paula said. She couldn't believe it. Her eyes went to the horse, who was now placidly nibbling at the big ball of netted hay hanging by his door, and then back to the little couple. Her voice rose again. "You . . . you *own* that horse?"

"Well, we own half of him—" Heddy began, her eyes going to John-Henry, who was standing behind Paula.

"Half of him!" Paula cried in sudden fury. "And what fool owns the other half? Oh, Grandma, this is too much! How could you have done such a stupid thing?"

She was so enraged that she couldn't say anything more. Whirling around, she nearly rammed into John-Henry. Roughly, she brushed by him and started toward the car. She felt hurt and betrayed. Why had Heddy done this? It was bad enough that she had lied about coming to the track, but to have actually bought a racehorse without saying anything . . . ! Paula was so angry she was close to tears. All she could think about was getting away from here before she broke down completely.

Unfortunately, she hadn't reckoned on John-Henry.

He caught up with her before she reached the car, stopping her with a hand on her arm.

"What are you doing?" she cried. She tried to snatch her arm away, but he held her firmly. "Let me go!"

"Not until you go back there and apologize."

"Apologize!" Infuriated, she tried to free herself again. "What are you talking about? *Let me go!*"

"You're acting like a child. Stop it!"

"How dare you!" Really furious now, she glared up at him. "Look, John-Henry, this isn't any of your business, so I'd appreciate it if you'd just butt out!"

"Not until you apologize to your grandmother," he said, his voice hard. "How could you have said those things?"

"How could *she?*" Paula cried. "All this time, letting me think that she was going to the Senior Center when she was really coming here!"

"She doesn't have to tell you where she is every minute of the day!"

"She doesn't have to lie to me, either! She knows how I feel about the track!"

"So what? You don't have the right to dictate to her. She has her own life."

She knew he was right, but that only made her angrier. "And you don't have the right to dictate to me!" she said in a fury. "Now, let go—"

"No, because I'm involved, too."

"Oh, sure! How?"

John-Henry was so angry now that his eyes were like deep blue slate. "I'm the fool who owns the other half of No Regrets."

"I don't believe you!"

"I can show you the contract Heddy and Otis and I signed, if you like."

"The contract?" she cried, wondering if it could get any worse. "What contract?"

Quickly he told her about the arrangement. Long before he'd finished the story, she was furious again.

"You were involved in that...that stupid scheme all this time, and you didn't say anything? How could you, John-Henry? You knew how I felt. We talked about it! Now I find out that you not only participated in this charade, you actually encouraged it!"

"She did it for you, Paula."

"Oh, please!"

He was losing control himself. "It's true. She did it because she wanted to be financially independent, just like you do!"

"And she thought the best way to do that was to go into partnership with that old man and buy a nag of a racehorse? Don't make me laugh!"

"You have a right to be angry," he said, his teeth clenched. "But you don't have a right to be mean and hurtful to two old people who wanted to make their own way and not depend on anyone else." He was so angry now himself, he had to stop for a moment. "Does that sound familiar, Paula? It should, since you've said the same damn thing to me!"

Her eyes flashed. "It's not the same!"

"Tell me the difference."

"I don't have to tell you anything, not when you've lied to me, too!"

"I haven't lied!"

"Oh, yes, you have. You've known all about that stupid horse right from the beginning, haven't you? You had all sorts of opportunities to tell me, but no—you didn't say a word. What do you call that?"

"Heddy wanted to surprise you," he grated. "She made me promise to keep it a secret."

"A secret! Well, you both certainly succeeded at that! I'm surprised, all right."

"I did want to tell you."

"Oh, right. But you were intimidated by my grandmother, who stands barely five feet tall. I can certainly see why you didn't say a word."

"I said I was sorry."

"Sorry!" She felt nearly overwhelmed by bitterness. "Well, so am I, John-Henry, so am I. And to think that

I almost called you to ask your advice about franchising!''

Without trying, she had alerted his banker's instincts. Momentarily distracted, he said, "Franchising? What about it?''

"Oh, what do you care?'' she cried. She was so hurt that she wanted to hurt him, too. "For that matter, what business is it of yours? I paid my loan back. You've got no say in what I do.''

"Damn it, Paula, that wasn't what I meant, and you know it!''

She looked at him furiously. "I don't know you anymore, John-Henry. I don't think I ever did. If you could do something like this, you're not the person I thought you were at all.''

"You've changed, too,'' he shot back. "The person I see now is not the same one who came to my office all those months ago, filled with hope and promise and determination.''

Stung, she snapped back, "That's not true! I'm exactly the same person I was. No, I take that back. Maybe you're right, after all. I'm more successful now. Is that what threatens you?''

He was trying his best not to lose his temper. "I'm not threatened, Paula—just bewildered. And so is Heddy. She doesn't know you, either.''

Paula clenched her fists. "Leave my grandmother out of this!''

He was desperate to make her understand, to help her see what she was doing to herself, to Heddy...to them. "Why?'' he said. "She's the person you said you were doing all this for, isn't she? Concern about your grandmother was the reason you wanted to start the first store—or so you said, when you came to my office that day.''

She stiffened. "That *was* the reason!"

"Maybe then, but not now. You think about it, Paula. We had something going, you and I, but you let it go. It just wasn't as important as expanding your stores, making more money, achieving greater success."

"And what's wrong with ambition?" she cried.

"Nothing, unless it changes you in some fundamental way, and becomes the most important thing in your life."

"Oh, what do you know about it?" she said bitterly. "You've never had to work for anything in your entire life!"

Something changed in his eyes, making her want to call back her hasty, angry words, but it was too late. "That's not true," he said. "I did have to work at something long ago, and I became obsessed, just like you have. It cost me dearly, Paula, just like it's going to cost you."

"You don't know what you're talking about!" she snapped. But even she could hear the uncertainty in her voice.

His eyes held hers. "Yes, I do," he said. "And you know I do."

She tried to close her mind against the fear she felt rising in her. She couldn't understand it. What was she afraid of? Of losing John-Henry? But she'd never had him. Of losing her grandmother? But she and Heddy would make it up, somehow. Of losing her stores? But if all else failed, she had the franchise deal.

"I haven't changed," she said again, weakly.

"Haven't you? That scene just now at the barn was proof. The Paula who came to my office all those months ago would have laughed at the story of No Regrets. She would have been amused by his fondness for her cook-

ies. She would have applauded her grandmother's determination to help out, if not to make it on her own." He
paused. "She would have been touched that Heddy was
trying so hard not to be a burden."

"She's not a burden!"

"Then why don't you have time for her anymore?" he
asked, and didn't add the question that seemed to vi-
brate between them, demanding an answer. *Why don't
you have time for me?*

She didn't know; she felt so confused. Was it wrong to
want to get ahead, to become so financially secure that
she and Heddy would never have to worry about money
again? Was she being too greedy, wanting to add to her
stores, to lend her name possibly to a franchise?

Because she had no answer, she became angry again.
"You don't understand," she said fiercely. "You've
never had to face the problems I've had to, so how can
you possibly pretend to know what I feel?"

His eyes held hers. "I know what I feel," he said.
"You're not alone, Paula, even if you think you are. You
have people who love you, who want to help. You don't
have to do it all yourself."

But for some reason, that frightened her even more.
"Yes, I do!" she cried. "I've learned the hard way that
the only person I can depend on is myself!"

He seemed about to say something, but then he just
shook his head sadly. "I'm sorry you feel that way,
Paula."

"I am, too, but we all have to do what we think is
right." She glanced angrily in the direction of the barn.
"You bought a half interest in an ugly, old racehorse, and
I'm going to franchise my stores."

"You've decided, then?"

She hadn't. In fact, until she blurted out that hasty statement, she hadn't made up her mind at all. Now it was too late, and she was too proud to back down. "Yes, I have. They're my stores, and I'm going to New York at the end of the week to sign the deal."

"Then I guess there's nothing more to be said."

"No," she said coldly, "there isn't."

She couldn't say anymore. Tears were crowding the back of her throat, threatening to burst through, and she would not cry in front of him. Turning on her heel, she started for the car again. This time he let her go. She was just reaching for the handle when he called out to her one last time. She looked angrily over her shoulder. "What?"

"No Regrets has his comeback race this Saturday. I know Heddy would love it if you were here to help cheer the horse home."

She looked at him bitterly. "You cheer the horse home, John-Henry," she said. "You're Heddy's partner, not me."

And on that cruel note, she started the engine and drove away.

CHAPTER FOURTEEN

WHEN JOHN-HENRY hardly touched his food at dinner that night, Henrietta pushed away her own half-finished plate without comment. But when he made himself another drink after they had retired to the living room without asking if she wanted her usual "dollop" of brandy with her coffee, she decided it was time to say something.

"Trouble at the bank, dear?" she asked.

She thought for a moment that he hadn't heard her. Then he started and glanced her way. "I beg your pardon?"

Now she was beginning to get worried. This wasn't like John-Henry, who was rarely moody. "I asked if there was trouble at the bank, dear," she repeated.

Sighing heavily, John-Henry stared down into his untouched drink. "No, no trouble at the bank."

Ah, now she thought she knew. "I'm relieved to hear that, dear," she said, and waited a moment. "Then it must be Paula."

The glass slipped from John-Henry's hand. It crashed onto the glass-topped coffee table, and he jumped up, uttering a vivid curse under his breath. Calmly, Henrietta handed across the napkin she had on her lap. "Here. As long as it stays off the rug, no harm is done."

Red-faced, John-Henry wiped up the spill. "Why did you mention Paula?" he asked angrily, when he sat down again with a fresh drink. He still hadn't asked Henrietta if she wanted her brandy, and she sighed. Men were so difficult at times.

"Well, why not, darling?" she asked reasonably. "I like Paula. I did so enjoy her when she was here. We never were able to set a date for dinner, and I wondered when I might see her again."

Frowning fiercely, he glanced away. "Who knows? For all I know, she could be moving to New York. Someone there has offered to franchise her stores."

"My, my. That was quick progress," Henrietta said, hiding her surprise. "Is she ready for that?"

He looked even more irate. "No, of course not. But no one can talk any sense into her—certainly not I. She wouldn't listen to me now if I were the last man on earth."

Henrietta gracefully put aside her cup. "Darling," she said gently. "Would you like to talk about it?"

And so John-Henry did. When he finished, nearly an hour later, Henrietta felt a little overwhelmed by the confused story of mixers, and racehorses, and contracts, and little old ladies who stormed banks, and dark-eyed young women who were too stubborn to listen to anyone.

"You love this young woman, don't you?" she said when he was done.

He had never been able to lie to her; it was useless to try, and what did it matter anyway? He had botched things up so hopelessly that Paula would never forgive him, so he might as well admit how he felt—how he would always feel. Not that it would do any good.

"With all my heart," he said.

She wasn't surprised. "And how does she feel about you?"

He didn't know how to answer that. For a time he had thought that Paula loved him, too. She was too honest to fake her emotions, angry or passionate or sad, and whenever he remembered that glorious afternoon and night they'd spent together, he knew they'd both felt the same way. But so many things had happened since then that he couldn't be sure about anything anymore.

"I don't know how she feels," he admitted unhappily. "I thought that all she needed was some time to sort things out. She's achieved so much in such a short time that her success has overwhelmed her. And now, with the franchise offer..." He stopped, shaking his head.

"Do you think she'll take the offer?"

"She says she's flying to New York at the end of the week to sign the contract."

"Then there's not much time, is there?"

"Time for what?" he said angrily. "Paula made it very clear that we're not right for each other." He looked bitter. "She insists our backgrounds are too different."

Henrietta paused. "Have you told her about that?"

John-Henry shook his head. "What good would it do? Or what difference would it make? Paula has a need for security that she won't let me provide, period. How can I fight that?"

"So you're just giving up?"

"I didn't say that!" he snapped. "But damn it, I have my pride!"

Yes, Henrietta thought sadly. *And so had she, once.*

John-Henry was too annoyed to sit still. Getting up, he went to the window and pulled the curtain aside to stare blindly out at the night. "I don't know what to do," he said. "I'm at my wit's end." He looked over his shoulder. "You don't know how stubborn she can be!"

"Camilla was stubborn, too," Henrietta commented.

"Camilla was a selfish—" he started explosively, and then collected himself. "Camilla never had a thought for anyone but herself in her entire life," he said, tight-lipped. "She was totally engrossed in Camilla. Paula isn't like that at all—or at least, she wasn't, when we first met. That's what attracted me initially, her concern for her grandmother. Providing for Heddy was her main goal in the beginning. But . . ." He stopped, pain flashing across his handsome, troubled face. He made himself continue, his expression becoming set and tight. "Ambition has become uppermost for Paula. It's as though she can't achieve enough. And it's making her lose that generosity of spirit that made her so . . . so lovely in the first place."

Despite himself, his voice caught at the end, and he turned back to the window, muttering a curse. Henrietta waited a moment, and then she said, "So what are you going to do?"

"I don't know. I'm too angry with her to think straight. I'll wait until she gets back from New York—"

"That might be too late . . ."

"I know," he said. "But what can I do? Kidnap her so she won't go? Hijack the plane?"

Wisely, Henrietta made some soothing remark. John-Henry was upset now; it would serve no purpose to agitate him further. But her expression was thoughtful as she watched him leave a few minutes later, and by the time she closed the front door on the Jaguar's disappearing taillights, she had reached a decision. It would mean exposing old wounds she had thought she'd buried long ago, but if it worked, it would be worth it. Her son's happiness was more important to her than any pain she might feel, and she couldn't bear to see him so tortured, especially now. After five interminable years he had finally begun to forgive himself for Camilla and to begin trusting his instincts—and himself—once more. Camilla had hurt him deeply, but Paula had made him come alive again, and Henrietta was not about to stand idly by and see her beloved son lead an embittered life. She had regrets aplenty, and she didn't want that for John-Henry. She loved him too much, and she had waited a long time for someone like Paula Trent to rescue him.

WHEN THE PHONE RANG Thursday night as she was packing for her trip to New York, Paula answered it eagerly, hoping it was Heddy. They'd had only one stilted conversation since that awful day at the racetrack earlier this week, and she was so hurt over what she considered her grandmother's betrayal that she hadn't really forgiven her. She had gone over to apologize for her behavior, and ended up feeling hurt all over again.

"You weren't ready to hear it," Heddy had told her gently, when they were sitting over tea in her grandmother's little kitchen. "I'm sorry, Paula, but you weren't. I don't think you are yet. You're still angry, aren't you?"

She tried to deny it, but she never could fool Heddy, and in the end, she said stiffly, "You didn't trust me, Grandma. That's what hurts."

"And what would your reaction have been if I had told you?" Heddy asked.

But they both knew the answer to that, and because Paula felt so angry at the obvious, she cried, "It isn't fair! You know how hard I've been working to make the stores a success. Why do you think I've done that, if it wasn't for us?"

"Paula, I appreciate all you've done—all you're trying to do," Heddy said, putting her hand over Paula's. "And

I know you work hard. Too hard, as I've tried to tell you so many times. But..." She hesitated, "If you're doing this just for me, I wish you wouldn't. I'm happy as I am, dear. I don't need much—"

"But what about the future!" Paula cried in distress.

"The future will take of itself. It always has."

Oh, how could her grandmother, always so perceptive and shrewd in so many things, say something so naive and foolish? Paula had asked herself. Hadn't they seen for themselves that anything could happen? The future didn't just take care of itself! It had to be planned for, guarded against! Suddenly, angry all over again that Heddy could be so trusting when she, Paula, knew how fleeting security was, she said something she never would have said last year, something that, even as she was saying it, shocked her and made her despise herself. But she couldn't stop; some inner demon made her say it to the last cruel syllable.

"And you think that stupid racehorse will provide you with everything you need, do you, Grandma? What if the horse can't run? What if something happens to him?" Her voice rose shrilly. "Then you'll see that I was right all along! I'll be able to provide for you, because I've worked and I've saved and I've planned. I won't have pinned all my dreams on an ugly, has-been racehorse who isn't worth a damn!"

And then she'd run out, tears streaming down her face, blurring her vision so that she could hardly see to drive home. She hated herself for saying such awful things, but she was angry with her grandmother, too. How could Heddy have lied to her? And after all her hard work!

Pride and hurt carried her through the horrible week, but she was grim and tight-lipped at work, forcing herself to keep out of sight doing paperwork after Rodney gently told her she would scare all the customers away if she served them looking so irate.

Angry with Rodney, as well, she spent every day seething, just waiting for the end of the week when she could forget Oklahoma City existed and fly off to New York. The people at FFI had made reservations for her at some posh hotel; they had even arranged for her to see one of the big musicals on Broadway. She had never gone away by herself, on such important business, and she wanted to feel excited and proud. Instead, all she felt was out of sorts, angry and disappointed. It was no fun going alone; if she'd been on better terms with Heddy, she would have asked her to come along.

Or asked John-Henry to go, she thought, and quickly banished that idea from her mind. She didn't want to think about John-Henry; she was even more furious with him than she was with Heddy. How dare he say all those horrible things to her about ambition having changed her, making her hard and narrow-minded, when all he'd done was lie to her along with the others?

And there was another thing, she thought, deliberately fueling her anger so that she wouldn't have to stop and examine things too closely. How dare he criticize her business decisions? He'd made it sound as though franchising was a mistake, when instead it was a wonderful opportunity, a tribute to her success. How many other little businesses got noticed by a big company like FFI? How many other small shops had been approached to franchise?

Now she was going to New York to clinch the deal, and she couldn't be happier, she told herself defiantly. So what if John-Henry objected, or her grandmother was unhappy, or even Rodney wondered if she was moving too fast? She knew what she was doing. These were her stores, after all, and the franchise offer was an opportunity she couldn't pass up.

Then why did the little voice inside her keep asking if she was making a mistake? Why did she feel so tense and unhappy when she should be elated? Was it the right decision?

It was too late now, she told herself as she answered the phone. "Hello?"

"Hello, Paula," said a voice she instantly recognized. "This is Henrietta Hennessey. I hope I'm not calling at a bad time."

Paula looked around her disorganized bedroom, with clothes piled in three places: those she had decided to take, those she was considering and those she was probably going to give to charity. She still hadn't begun to pack and her plane was due to leave at noon the following morning.

"No, no, of course it's a good time. How delightful to hear from you, Mrs. Hennessey. How have you been?" Paula said, her fingers tightening on the phone. Why was Henrietta Hennessey calling her? Had John-Henry put her up to it? If he had, she thought fiercely, she couldn't imagine why. The only communication she intended with him was a triumphant, "Take That!" telegram when she got home from New York.

"Well, I won't keep you, Paula. I just called to ask a favor."

A favor? Paula thought suspiciously, and said, "Of course. Anything. What is it?"

"Could we meet tomorrow?" Henrietta said. Then added quickly before Paula could protest, "I know you're leaving for New York, but I did have something I wanted to...to say, if you could spare me a few minutes."

Why couldn't Henrietta say whatever it was over the phone? "I'd really like to oblige, Mrs. Hennessey," she said. "But as you mentioned, I am getting ready for a business trip, and I—"

"I promise I won't take much of your time, Paula," Henrietta said. "And I could even take you to the airport, if that would be more convenient."

"Well, I—"

"Please, dear," Henrietta said. "I do think it's important, or I wouldn't have bothered you."

Well, she couldn't say no to that, could she? Feeling manipulated, Paula said, a little ungraciously, "Well, all right, if you insist. But my flight leaves at noon—"

"Oh, that will be plenty of time," Henrietta said. "What time shall I pick you up, then?"

Sighing, Paula told her ten o'clock and hung up. It took her until midnight to finish packing and writing her instructions to Rodney about the stores, and asking him to drop off her car at the airport, but even then she couldn't sleep. She lay awake until nearly two o'clock, wondering why Henrietta had called, and what was so important that they had to meet right away.

"You'll find out in the morning," she muttered to herself for the hundredth time, pounding her pillow. "Now go to sleep!"

MORNING FINALLY CAME and, precisely at ten, so did Henrietta Hennessey. She was wearing a cream-colored silk suit, with low heels and pearls, making Paula, in her travel outfit of slacks and sweater, feel instantly dowdy. Quickly stuffing her dilapidated little suitcase into the back of the car, out of sight, she climbed into the gleaming old Cadillac and looked expectantly at Mrs. Hennessey.

She started the car and as they pulled smoothly away from the curb, Henrietta smiled. "Thank you for agreeing to see me, Paula. I appreciate it more than I can say. I know how busy you are."

"Actually, at the moment I'm more curious than anything," Paula said, and decided to get right to the point. If Henrietta intended to talk about John-Henry, she wanted to get one thing straight immediately. She wasn't going to discuss John-Henry, period. Especially, she thought, with his mother. "What did you want to talk to me about?"

Henrietta smiled again. "Direct as always," she said, with an approving glance. "I do admire that about you, Paula." Her smile disappeared. "But would you mind if I did this my own way? I'm beginning to realize that it's a little more difficult than I anticipated."

Now Paula's curiosity was really aroused. Wondering what it was all about, she shrugged. "As you like," she said, and realized suddenly that they were heading into a poorer rundown section of town. The Cadillac seemed completely out of place on rutted streets, with houses showing increasing neglect. Fences surrounding weed-choked lawns leaned and sagged; porches canted alarmingly, often with one or more posts missing. Here and there were empty houses with broken windows, and once Henrietta had to brake sharply when an emaciated cat, with one ear missing, darted out in front of the car and then ran, yowling, into an alley.

"My goodness," Henrietta murmured, "I hadn't realized..."

Paula was feeling very uneasy, imagining shadowy faces behind grimy curtains watching them as they drove slowly by. "Mrs. Hennessey," she said nervously. "Do you think we should be here? Are we lost?"

"No, we're not lost," Henrietta said with a sigh. She sounded so sad and dejected that Paula gave her a quick glance. "We're right where we're supposed to be."

Before Paula could ask why they were here, Henrietta stopped the car in front of the most wretched-looking house Paula had ever seen. Three sagging steps led up to a porch with rotted rails; the front door had long ago been kicked out; not a window remained intact. Graffiti covered the exterior walls, and piles of trash were piled in the corners. Paula caught a glimpse of the dark interior—battered walls, dangling wallpaper, more piles of trash, and could only imagine what the rest of the place looked like.

Outside, the patch of grass, what there was of it, had died long ago, and a single dead tree spread skeletal limbs over the drooping roof. Hanging from one of the branches was a frayed rope tied to a long-deflated inner tube—a child's pitiful swing. The only thing with life or color at all was a stunted rosebush in the corner; it struggled bravely in the dirt and damp, with one yellowed leaf still clinging to a branch.

"My rosebush," Henrietta exclaimed. "I can't believe it's still here after all these years!"

Startled, not sure she had heard right, Paula glanced quickly across the seat. "I beg your pardon? Did you say—?"

She broke off as Henrietta turned to her and she saw the tears in the woman's eyes. "Welcome to our first home, Paula," Mrs. Hennessey said. "John-Henry and I spent the first five years of his life here."

Paula didn't know what to say. "I . . . I don't understand."

Henrietta glanced at the dilapidated house again. Her voice faraway, as though reliving old memories, she said,

"John-Henry doesn't know it—he wouldn't approve, I know—but I come here sometimes . . . to remember."

"Remember?" Paula said. She was still having trouble thinking of the elegant and gracious Henrietta in such a place. Even though it had been—what? Thirty-five years—it was obvious that the little house before her had never been much more than what it was—a small shack in a bad section of town. Why hadn't John-Henry said anything?

As though Henrietta had read her mind, she said, "John-Henry never told you about his early beginnings, did he?"

"No," Paula said with a slight shake of her head. She still didn't understand. "He never mentioned it."

Henrietta nodded. "That's because of me. He knows how painful it is for me to remember my life here. He wanted to spare me the . . . the humiliation."

Again Paula hesitated. But Henrietta had brought her here for a reason, and she had to say it. "But you brought me here."

"Yes. I wanted to show you that . . . that things aren't always what they seem, my dear. Sometimes you have to remind yourself where you've been, in order to know where you're going. And sometimes," she went on sadly, "you have to remind yourself to know what you've missed."

"But you have a beautiful home now—"

"As you see, it wasn't always that way," Henrietta said, looking back at the house again. "And the truth is that my life would have turned out very differently if I hadn't valued security above everything else."

Paula felt a pang. "I . . . don't—"

"Let me tell you my story," Henrietta said gently. "You see, when I was very young, John-Henry's father and I fell in love. Oh, he was a handsome man—" she sighed, remembering "—in fact, John-Henry looks so much like him that sometimes I swear my Johnny is looking at me right from his eyes." She looked away again, her voice low. "But Johnny was poor, uneducated. Oh, he was clever with his hands; he could do anything. I wanted him to go to school, to get an education, but...but he just laughed. He wasn't meant for school, he'd tell me. He was meant for better things. He wanted to see the country, go around the world. And he wanted me to come with him."

She stopped, and after a moment, Paula said gently, "But you didn't."

Henrietta shook her head. "No. I wouldn't go. I couldn't imagine myself living such a life—rootless, without my own roof over my head. And even though I, too, longed to see all those wondrous things Johnny talked about, I didn't have the courage to go off, willy-nilly, without a thought for the future. I wanted a house, furniture, savings—my own things around me. I didn't want to wake up in the middle of a field some morning and realize that all we had between us was a crust of bread."

Henrietta had painted such a vivid picture that Paula could almost see it. "But then something happened," she said.

Henrietta smiled sadly again. "Johnny left. Oh, I knew he would. I thought he'd come back, but he didn't. I heard some time later that he had been killed crossing some river in South America. Until then he had been having the time of his life. I know he didn't regret a minute."

"But what about John-Henry?"

"Johnny never knew about the baby. I didn't tell him."

Paula was shocked. "You didn't?"

"No, because I knew it wouldn't have changed anything. Johnny would always have been...Johnny. He wasn't ambitious, he never would have given me the security I craved."

Paula was silent for a moment, staring at the rundown little house. Finally she asked, "Why are you telling me these things?"

"Because you and I are kindred spirits, Paula," Henrietta said simply. "I knew from the moment I met you what was important to you and what wasn't. And I am fond enough of you not to want you to make the same mistake I did. Seize the moment when you have it, or it might not come again."

But wasn't that what she was doing? Paula wondered. Why was it wrong to plan your life, to be ambitious, to want security?

"But you married Claude," she pointed out.

"Yes, I married Claude," Henrietta said, sighing. "And Claude was a wonderful man, kind, considerate, a good father to my son. He loved me dearly, he gave me the security I so desperately craved, and I was fond of him. But it wasn't the *passion* I felt for my Johnny, and when I look back on it now, I realize what my choice should have been." She turned somberly back to Paula, reaching for her suddenly cold hand. "You love my son," she said quietly, intensely. "You don't have to deny it. I see myself in you, all those years ago. I *know* what passion is. And John-Henry loves you, more than you know." Her fingers tightened on Paula's hand. "Don't have regrets, my dear, or spend your life thinking or wondering what might have been."

THEY WERE BOTH SILENT on the way to the airport, Henrietta sad and preoccupied, Paula not knowing what to think. When they embraced quickly at the terminal, Paula said, "Thank you, Mrs. Hennessey. I know how difficult that was for you."

Her eyes shadowed, Henrietta put her hands on Paula's shoulders. "It's always difficult to take out the ghosts of the past, Paula," she said. "But I was glad to do it for you." She smiled fleetingly. "It was worth it if I can save you from the regret I've lived with all these years."

And with that, she bent and kissed Paula's cheek. "Safe flight, my dear," she murmured, and watched as the plane lifted off.

Feeling let down and exhausted from her ordeal, Henrietta drove home slowly, hoping she had done the right thing. She still wasn't sure that night when John-Henry stopped by with some papers for her to sign. He looked just as unhappy as she felt, and, as they were having coffee in the living room, she looked down at the cup she had just poured. Wishing it were brandy instead, she said, "I'm afraid I've done something today you're not going to like very much, darling," and proceeded to tell him the entire story.

John-Henry listened to what his mother had done, his expression growing more grim with every word. When she finished, he very carefully put his cup on the coffee table and stood. "Good night, Mother," he said, and turned toward the door.

"Where are you going?" Henrietta asked.

"To New York," he replied tersely. "This has gone far enough. I don't need my mother, of all people, to plead my case. I'll do it myself!"

"But darling," she said, following him quickly. "You don't know where Paula is staying—"

Tight-lipped, he said, "That doesn't matter. I'll call every hotel in Manhattan if necessary. If that fails, I'll hire a private detective. I'll find her!"

"But what about the race tomorrow? Isn't Heddy expecting you?"

He had forgotten about that, and he muttered a curse. He couldn't let Heddy down; she was counting on him. Which one would it be: grandmother or granddaughter? Why did he have to choose? Damn it, why was Paula so stubborn?

And why was he still here, in Oklahoma, when he should be in New York, going after Paula?

"Darling, I know you think I've interfered enough," Henrietta said, refusing to wilt in the face of his angry glance, "but you can't force Paula to choose, don't you see? She has to come to the decision herself."

He was so torn he didn't know what he should do. Instinct told him to charter a plane and find Paula even if he had to tear Manhattan apart. But maybe his mother was right. "What if she makes the wrong decision?"

"She won't," Henrietta said quietly. "She's not Camilla, John-Henry. Trust her. You'll see."

Trust her, he thought, on the way home. But that's what he had tried to do. He had made so many mistakes with Camilla. He had been so young when he married her, so blindly in love with the image he'd had of her that he had to possess her or die. What a fool he had been! Terrified that she would get bored and leave him, he had become increasingly wild and reckless himself, until the game got out of hand.

Camilla hadn't died alone in that speeding car; she'd been with her lover that day, and they'd been racing off to some hidden motel. He hadn't found out until he got to the hospital, but by then it was too late. Much too late.

He'd learned his lesson, in spades, John-Henry thought. He had tried everything he could to hold Camilla, and the result had been tragic. So he'd tried to do just the opposite with Paula, and now she was off to New York. Would she come home again? Would she come back to him?

When you love something, set it free. If it comes back to you, it was meant to be.

And if she doesn't? he wondered, and clenched his hand on the wheel in agony.

CHAPTER FIFTEEN

AFTER HER EXPERIENCE that morning with Henrietta Hennessey, Paula was too deep in thought to enjoy New York. The flight passed in a daze, and she was so preoccupied she barely appreciated the impressive sight of a glittering Manhattan Island. As the taxi took her to her hotel, she had a vague impression of noise and traffic and people hurrying across the streets even against Don't Walk signs. When she paid the driver in front of the hotel and looked around, she realized that the tall gray buildings that surrounded her blocked out much of the sky. Her hotel room had a single bed, old-fashioned wainscotting and pipes that creaked, and it was the pipes that broke through her thoughts. They reminded her so much of home that she immediately sat down and called Heddy intending to say how sorry she was.

But her grandmother didn't answer the phone, and as Paula hung up, she imagined they were all—including John-Henry—out at the track pampering that horrible, ugly, good-for-nothing racehorse.

That thought made her angry again, and she sat at the little table by the window until long after dark, drumming her fingers and listening to the sounds of traffic below. She could hear it even nine stories up, and as she opened the window and gingerly looked down, the thought occurred to her that she probably had one of the last hotel rooms in New York with windows that actually opened. On the table was a basket of fruit and a bottle of champagne, compliments of FFI, who had provided everything except company to help her celebrate. She had never felt so alone.

If John-Henry really loved me, he would have come after me, she thought mournfully.

And then: *If you really loved him, you wouldn't have gone.*

Angrily shutting out both thoughts, she called room service to order a dinner she didn't have the appetite to eat, watched a silly movie on cable to keep her mind off everything else, and then went to bed. Despite her depression, she had to be on her toes for the meeting tomorrow. So much depended on it, but once under the covers, she couldn't sleep. Now that she was here, now that she'd come all this way and had practically committed herself to that big food chain, she was even more uncertain about what to do.

If only she had someone to talk to! she thought, feeling sorry for herself. But no, everyone she knew—whose opinion she valued—seemed to have forgotten her tonight. They were probably still out at the track, rubbing the horse down, or whatever it was you did before a horse raced. Did they really think that sorry creature would win tomorrow?

Oh why was she thinking about that?

MORNING FINALLY CAME. Feeling keyed up and nervous, Paula took a taxi uptown to the address she had been given, and took a deep breath before she went in. The giant Freedom Foods International building towered above her, a monolith of glass and stone, making her

wonder again what she was doing here alone. But, she
told herself, she was the owner of Sweet Temptations,
and it was up to her alone to cut the deal.

A little while later, seated in a huge conference room
with a gleaming rosewood table that seemed as big as a
football field, she wondered if she was going to be cut up
instead. In addition to the dozen or so male executives,
there were two other women in the room, both of whom
ignored her except for a brief, sharp nod of introduction. They retired to the other side of the room, where
each became immersed in communication with her lap-
top computer. They wore almost identical gray suits
without ornamentation, and Paula didn't know which
was more severe: their asymmetrical haircuts, or the
harsh red lipstick that seemed to be the only color in their
pale faces. Why were they so unfriendly?

Beginning to be more and more certain she had made
a terrible mistake, Paula tried not to glance down at the
simple suit she had bought for the occasion. She had
thought she looked businesslike and professional when
she dressed this morning, but now she wasn't so sure. All
these high-powered people kept glancing covertly at her,
and she wondered if despite the suit, she had country
bumpkin written all over her. Wishing they would get
started, she pasted a weak smile on her face and tried not
to make too much eye contact.

To her relief, the meeting got under way. Paula didn't
see anyone come in, but there was a sudden stirring, a
tenseness that rippled through the room, and suddenly
the executives parted like the Red Sea, and standing at the
head of the table was a silver-haired man, who gave her
a wintry smile as they were introduced. His name was

Lymon Freedom, and he was president and owner of Freedom Foods.

"Nice to meet the young woman who so impressed my wife," he said, gesturing her to be seated.

"Your wife, sir?" she said, trying to hide her confusion. She didn't know what he was talking about.

He seemed surprised that she didn't know. "Yes, didn't Gerry tell you? That's why we contacted you. My wife, Bettina, was visiting her aunt in Oklahoma City last month, and happened to pass by one of your stores. She was so impressed with the product—and the service—that when she came home, she insisted that we get in touch. Well, we did. And here you are. Are you ready to talk about franchising?"

She never imagined it would all go so fast. Before she knew what was happening, everyone at the big table, it seemed, was throwing facts and figures and data and survey results and demands at her. Although she had tried to do her homework before she came, so she'd know what they were talking about, she realized belatedly that she should have brought someone with her—her accountant, or, she thought in panic, a good lawyer. These people were talking so fast her head was spinning.

But out of all the babble, one thing became penetratingly clear. If she was to franchise her name and her precious recipes, there was no way her stores would remain the same.

"Franchisers depend on precise limits," someone told her severely.

"We must keep control of standards," someone else said.

From down the table came the edict: "The product has to be a certain size and a certain thickness."

"Well, my cookies are about this thick and about this wide." she said, showing them with thumb and forefinger.

"Not good enough," one of the red-lipped women told her severely. "We'll have to be more precise than that. Marketing surveys indicate the perfect cookie is one-quarter inch thick and two inches in diameter. No more, or less."

"But my cookies are bigger than that—" she started.

They didn't let her finish. "And we have to standardize all the ovens," someone else stated. "The cookies have to be baked at so many degrees—"

"—and served on a napkin of standard measurements—"

"Which is milled from number 10 paper—"

"And—"

"Stop!" she cried. What was she doing here? She didn't belong in a thirty-four-story building, listening to these people flinging facts about as though they had meaning. These were her stores they were talking about, *her* stores! If she gave them up, everything she had worked for, everything she'd planned, everything she'd dreamed, would be gone. They would make something plastic and impersonal and...and *standardized* out of her cookies, and nothing would be the same.

Oh, John-Henry had been right! He had been right all along! She *had* allowed ambition to consume her; she just hadn't realized it until now, when someone started talking about number 10 paper. What did paper matter when they were talking about cookies?

Her eyes wide, she looked around the table. They didn't understand her anymore than she did them, she thought. Had anyone here ever gotten up at six in the morning to make a batch of oatmeal-raisin? Had any-one babied an ancient old mixer because it was the only one that could blend the ingredients to the right consist-ency? Who among these graysuits had ever experienced that delighted smile that spread across the customers' faces when she handed them a free sample and they bit into one of her cookies for the first time?

All that would be lost, gone, if she sold her name and her recipes to FFI. Why hadn't she listened to John-Henry? She was a cookie-maker, not a business mogul! She'd been a fool to leave behind everything that mat-tered to her to come and try to talk cookies to people who were only interested in standards. And why should she promise to make all her cookies exactly one-quarter inch thick and two inches in diameter? Where was the fun in that?

Fun, she thought. That's what she had been missing these past few months. In the beginning, she had been excited, thrilled at her success; lately, it had just been something she rushed blindly after. When had the fun gone out of it?

"I'm sorry," she said, realizing they were all staring at her. "I just can't do it. My cookies aren't precise. They aren't meant to be standardized. They're meant for peo-ple to enjoy!"

Everyone looked scandalized. "But that's not the way to franchise! All the product has to be the same! That's the whole point!"

"Then you'll have to find someone else," she said, becoming suddenly aware of the hour. If she left now, could she get back in time?

"I'm sorry," she said again, looking pleadingly at the white-haired Mr. Freedom. "I hope you understand. I can't do it, not even for the money you mentioned."

He stared back at her for a moment, his face expressionless. Paula had, after all, just refused an offer that wasn't made every day. All the executives seemed to hold their breaths, obviously expecting a tirade.

Paula was oblivious to the growing tension. She stared at the president, begging him to understand. Finally, to the obvious consternation of everyone else at the table, he smiled and stood with her. He held out his hand. "I do understand," he said quietly. "And I admire you. It's not everyone who can refuse that kind of money because they have standards of their own." He glanced around the stunned table.

"I wish..." he murmured, and then shook his head. "Well, it doesn't matter," he said, and smiled again as he walked Paula to the door. "I wish you good fortune, my dear and—"

"And?" she said, relieved that it had gone so well after all, anxious to be out the door and on her way and gone. She had somewhere to be, and time was running out. After all this, she couldn't be late.

"Send me a box of cookies now and then," the president said with a wink. "Otherwise my wife will divorce me for failing to make this deal."

Paula laughed. "I wouldn't want that," she said, excitement suddenly flashing across her face. "But you've given me an idea. Instead of franchising, maybe I'll start a mail-order service. I could promise express delivery."

Mr. Freedom was still holding her hand. Laughing with her, he gave her fingers another warm squeeze. "I wish I had about ten like you on my staff. Goodbye my dear, and good luck. I hope you've got no regrets.''

"Just one," she said, her eyes sparkling. "But he's back home."

And with that, she sped away.

She caught the first flight out of New York, and spent the entire time willing the plane to hurry. Would she be on time? The trip seemed endless, but at last she was in her car and speeding down the turnpike to Remington Park. With no time to talk the gate guard into letting her in the ''backside,'' she raced into the grandstand like everyone else, her heart in her throat. Was she too late?

Grabbing a schedule from one of the sellers, she quickly scanned the races. No Regrets was listed in the sixth, she saw, and gasped a breath of relief. The tote board told her it was two minutes to post time for that race, so there was no time to find Heddy or Otis or John-Henry, even if she knew where to look. They were probably with the other owners or trainers. She didn't know; she had never paid attention to what really went on here. She didn't even know if they had special boxes, or just stood at track level like everybody else. Pushing her way through the crowd, she tried to find a place by the fence.

She was still jockeying for position when the horses came out onto the track. No Regrets couldn't be missed; in a field of bays and chestnuts, he was the only flea-bitten, lop-eared gray. But he pranced along, as high-stepping as the rest of the horses, and as she watched him go by, tears came to Paula's eyes. She had put all her energy into her stores; her grandmother had pinned her hopes on this rawboned big gray horse. She'd accused Heddy of being foolish, silly, and naive, but how wrong she'd been. They'd both had dreams. Hers had come true; now it was Heddy's turn. Would the horse run his race, as they all must do in the end? Unconsciously, she clenched her fists. *He had to run,* she thought fiercely, and felt her heart begin to thud.

"The flag is up!" the announcer cried a few minutes later, as Paula jumped up and down, trying to see what was going on. The gate was opposite, on the other side of the infield, and she couldn't see a thing. Did the flag mean they were ready to run? Suddenly there was a clang as the gate doors opened. Ten thousand pounds of thoroughbred hit the ground at a dead run, and over the loudspeaker came the triumphant cry: *"And they're off!"*

Paula's heart was pounding so hard that she couldn't hear the race being called. She was so excited that, despite the display on the huge two-story video screen at the end of the track, she couldn't pick No Regrets out of the close-running pack.

"Where's the gray?" she screamed, turning to the man standing next to her. The words died in her throat. It was John-Henry.

There wasn't time to say anything; the look in his eyes said it all, anyway. Gesturing with his head, his eyes not leaving her face, he said, "Trailing at the back."

What did that mean? Was he going to lose? Oh, no! It couldn't be! Paula thought, and grabbed onto John-Henry's arm. She had so much to say to him, but not now. Not now! Knowing he would understand, she turned away, screaming herself hoarse, as though No Regrets would hear her and respond.

"Where is he?" she screamed again, clutching John-Henry's arm even tighter.

John-Henry looked up at the big television screen and said something, but his reply was lost in the sudden surge from the stands as the horses came around the turn. Everyone in the grandstand got to their feet, and the murmurs became a swell, and then a clamor, and then a roar, as thousands of voices started yelling their horses home.

People surged to the fence, pushing Paula out of the way. Somehow she got separated from John-Henry, but she fought her way back to her place, grabbing onto him as he was turning to look for her. "What's happening now?" she screamed.

He pointed quickly at the big video screen again. "They've turned for home!"

"Who's in front?"

"A horse named Sea Cane."

"No! It can't be!" she wailed. "Where's No Regrets?"

The noise around them was deafening. "I don't—"

"Where *is* he?" she screamed.

Now the announcer was shouting, too. Paula suddenly became aware of the thunder of hoofbeats coming toward her. Shoving some hapless spectator out of the way, she pressed against the rail, trying to see.

"Good heavens," she murmured, when she saw the field streaking toward the finish line, only a few feet beyond her.

The announcer changed pitch. *"And it's Sea Cane, and Follow Through, and Tapestry Gent by a length, and here comes, and here comes..."*

"Who?" Paula screamed, straining to see.

"And here comes... No Regrets between horses!" the announcer cried. *"And it's Sea Cane and No Regrets, Sea*

Cane and No Regrets, Sea Cane and No Regrets... battling it out to the finish. And it's..."

The crowd was going crazy; Paula couldn't hear the announcer. Before her eyes, the horses streaked by, blurs of speed, legs and necks and heads and jockeys plying whips. She saw a blotch of gray—she thought, and looked in panic at John-Henry.

"What...what happened?" she croaked. She had lost her voice from screaming, and because her hair was in her eyes, she couldn't see.

"I don't know," he said excitedly, and pointed to the tote board, where the Photo sign was lit.

"No!" she cried. Even she knew what that meant. "Oh, no! Was it?"

"We'll just have to wait," John-Henry said. "It's between Sea Cane and that good-for-nothing, ugly, lop-eared old gray."

Even through her excitement she reddened. Embarrassed, she muttered, "I never should have said that."

He looked down at her, his eyes a blaze of blue. "We both said things we didn't mean," he said. "How did the trip to New York go?"

"It didn't. I told them I couldn't franchise."

"Why?"

She bit her lip. Even though they were surrounded by the milling crowd, eager and anxious racegoers holding on to crumpled tickets waiting for the official results, they might as well have been alone. "Because you were right," she said, looking up into that handsome face she loved. "I did allow my ambition to get the upper hand." She glanced away. "I feel so ashamed."

John-Henry put a hand under her chin and turned her to look at him. "What made you come back?"

Tears filled her eyes. "I realized that everything—everyone I loved—was here...right here, at the racetrack I've always despised. I had to see No Regrets run his race. I had to apologize to Heddy. And I had to tell you—"

But just then a roar went up from the stands. Paula turned. "What is it?"

He glanced toward the tote board. When a broad smile broke out across his face, she clutched his arm. "Did he win?"

"Second."

"Second!"

He looked at her. "Not good enough?"

But she had learned her lesson and didn't hesitate. "It is for me," she said fervently. "I *know* how hard it is to run."

Laughing, he put his arms around her and lifted her off her feet. "That's the Paula I love," he said, giving her a fierce hug. "Come on, let's go find Heddy and Otis. They'll be at the holding barn."

She hadn't the faintest idea what the holding barn was, but she was eager to see Heddy. And Otis and No Regrets. She had a lot of apologizing to do.

"Where is this place?" she asked, and followed John-Henry as they wound their way to where the officials kept the top three finishers in every race until they were examined and had passed drug tests. The guard nodded at John-Henry and let them go inside. Suddenly there was Heddy, rushing up to her with her arms open wide.

"Paula! You came after all!"

Paula returned the hug, laughing and crying at the same time. "I wouldn't have missed it, Grandma. It was a splendid race! I'm so proud of you—and Otis—" she said, seeing the little man standing to one side.

Blushing, Otis muttered, "I always said, there never was a lop-eared horse couldn't run."

"And you were right," Paula said. "He was wonderful! It was so exciting!"

Heddy's eyes were sparkling. "'Did you see the whole race?"

"From start to finish."

Heddy drew back. "But you were in New York."

Paula smiled shakily, tears still on her cheeks. She looked briefly beyond Heddy to where John-Henry was standing. She addressed her grandmother, but it was really to him she was speaking when she said, "I came home, Grandma. Where I belong."

"And I'm glad, darling," Heddy said, giving her another big hug. Then she looked up into Paula's face, and winked. "But I knew you would."

"Oh, Grandma, can you ever forgive me?"

"It's already done. There wasn't nothing to forgive anyway. You just had to find your own pace."

"Well, I found it now," Paula said, her eyes still on John-Henry.

Heddy followed the direction of her gaze and smiled again as she gave her granddaughter a little push. "You go on now. Otis and Fernando and I have to get our horse back to his stall. You come along later. We've got a cookie party all planned. No Regrets is going to get all he wants tonight, for a job well done!"

But Paula hesitated. "You don't mind that he ran second?"

Heddy laughed. "I wouldn't care if he ran second all his life. He ran his heart out for us today. What more can a body ask? It's the trying that counts, not the race. Haven't I taught you that?''

Paula looked down into that beloved face, tears springing into her eyes once more. ''Yes, you have, Grandma,'' she whispered, giving her little grandmother a heartfelt kiss. ''I guess it just took me a little longer to learn than it took No Regrets.''

Heddy patted her shoulder. ''You learned it, that's the important thing,'' she said, a little misty-eyed herself. ''You go on now. And don't forget the cookie party.''

''I wouldn't miss it for the world,'' Paula said, and approached the holding stall, where No Regrets was standing with Fernando at the halter. She wasn't allowed to touch the horse, or get near him until he had been cleared, but she felt a lump in her throat as she looked at him. He was still breathing hard, his nostrils distended, his coat wet with sweat. As she stared at him, she wondered how she could ever have thought he was ugly; right now, he seemed the most beautiful horse in the world to her, and as she looked at him, she whispered, ''I'm going to make you a special batch of cookies, your favorite kind—with carrots. How about that?''

When he nodded his head as if he understood, Paula laughed and turned to look into John-Henry's eyes.

''John-Henry, I—'' she started to say, but he just shook his head and smiled.

''We'll have all the time in the world,'' he said. ''But for now, I just want to know one thing.''

''What?''

''Any regrets?''

''Just one,'' she said, and then smiled when he looked anxious. ''That it took me so long to realize what was really important to me,'' she said softly.

John-Henry let out the breath he had been holding. Now he could believe something he'd only dared dream. Against all his instincts, he had let Paula go, and she had returned on her own. He knew what she felt by the look in those beautiful, expressive eyes. It *was* meant to be, he thought, and held out his arms.

Paula didn't hesitate. She flew into his embrace and buried her face against his chest, hugging him fiercely as he threw back his head in an exultant laugh. The big gray horse behind them had run his race and would come back to run again. For all of them, the fun had just begun.

COMING IN 1991 FROM
HARLEQUIN SUPERROMANCE:

Three abandoned orphans,
one missing heiress!

Dying millionaire Owen Byrnside receives an
anonymous letter informing him that twenty-six years
ago, his son, Christopher, fathered a daughter. The
infant was abandoned at a foundling home that
subsequently burned to the ground, destroying all
records. Three young women could be Owen's long-
lost granddaughter, and Owen is determined to track
down each of them! Read their stories in

#434 HIGH STAKES (available January 1991)
#438 DARK WATERS (available February 1991)
#442 BRIGHT SECRETS (available March 1991)

Three exciting stories of intrigue and romance by
veteran Superromance author Jane Silverwood.

SBRY

This April, don't miss #449, CHANCE OF A LIFETIME, Barbara Kaye's third and last book in the Harlequin Superromance miniseries

Hamilton
H·O·U·S·E

A powerful restaurant conglomerate draws the best and brightest to its executive ranks. Now almost eighty years old, Vanessa Hamilton, the founder of Hamilton House, must choose a successor. Who will it be?

Matt Logan: He's always been the company man, the quintessential team player. But tragedy in his daughter's life and a passionate love affair made him make some hard choices....

Paula Steele: Thoroughly accomplished, with a sharp mind, perfect breeding and looks to die for, Paula thrives on challenges and wants to have it all...but is this right for her?

Grady O'Connor: Working for Hamilton House was his salvation after Vietnam. The war had messed him up but good and had killed his storybook marriage. He's been given a second chance—only he doesn't know what the hell he's supposed to do with it....

Harlequin Superromance invites you to enjoy Barbara Kaye's dramatic and emotionally resonant miniseries about mature men and women making life-changing decisions.

HARLEQUIN Temptation

Lovers Apart

FOUR CONTROVERSIAL STORIES! FOUR DYNAMITE AUTHORS!

In this new Temptation miniseries, four modern couples are separated by jobs, distance or emotional barriers and must work to find a resolution.

Don't miss the LOVERS APART miniseries—four special Temptation books—one per month beginning in January 1991. Look for...

January: **Title #332**
DIFFERENT WORLDS by Elaine K. Stirling
Dawn and Michael... A brief passionate affair left them aching for more, but a continent stood between them.

February: **Title #336**
DÉTENTE by Emma Jane Spenser
Kassidy and Matt... Divorce was the solution to their battles—but it didn't stop the fireworks in the bedroom!

March: **Title #340**
MAKING IT by Elise Title
Hannah and Marc... Can a newlywed yuppie couple—both partners having demanding careers—find ''time'' for love?

April: **Title #344**
YOUR PLACE OR MINE by Vicki Lewis Thompson
Lila and Bill... A divorcée and a widower share a shipboard romance but they're too set in their ways to survive on land!

LAP-1

Coming in March from